HEARTSONG

D1452157

HEARTSONG

A.E. WASP

HeartEyes Press

Copyright © 2021 by A. E. Wasp

All rights reserved.

This book was inspired by the True North Series written by Sarina Bowen. It is an original work that is published by Heart Eyes Press LLC.

No part of this book may be reproduced in any form or by any electronic or mechanical means, including information storage and retrieval systems, without written permission from the author, except for the use of brief quotations in a book review.

This book is dedicated to anyone who's ever felt like they needed to hide who they are in order to survive. You deserve to be yourself, you deserve to be seen, and you deserve to be loved exactly as you are.
May your heart find the song it was born to sing.

ACKNOWLEDGMENTS

I need to give a huge special thanks to Emily Lepping, who made the mistake of talking to me on Twitter and ended up spending hours beta-ing, proofreading, and virtually holding my hand while I wrote this book. Without her, this book probably wouldn't have been finished.

As always, thanks to Angela Bricker who takes time out of her important day job and busy life to proofread my messy documents and tolerates me changing chapters she's already proofed.

Thanks to everyone on Zoe Jay's discord server for letting me hang out with you, introducing me to a never-ending list of interesting things, and sprinting with me to keep me going. You guys are the best.

And a huge thank you to Sarina Bowen for giving me the opportunity to play in her sandbox.

Troy and Dmitri's story is in Incoming, the first book in my small town romance series, Veteran's Affairs. The story of the fateful Christmas Even is in the sequel, Christmas Outing.

SEAN

There're three things you need to know about me: I'm a hillbilly, I'm gay, and I'm not normal. Lord knows there's nothin' I can do about the first two, but I'm gonna fix that last one or die trying.

Step number one of Sean Johnson's Guaranteed Plan for Being Normal ™ is the biggest and most important; get the H-E-double-hockey-sticks outta West Virginia.

There's no way to feel normal when every time you go to church, or work, or even the dang grocery store, it feels like all eyes are on you and everybody's whispering behind their hands about you.

I don't go to church anymore, but a man's gotta eat. Work is mostly fine. I help my best friend and his dad build houses, and they don't let anyone talk crap about me or anyone on their sites. It's good, honest work.

But I'm tired of feeling judgmental eyes on me all the time, wondering if people are talkin' about me. Small towns have long memories. And I want more from life. A bigger life. I know, who the hell am I to think I can have that? What makes me so special? Why can't I just want a normal, easy life?

The answers are, respectively, no one, nothing, and Lord only knows but I don't. There are just some things I was born wanting and no amount of trying can beat them out of me.

That's why, two-year degree from Pierpont Community and Technical College in hand, I packed up my old truck and left town without saying goodbye to anybody except my mom and grandma. I'm headed to Vermont to finish my bachelor's degree and get started on my new life.

Eighteen hours after leaving home, I'm almost there, but Mother Nature is not making these last few hours easy. It's pouring down rain and I'm hanging on to the steering wheel, fighting the wind, and following the taillights of the Subaru Outback in front of me to avoid going into a ditch. The Outback is going faster than I'm comfortable with, and I lose their lights around a corner.

Dang. It kind of feels like I'm losing a friend. I've been behind that Outback for the last three hours. *Bye bye, mysterious stranger. Drive safe. You might want to slow down a hair.*

My phone buzzes with a text from my mother. I ignore it, the way I've ignored the last five. I spoke to her this morning, she'll survive a few more hours.

I hope this Cooper Hill dude my uncle Troy hooked me up with is patient. I'd texted him after I cleared the accident and he said it was fine, but now I'm running even later.

Great first impression, Sean. Excellent start. A rainstorm is an act of God, though, right? Not my fault. And it could be worse. At least the truck is holding up. I pat the dashboard. *Good job not falling apart, Rusty.* I hear twenty-five makes you a classic.

The Google maps lady is telling me to turn right in a half a mile, but Cooper's last text said to ignore her and just go straight until I see the entrance to the strip mall. Which would be great if I could see the driveway.

Maybe the traffic light coming up will turn red when I get there, and I'll risk a glance at the map. Obligingly it does. Oh hey, look who's waiting for me at the light. Hi, Mr. Subaru, nice to see you again. Or Ms. Subaru. I don't wanna make assumptions.

A glance at the map shows me I should be right in front of the diner. The light turns green and the Outback guns it off the line, water spraying up behind it. Rusty and I take off more sedately, in deference to her age.

My eyes flick to the right, looking for the driveway, and flick back just in time to see the Outback slam on its brakes, nose dipping down and back up, chassis swaying as the car lurches left into the oncoming traffic lane. A dark blob goes flying off the car's right fender. The Outback jerks back into the right lane and then the fucker takes off like a bat outta hell, taillights disappearing into the storm, leaving a mound of something in the middle of the road.

He hit something, that's for sure.

Two glowing circles in the middle of the lump reflect my headlights back at me. Eyes, my brain supplies, and I'm yanking Rusty hard to the right before I consciously decide to. The truck bounces over the curb and slews sideways down a steep, muddy ditch. I twist the steering wheel to the left to keep from tipping sideways, and Rusty slides through the mud, brakes locked up, until she's stopped by a clump of scraggly bushes.

"Fuck me! Goddamn it!" If the truck is messed up, I'm so screwed.

Heart beating a hundred miles an hour, I grab a flashlight and my baseball cap like it's going to keep me dry in the torrential rain and push the door open. Across the parking lot, the neon glow of the Dew-Over Diner's sign, the place where I'm supposed to be meeting Uncle Troy's friend, mocks me with its promise of warmth and shelter.

Well, at least I found the place. Sure hope the guy didn't witness my grand entrance.

Thin flashlight beam leading the way, I jog back to the stationary lump in the road. Oh, that's definitely a dog. A small, soaking wet lump of dark curly fur, and it's not moving. Dang it. Praying I don't get hit by a car myself, I crouch down near the dog. "Hey, baby," I coo. "It's okay. How you doin'?"

The dog's eyes open and it looks at me. I'm pretty sure the look says *Doing pretty crappy, Sean. How do you think I'm doing?*

"Stupid question. I'm sorry. I'm just goin' to check you out, okay?" The dog gives a weak thump of her tail. Her chest rises and falls rapidly beneath my hand.

There are cars headed in my direction now, so I swing the flashlight, hoping they'll see me. I've got to get her out of the street. As the cars approach the stoplight their headlights wash over us, turning everything black and white, and I get a better look at the dog. Oh, man. She's so small and her feet are so big. "You're just a baby, ain't you?" Between the rain and the night, it's impossible to tell how injured she is. If there's any blood it's either invisible against her dark fur or being washed away by the rain.

The light turns green. We have to move now.

"Sorry, baby," I say. "This might hurt." She yelps loudly as I scoop her into my arms. "Please don't bite me." I scurry off the road, the cars close enough behind me that I get splattered with muddy rain from their tires and feel the wind of their passing on my back. Slipping in the mud of the ditch, I make a beeline for the diner. I'm sure it violates like seventeen health codes to bring her inside but she needs help and I don't have a clue who to call or where to take her even if the truck wasn't in a ditch.

Head down against the driving rain, body hunched over the injured dog, I don't see the taillight of the car pulling out of a parking spot until it's almost too late. *Oh fuck.* I close my eyes, turn the dog away, and brace for the impact.

Strong hands clamp down on my upper arms and yank me back. My back slams against a hard, broad chest, and then all three of us, me, my rescuer and the dog, are stumbling into the back bumper of a minivan.

The hands around my arms tighten and I lean against this stranger's body for a second. The guy is almost the same height as me, but much broader, his chest wide and warm against my wet back. The feel of stubble against my cheek and warm breath blowing over my ear make me shiver.

"Sean?" he says, voice deep and smooth.

Oh, holy hell. Can it be?

"Cooper, get the hell in here!" a second man calls from behind us.

A'course it is.

I straighten up and try to pull away. I swear his hands tighten on my arms, tugging me back against him for a glorious but far too brief moment before he lets me go. When I look over my shoulder at him, our eyes meet and my words lock in my throat as a sizzle of electricity shoots down my spine. It's so real, I swear lightning must have touched ground somewhere. By the way his eyes widen, Cooper feels it, too.

I can't hear anything except our breathing and the rain pounding on the gravel parking lot, soaking my thin T-shirt, and plastering Cooper's hair to his head.

In my arms, the dog whimpers, and still I can't look away from Cooper's piercing gaze. What the hell is going on?

He starts to speak, and I sway toward him, holding my breath.

Those dark, intense eyes narrow and he scowls. "Don't you fucking know how to drive?"

Speechless, I reel back and he grabs my arm again to keep me from losing my balance.

"Jesus Christ," the older man says. "Don't either one of you idiots have the sense God gave a goose? Get the hell inside."

Cooper drops my arm like it's scalding him, and I tear my gaze away from his angry face. An older guy with dark-brown skin, gray beard, and salt-and-pepper dreadlocks tied behind his neck waves at us from the open doors of the diner.

Grateful for the save, I walk carefully to the doors and into the diner.

"What happened?" the man asks as I pass him.

"This kid hit a dog and then almost got hit by a car himself," Cooper answers from behind me.

"Are you always such a dick or is today special?" I snap at

him, adrenaline and whatever that electric jolt was playing havoc with my nerves and my composure.

A middle-aged waitress hurries out from behind a counter holding an armful of towels. "Here you go, Dewey."

"Thanks, Debbie," Dewey, says, motioning her toward an empty booth. She spreads the towels out on the table with a brisk efficiency.

Dewey turns to me. "You the one who hit this dog?"

I ignore them both. The dog is the only one who matters right now. "Just gonna put you down on here, sweetheart," I tell her. She might be a he, but I can't keep referring to her as "it" even in my head. Laying my hand on her wet head, I take a few, deep, calming breaths before turning back to my accusers.

"*I* didn't hit her," I explain slowly and carefully. "It was some douchebag in an Outback. Hit-and-run," I say, my voice getting higher and less controlled as the anger hits me on top of everything else. "Who does that?" I drop down on the bench.

Water streams off my clothes to puddle on the floor. My soggy sneakers squeak on the linoleum as I slide closer to the dog. Should I try to dry her off? I hate seeing her soaking wet, but I can't tell where she's injured and I'd hate to hurt her.

Cooper leans over the table, close to me. "Is she hurt?"

"Well, I'm no vet, but I reckon that ain't right," I say, pointing to her back leg. It's bending in a way legs are not supposed to bend, and it looks, well, crushed is the only way to describe it. Poor baby. It hurts me almost like a physical pain to watch her suffering.

"No, it doesn't," Cooper agrees. There's a few seconds of awkward silence between us where I can hear Debbie on the phone talking to someone about the dog. Cooper finally breaks the silence. "I'm sorry."

Our heads turn at the same time and our eyes meet again. This time our connection hits me more like molten heat than electricity. Still strong, but I can breathe around it. The rest of the diner fades away as the heat spreads slowly through my body, and all I can see is him.

Now I can see the laugh lines spreading from his mahogany eyes, and the thick honey-gold fan of eyelashes surrounding them. His strong jaw is covered with golden-brown stubble that I want to feel rubbing against my inner thighs. When his lips aren't pressed tightly together with anger or annoyance, his mouth is lush and eminently kissable. His shoulders are so broad and I doubt I could get both hands around his biceps but, God, do I want to try. I don't let myself go further down his body, not sure I could survive it.

I'd feel worse about my blatant ogling if he wasn't checking me out the same way.

As I'm cataloging each of his unnecessarily sexy features, Cooper's taking his own inventory, his gaze blazing a trail of fire as it glides from my eyes to my lips and to my chest.

When our eyes meet again, his pupils are blown far too wide for the brightly lit diner.

I swallow around a suddenly dry throat.

I may be twenty-three years old, but my experience with men is, well, let's just say mostly theoretical. My experience with a man like Cooper looking at me like *that* is nonexistent. It can't possibly mean what I want it to mean. No way is this man who looks like he could lift a small car by himself looking at me like I'm some kind of snack. I'm just your basic scrawny white boy. Now Cooper, he's worth looking at, with his broad shoulders and extremely buff arms.

My brain is trying to tell my dick to stand down, despite it being more than ready to take Cooper up on his offer. My nipples, already pebbled from the cold rain, agree with my dick. Somehow they get harder, making a valiant attempt at poking through my T-shirt. *Fabulous. Great fucking timing, body.* I shift to make sure my crotch is hidden from his eyes by the top of the table.

I feel the heat radiating from his body over every inch of

exposed skin on my body, my wrists, my throat, my face, and I shudder so hard he has to notice.

"Jesus Christ," Dewey mutters under his breath. Cooper and I both start and sound pours back into the world like someone broke a spell. Dewey snorts and shakes his head. "Idiots."

Exhaling, I run my fingers through my hair, pushing the dripping strands away from my face. Cooper finds something down the far end of the diner fascinating, and turns away, hand rubbing the back of his neck.

Again I ask, what the hell?

"Cooper," Debbie calls, holding the phone out. "Dr. Moore wants to talk to you."

Cooper steps away to speak to the vet, and Dewey hands me a dry T-shirt with the name of the diner on it and a clean dish towel. "You're cold, take this."

As I pull off my wet shirt and quickly dry off, I feel Cooper's eyes on my scrawny hairless chest. I bet he's not hairless. I bet that broad chest is covered with the perfect manly amount of hair.

Trying to ignore Cooper, I tell the dog how I'll get the bastard that hurt her. I promise she can bite whoever was driving that Outback as I pull on the dry shirt. Don't think I didn't memorize that license plate after staring at it for a hundred miles.

"I'm not seeing any bleeding but she's been in the rain. Her back leg is pretty mangled, though," Cooper says into the phone. "Yeah. I can do that." He looks around the room. "Yes, I'm at the diner. Dewey's here. He'll help." He looks at the older man, who nods in agreement. "Yeah, great. I'll meet you there. Thanks so much." Cooper hangs up. "Dr. Moore says he'll meet us at his clinic back in town. And we need to make a stretcher of some kind and to wrap something around her, to immobilize her. Like a towel or a blanket."

"I think I got something," Dewey says and disappears into the back room.

"You are Sean, right?" Cooper asks me, a deep frown line between his dark eyebrows.

I nod. "Yeah, and I reckon you're Cooper."

He nods.

Great. This is Uncle Troy's buddy. The man I'm supposed to be living with while I'm in school. If he's going to be looking at me like that the whole time, things are going to be interesting. God, I hope he does.

Oh God, what if he does?

Cooper gently pets the dog's head and talks to her. He tells her she's a good girl and she's doing great. The puppy stares at him, eyes wide and trusting.

I feel you, dog. If Cooper told me I was a good boy in that same voice, well, it wouldn't be my tail that was wagging. I'm just saying.

Dewey comes back with a big plastic tray and another T-shirt. "Pull it over her and the tray. It will keep her still. It's what I had to do to give my asshole cat his meds."

We pad the tray with some clean dishtowels, and then Cooper and Dewey hold the tray at the end of the table. "I'm going to have to move you, honey," I tell the puppy. Her eyes are still glassy but her breathing has slowed a bit. She lifts up her head and snaps listlessly at me. "I know. It's going to hurt. I'm sorry." Keeping a hand on her side, I slide her onto the tray. Then I roll her up in the apron she's been lying on. Dewey slides the T-shirt up over the end of the tray and the dog. She struggles briefly, yelps, and then gives in.

"Good girl," Cooper says, scooping up the dog and the tray like they weigh nothing. "Let's get her into my truck."

"Got you some coffees to go," Debbie says. She's holding a cardboard tray with two cups on it.

Cooper seems surprised. "Thank you. I'll pay for it tomorrow."

She waves him away. "On the house. You just get that poor baby taken care of."

"Yes, ma'am," I say, taking the coffees. "Thank you."

"Come on," Cooper grunts.

"Oh, my truck," I say to Dewey, who I assume is the owner of the diner. "It's in the ditch. Is it okay for me to leave it there?"

"Don't worry about her," Dewey says, laying a heavy hand on my shoulder and giving me a comforting squeeze. "I'll take care of it."

"Thanks," I say. "Keys are in the ignition. The parking brake don't work," I warn him.

"I'll take care of her. Go," he says to both of us.

We go.

Thankfully there's a break in the rain as I follow Cooper to a new blue pickup a few spots down from the door. I'd like to be a tiny bit dry for a minute.

"Hey, you have a 150, too?" I ask as if it's the most incredible coincidence in the world. It's a truly brilliant observation considering it literally says that on the back of the truck. Cooper gives me a grunt that I choose to interpret as *Yes, I do. Good of you to notice.*

Opening the door, I put the coffee down on the seat and slide in. Once I'm buckled up, Cooper hands me the makeshift dog stretcher.

Unlike when I start my truck, music doesn't blare from the speakers as soon as the engine starts. Which means Cooper is either a freak who doesn't listen to music while he drives, or he's a responsible adult who shuts off the radio every time. After a few silent minutes, I conclude he must not like music.

"Is it far to the vet's office?" I ask.

"About twenty minutes."

The silence in the cab isn't quite awkward, but it isn't quite comfortable either. It feels oddly charged. Seeing Cooper in real life is different from seeing his picture. Troy didn't give me too many details. Just that he is a few years older than Troy, he's a "good guy," and he was a staff sergeant in the army. I not sure what that last part means, but Troy likes him so I'm willing to give him the benefit of the doubt. And not just because I think he's hot. Though I do.

I might be imagining things, but I keep feeling Cooper's eyes on me. As a rule, my gaydar sucks, but I swear he's checking me out. Could Cooper be gay?

Troy hadn't said either way, but it's not like I can ask Cooper right out. There's nothing about him that screams *I'm into men.* He looks like a construction worker or lumberjack or something manly like that. Maybe he's bi?

At the next red light, Cooper throws another of those glances my way, and I whip my head around, catching him in the act. "What?"

He doesn't look away. "You're not what I expected."

"Ha. That's not what I expected you to say, so we're even. What'd you expect?"

"From the way Troy was talking about you, I thought you were seventeen," Cooper says. "Thought I was signing up for some kind of babysitting."

Great. Freakin' awesome. Just what I need, another person who thinks they have to take care of me. Guess I'd only been imagining he was into me. Of course, I was. Look at him and look at me. Why would he want me? Instead of answering right away, I murmur something soothing to the puppy. She's not struggling, but her breathing is still too fast for my comfort.

"From the way my family treats me, you'd think I was. But no, sir. I'm twenty-three."

"Really?"

I gotta admit, I'm a mite offended. I know I'm on the scrawny side, especially compared to him, and looking like a drowned rat isn't helping either, but I didn't think passing for twenty-three was such a stretch. "Is that so hard to believe?"

"Not at all."

Well, that's good to hear, at least.

"You're not that much younger than Troy, are you?"

"Six years. My mom is ten years older than him." I'll let him do the math. "How old are you?"

"Old. I just turned thirty-five," he says as if he's older than Methuselah.

"Don't give me that. You're younger than my mom and she was a teen mom."

"Younger by how many years?"

"Four," I confess quietly.

He snorts. "That's what I thought. Still, for the record, I don't think twenty-three is a kid. I said Troy made it *sound* like you were." He gives me a sideways glance again, the one I feel like heat on my skin. "I can see you're all grown up."

Dayum. Between that look and the tone in his voice, I'm glad there's a puppy on a tray covering my lap. I definitely feel some kind of connection between us, but what does it mean?

Cooper keeps talking, unware of my internal crisis. "You're older than the new recruits I work—worked—with. I swear those eighteen-year-old enlistees looked younger and younger every year." He shakes his head at the audacity of youth to be young.

"Tell me about it," I say. "I'm worried that I'm going to look like a grandpa next to the freshmen in college." I'm not going in as a freshman, but still, by my age a lot of people are already two years out of college. I hope I won't stick out too much. Am I going to have to hang out with a bunch of eighteen-year-olds? Will they ask me to buy beer because I'm older?

"I think you'll be fine," he says. "Lots of people go to college later. I'm thinking of going myself."

"Yeah?"

"Yeah. I mean, I have to do something now that I'm out. And I have the GI bill money."

"I think Uncle Troy is using that for his schooling," I say. "Does it cover a lot?"

"Tuition and fees, a monthly housing allowance and a stipend for textbooks and supplies for up to three years," he says.

I whistle. "Damn. That's a good deal."

"Yeah, well, I did work for it," he says darkly. "Believe me, I earned it."

I throw up a hand to stop him. "I'm not saying you didn't. I'm just jealous."

"Don't be," he says.

"You sound like Uncle Troy."

"He's a smart man," Cooper says.

2

COOPER

With Sean riding shotgun in my truck, his body heat, and the scent of whatever cologne or body wash he uses filling the confined space, it's damn hard keeping my eyes on the road. No matter how hard I try to ignore him, he draws my attention like iron filings to a magnet. It's a damn miracle we don't hit another animal.

Only once or twice before have I felt this instant connection with another person. They walk into the room and something between us clicks. It's like the universe is telling me *pay attention, this person is important.* I felt it tonight.

My eyes met his and I knew down to my bones that my life would never be the same.

This attraction isn't just physical, though he is striking looking, with high cheekbones, thick hair darkened by the rain, and incongruous, piercing ice-blue eyes that contrast beautifully with his tan skin. What draws me is the haunted look I saw in the depths of those beautiful blue eyes. I know I'd see it again, if it weren't dark in the quiet closeness of the cab, when he looks from the dog to me. It's there in the way his hand hovers over her, as if he needs to touch her, to comfort her, but is too concerned that his touch will add to her pain.

They're the eyes of someone who's seen too many bad things, too young. The same look I saw in kids in warzones. Need burns in me to chase that look out of his eyes, to take the burden of whatever pain he's concealing from him.

If I could wrap myself around him, shield him from the bad things in the world, I would. But even if he were mine to protect, I couldn't.

Mine to protect? Where the hell did that come from? I don't think crap like that. I'm not the possessive type. Oh my God, I'm losing my mind after only a half hour around him. What's going to happen when he's living and working with me, in my house, twenty-four seven?

Nothing. Nothing is going to happen. For fuck's sake, I don't even know if he's into men. For all I know he's the straightest guy in his school, though my gaydar is honed to a fine instrument out of necessity, and it's telling me Sean is definitely gay.

What it doesn't tell me is what he thinks about me. Probably that I'm a dick, given how in the short time he's known me I've either grunted or yelled at him.

I take a deep breath. Then another. Unfortunately, all that does is draw more of his scent into my lungs. I hit a pothole and the puppy gives a sharp yip. *Get your head in the game, Hill. There'll be time enough for fantasizing about gorgeous young men when you get home.*

———

The small parking lot behind the vet's office is mostly empty on this rainy weekday night.

Dr. Moore, a kind-looking man in his thirties with a bit of an absent-minded air to him, meets us at the door with a gurney. "Come in. Come in." He takes the dog, tray and all, from Sean. "Oh, you are a sweet thing, aren't you?" He hits the automatic door button and pushes the gurney through.

We follow him to an examination room, Sean's eyes never leaving the puppy.

"What do you think, Doc?" Sean asks after a few long seconds of silence.

"Oh," he says, looking up from his examination of the puppy as if he's forgotten we were there. "It's, ah, the leg doesn't look good. I'm going to have to examine her more closely, of course." He's covered the dog with a warm blanket, only uncovering what he needs to see. The puppy is breathing heavily, eyes closed.

The doctor presses on the dog's side and she yips, legs scrabbling against the metal examination table. "Sorry, girl," Dr. Moore says, laying a gentle hand on the puppy.

"Can't you give her some painkillers or something?" Sean asks, the dog's pain hurting him, too.

Dr. Moore shakes his head and continues his examination.

"He needs to hear if she complains when he touches somewhere, so he can see if it hurts," I explain. "Same way medics do it. A head to toe examination running your hands over every inch of the body. Fingers can feel things eyes can't see."

Dr. Moore nods in agreement. "And I need to make sure she doesn't have a concussion before I give her anything. You two don't have to stay. I can tell you right now, this baby will be staying overnight. We'll take good care of her."

"What about her leg?" Sean asks.

The doctor's head lifts and his eyes meet mine briefly. I know that look. I've seen that same look exchanged between two medics over my own body. It's not good. "I'll do what I can," he says. "Go home."

"Do you need any help?" Sean asks.

The doctor shakes his head. "My partner's here."

"Um," Sean asks nervously. "Who...the bill...I mean. This stuff is expensive, right? I don't have a lot, but, I, uh...I don't want you to like, y'know..." He makes a vague hand gesture indicating nothing specific, but I know what he means. He doesn't want them to put the dog to sleep if he can't come up with the money to pay for her care.

Dr. Moore gives him a tired smile. "Don't worry about that. We have people we can call and some organizations that have a small amount set aside for just such a situation. You should get home. You both look wet and wiped out."

"I am," Sean admits. "Long day."

Dr. Moore nods, his attention already back on his patient.

"Bath's ready," a man calls from the back. His accent gets my attention first. Australian? New Zealand, maybe. He comes into the room, and somehow, even though I know he's walking normally, it feels like he's sauntering. I like him right away.

"Thanks, Tai," the vet says. "Can you get contact information from these men?"

Tai comes over to the table and kisses the doctor on the cheek. "No problem." He turns to us. "Come with me, boys," he says. I follow him, but Sean seems stuck. Tai walks over and puts a gentle hand on his shoulder. "Come on, honey." He turns Sean slowly, guiding him forward with a hand on his lower back. "I know it's awful but there's nothing you can do now. Your baby's in excellent hands."

"She's not mine," Sean says, looking back over his shoulder. "I just found her."

"Well, we'll still call you when we have some information, okay? Just give me your numbers." Tai guides us to the reception counter in the waiting room and hands us a notepad and a pen.

We give him our numbers and I turn to leave. Sean is staring down the hallway, hands shoved in his pockets. "Come on," I say roughly. "Let the man work."

"We'll call," Tai reassures us. He locks the door behind us.

By the time we get back to the diner, Sean's truck is out of the ditch.

"Truck seems fine," Dewey reports. "Maybe a few new dents and scratches, but she's running."

"Thank you so much," Sean says. "I really appreciate it."

"Don't worry about it. Just bring this guy here more. Maybe he'll stay and talk a bit with you around," he says, pointing at me. "Like trying to get blood from a stone to get him to have a conversation."

Though he's smiling, he sounds hurt and it takes me by surprise. Sure, I've been coming here three or four times a week since I moved back a few months ago, and Dewey seems like an interesting guy I'd like to get to know better, but this is his place. He's got a business to run, and I'm not going to presume on his time or friendship by bending his ear with my boring stories.

Maybe he's a little lonely, too? Maybe Dewey wants someone to talk to as much as I do.

"I'm sorry," I say. "I just assumed you were busy. I didn't want to bother you."

Debbie laughs and Dewey rolls his eyes at her. "Never too busy to talk to a new person."

"Besides, I'm thinking we have a lot in common. Military?" he asks me.

I nod. "10th Mountain Division, 10th Sustainment Brigade, out of Fort Drum."

"Vietnam," he says. "4th infantry."

"That must have been rough," Sean says.

Dewey looks at him and raises his eyebrows. "Definitely not a cakewalk, that's for sure." He turns back to me. "Cooper, right? Don't be a stranger," he says on my nod.

"I won't," I promise.

"I can whip up some burgers if you want," Debbie says. "You're soaking wet and probably hungry."

Sean and I exchange glances. We're both wet and cold, and I think we're on the same page. "No, thank you," I answer for both of us. "I appreciate it, though."

"Then I'll get you next time," she says.

Sean exhales, and we head back out into the night.

I follow Sean to Troy's old truck. "Never thought I'd see the day Troy gave up Rusty. He loves this old thing. I can't believe it's still running." He'd had it when we were both stationed up at Fort Drum and it had been held together with spit and baling wire back then.

"He said she's good luck and that I need it more than he does," Sean says, dropping the tailgate. "Now that he's engaged and all."

"To Dmitri. Fuck!" I bark as pain like a knife stabs me in my shin. A shin I no longer have thanks to the below-the-knee amputation I had to have a year ago after the motor vehicle accident that ended my military career.

Sean stops with a hand on the tailgate. "You got a problem with Dmitri?" he asks. "Is it because he's a man?"

"What? No," I snap. I'd known Troy was gay before he did. Not that we'd talked about it in so many words, but I'd made sure he knew about me and that I was available if he wanted to confide in someone. "The engagement caught me by surprise, that's all. Troy told me once he couldn't see himself getting married."

Sean stares at me like he's trying to read something in my expression, his hand clenching and releasing around the tailgate. He glares at me, chin lifted defensively. "I'm gay. Is that going to be a problem?"

Hell, yes, it's going to be a problem.

Knowing he's gay makes it a lot harder to ignore this spark between us, and I have to ignore it. We both do. Neither of us can afford to risk our mutually beneficial arrangement on a hookup. Besides, Troy asked me to help Sean get settled in Burlington, not in my bed.

But I can't let him think I'm homophobic. "I'm gay, too."

That catches him by surprise. "Troy didn't tell me."

"It's not Troy's information to tell."

"Did you know about Troy when you were in the army together?" he asks.

I nod.

"Well, okay, then. Glad that's out there." He sits on the dropped tailgate, careful not to bang his head on the window hanging down from the roof. "We didn't know," he says. "About him being gay, I mean, until he came home for Christmas a few years ago with Dmitri."

"That must have been a surprise."

"Yes, sir, it was." His weak smile doesn't reach his eyes. "Almost as much a surprise as me coming out to the whole family that same night."

Sean has a stronger version of Troy's distinctive Appalachian accent. Troy used to call it his hillbilly accent and tried to hide it, but I'd always liked hearing him speak. Sean has a story-telling voice. I could listen to it all day. "Sounds like an exciting Christmas."

"You could say that."

"How'd your family take it?" I ask.

He slips off the tailgate and turns back to his truck to break our eye contact, propping the back window of the truck cap up with a stick. "My mom, she already knew," he says into the depths of the truck bed. "Uncle Paulie was fine. Uncle Davey not so much but he's kinda a dick in general. My grandparents came around."

"And your father?"

Troy yanked a blue plastic tote away from the wall. "I don't give a flying fuck what he thinks about anything. My life was—is —better when he stays the hell away from me and my mom."

Okay. So Dad is not a topic we'll be bringing up again. "Well, good for your mom, then. And it's good you have Troy. And Dmitri."

Kicking off his wet sneakers, Sean climbs into the truck with a soft grunt. I try and fail not to look at his ass as he does. In my defense, it's a nice ass. Small and tight.

"Everything okay?" Troy's old truck has an eight-foot bed, so there's plenty of room for Sean and his stuff. Boxes and storage totes are shoved against the sides and the sleeping bag he's kneeling on says he's slept in it on this trip.

"Just lookin' for some dry pants," he says. "These jeans are startin' to chafe." With a small sound of triumph, Sean pulls a pair of sweatpants out of a duffle bag, and backs out of the truck bed.

"You're going to strip in the parking lot?" I ask.

"Cover me." Hands on the button of his jeans, he flashes me a killer grin.

Oh, I'll cover him all right. Slowly, I turn, keeping my eyes on him as long as I can.

I hear the sound of his jeans being peeled off and dropping wetly to the ground. There's another soft sound that I know is his underwear slipping off his legs. Since he can't see me, I smile. They can't be that wet. Whether or not he knows it, he's flirting.

Damn, I want to flirt back so badly.

"Okay, I'm decent again," he says.

"You ready to go?" I ask. He nods. "Then follow me."

3

COOPER

It figures the first guy I'm bringing back to my place is cute, single, and totally off-limits. There's a laundry list of reasons I shouldn't encourage Sean's flirting, starting with the twelve-year age gap. But the gap in our ages is nothing compared to the gap in our experiences.

I've been on my own emotionally my whole life. Been taking care of myself physically and financially since I was old enough to earn a paycheck. When I turned eighteen, I signed up with the Army, expecting to be in until I was eligible for a full pension at twenty years, at least. I'd made it to seventeen before a freak rollover accident crushed my left leg, rattled my brain, and shifted a few vertebrae. I've been to hell and back and have the nightmares and scars to show for it.

According to Troy, Sean's never left West Virginia and probably hasn't suffered anything worse than a paper cut. His life is just getting started. He needs to find his own way, carve out his own life.

Is there someone in West Virginia waiting for Sean? If not, he's come to a great place to find one. Vermont in general, and Burlington in particular, is a pretty liberal place. Sean will have his pick of cute guys once he starts school. He'll probably hook up with someone that first week.

Not that my potential love life was a factor in my decision to move back to Burlington after separating from the Army. I just didn't know where else to go. Outside of Army bases, it's the only place I've ever lived. I grew up here, shuttling between loveless foster homes and uniformly depressing group homes.

To my teenage self, Burlington was a trap, a dead end, someplace I couldn't wait to leave. Now as an adult, it seems like a refuge. A beautiful, vibrant town surrounded by the great outdoors. I think I could build a life here.

I've found some new places to explore that hadn't been around when I was a kid. There's this inclusive wine bar and bookstore on Church Street called Vino and Veritas that I particularly like. It's cozy and welcoming. Good snacks and great local beers and cider. But most importantly, twice a month they hold an open mic night where I can get up on the small stage and play my guitar in front of actual people.

It's the kind of place I can picture myself killing a few hours after dinner with a group of friends. If I had any. I'm having the hardest time figuring out how adults make friends in the civilian world. Never before in my life have I had to intentionally seek out people to be friends with. For better or worse, military service gives you a built-in group of buddies. Hell, it's harder to get alone time than it is to find someone to hang out with.

I'm hoping the open mic nights might lead to something. I've spoken to a few of the staff and regulars once or twice, but nothing more than small talk. I've never been one for small talk, and, well, after some of the things I've seen, things I've done, casual conversation just seems so pointless. And there are things civilians just don't get.

I know I can come off as unapproachable. The guys used to say I had resting grumpy face. Integrating back into civilian life is more difficult than I thought it would be. Guess I should have paid more attention during out-processing when they were talking about how difficult it is.

But friends can wait and dating definitely will wait. My first priority is fixing up the house.

The main work I needed done was far too big for me to handle alone, even if I had been comfortable handling the plumbing, and I'd needed it done quickly. Most of my budget had gone into hiring contractors to put up some new walls, take out some others, and turn the old den and three-quarter bath into a master bedroom with patio doors opening onto the backyard and an en suite bathroom with enough space for a wheelchair and a walk-in shower rigged with a bench, handrails, and a hand-held shower head.

The rest of the jobs aren't as complicated. With my construction background, I should be able to handle the rest of the work myself with one other person. That's where Sean comes in. He needs a place to stay and I need a pair of hands. Pair of legs, more specifically. Some things, like climbing ladders and kneeling for long periods of time, are not as easy for me anymore.

The exterior is mostly fine. A handful of wood shingles need to be either repaired or replaced, and it could use a weather sealing. Most of the work will be in the interior, bringing it into the twenty-first century and making sure it's wheelchair and crutch friendly.

When I'd told her I'd be living alone, my occupational therapist had been all about "path of travel" and "ease of access." She also told me I need an "area of rescue," which meant there needs to be enough space in the bathroom and bedroom for someone to be able to get in and help me when I fall.

I fell a lot in rehab. Still fall every now and then. I'm an expert faller now.

Another fun reality check was the fact that there was a high probability of me needing to be wheeled out of the house on a gurney at some point, so I should make sure the doorways, both external and internal, are wide enough and that there aren't any tight turns between the bedroom and bathroom doors and the external doors.

At least it gives me an excuse for replacing the old back door with double French doors and building a deck and a walkway down to the beach. It's not indulgent if it's a medical necessity.

After all that, I need to find a job and figure out what I'm going to do with the rest of my life. Which is easier said than done, given the fact that all my military experience is in construction. No one is going to hire a one-legged contractor. Maybe I can get a supervisory position? Being a staff sergeant has to count for something in the real world.

Hell, maybe I should go to college, too. It would put off having to think about a job for a few years and maybe give me some kind of direction for the rest of my life.

Sean's headlights flash in my mirror as he drives over a speed bump. He came here to help me and get a start on the rest of his life. He doesn't need me panting over him. Sure would be easier to remember if he was ugly and straight. *Thanks for the heads-up, Troy.*

The roads get narrower and darker the closer we get to my tiny house on Lake Champlain. Overgrown bushes and plants make it hard to see the edges of the blacktop even without the rain that's started up again. Keeping my eyes peeled for the reflectors I'd nailed to the trees on either side of my driveway, I slow the truck to a crawl.

Finding the opening in the brush, I stop the truck, and call Sean.

"Hello?"

"I'm at the driveway. I'm going to pull up so you can go in first. We'll be using my truck more than yours. Pull as far forward as you can."

"Okay."

Access to my truck isn't the only reason I wanted Sean to go up the driveway first. By parking behind him, I end up closer to the side door, giving me less distance to navigate into the house.

Of the many things I hadn't appreciated pre-amputation, the ability to do things mindlessly was the one I missed the most. How many times had I jumped from the seat of a truck and run to wherever I wanted without a second thought?

Now every new surface requires a threat assessment and a determination of the best angle of attack. For example, the hard-packed dirt driveway running up the side of my house is usually a firm, fairly smooth surface, easy to navigate with crutches or the prosthesis. Tonight, however, hours of constant driving rain have turned slight depressions to large puddles and the hardest-packed dirt to slick mud.

Luckily, the rain has stopped for the moment, and I can see a clear path to the door. Turning my body so I can slide both legs out of the truck at the same time, making sure to distribute my weight evenly, I spare a thought for the cane behind my seat.

Before I can decide, Sean hops down from his truck, duffle bag in hand, and jogs over to me. "Hey," he says.

Pride wins. Screw it. The door is only a few feet from the truck and the first thing I did after I bought the house was have a small ramp installed. I'll be fine.

I toss Sean the keys. He snatches them one-handed out of the air.

"Nice reflexes," I say, and he grins at me. "Open the door. I'll be right in."

I make my careful way to the door, trying my hardest to keep my gait natural. A little voice in my head tells me I'm being stupid but I ignore it. Feeling the slick wood of the ramp under my foot, I make a mental note to get a handrail built before the snow falls.

Sean stops a few feet into the kitchen. This room, at least, is in decent condition. The appliances were new in the eighties, but everything works and since they were manufactured before planned obsolescence was a thing they'll probably work forever. There is plenty of counter and cabinet space.

"Cute," Sean says, dragging me back to the present. He looks out the window over the sink. Right now all we can see is darkness and raindrops.

"That looks over the lake," I say as I make my way past him.

"There's a lake?" he asks, sounding pleased. "I love lakes."

"*A* lake? It's not just a lake, it's *the* lake. Lake Champlain. You are going to be surprised in the morning. This property has a private lakefront beach. The sunsets are amazing." That private beach is the main reason I bought this house, despite it needing a bunch of work and having a second story I'll probably never use.

"I can't wait to see it during the day."

I can't wait to show it off. This house is everything to me. My first real home, something that is just mine. It might sound stupid, but this house is my independence. Once I've got it set up, I'll be able to live completely on my own. Though it would be nice to have someone to share my life with. A boyfriend. Maybe even a husband and kids one day. If there's one thing I learned growing up in foster care, it's how not to raise kids. But all of that is way in the future.

Getting the house fixed up is my priority. That's what I've got to focus on, not Sean's cute butt and sad, beautiful eyes. Why am I even thinking about his butt? Jesus, I'm around a good-looking guy for an hour and I'm already naming our kids. I'm an idiot. I might need to get laid. It's been way too long. Since before the accident. I definitely need to get away from Sean for a minute.

"Your room is upstairs. The door in the middle of the hallway," I say, sorting through a three-day old pile of junk mail like I'm going to find the secrets of the universe there, just to keep from looking at him. "It's got an air mattress and some sheets. Bathroom's at the top of the stairs. Towels in the bathroom." That was all I'd been able to get upstairs on my own. "We can get a real bed and mattress up there eventually. Why don't you go get settled?" I suggest, voice tight with frustration and the return of my phantom pains.

"Uh, yeah. Okay," he says.

I know it looks like I'm trying to get rid of him, because I am. I hold my breath until he's upstairs, listening to the floors creak beneath his feet, and don't completely relax until I hear the water running in the shower and know he won't be back down for a few minutes at least.

If I were alone in the house, I'd take my leg off, do my night-time routine, and hop around on crutches the rest of the night. But I'm not ready for Sean to see me like that. Not yet. I'm not planning on keeping it a secret forever; that would be impossible.

But that was before he flirted with me, made me feel things I haven't felt in a long time, and I'm not ready to let that go yet. One more day before he see me as old and broken. Helpless.

I'm not helpless. But I am hungry, and I bet Sean is, too. Making a mental note to keep an eye on that spot on the ceiling, I stand up and head for the pantry. A late night pancake snack sounds perfect.

I wonder if he'll take a shower to warm up. I can't help wondering what Sean looks like naked and wet.

An image of his face when our eyes met in the parking lot flashes in my mind. His eyes wide and scared, dark hair plastered to his cheeks. And once again, I get that feeling, like a punch to my heart, that this is either going to be a disaster or the best thing that's ever happened to me.

Maybe it's both.

SEAN

Get settled, he says. Funny, I'm feeling pretty unsettled right now.

Between the stress of driving in the storm, the whole thing with the poor dog, and the fact that I've been running on caffeine and gas station burgers for two days, I'm wound tighter than an eight-day clock.

My room is small and bare, and judging from the slope of the ceiling, the space used to be an attic. All that's in it is an air mattress, a night stand, and a floor lamp without a shade standing in the corner. The lock on the door is one of those push button ones, but it works. There's only one window, so not much of a breeze, but there is a great view of the lake. I should ask Cooper about putting in one of those roll-up fire escape ladders. Can't be too careful.

There's a small closet in one wall, but no dresser. Wonder if Cooper would mind if I put a dresser up here, and maybe a couple of shelves. If not, no biggie, it's not like I have a lot of stuff anyway. There's a suitcase and a few totes of books and knick-knacks in the truck. I'll empty it tomorrow.

I kick off my shoes and flop down onto the mattress, which is firmer than I'd expected. Damn, I'm tired and wired. What am I supposed to do for the rest of the night? My books are in the car.

Guess I could watch a movie on my laptop, but I'd have to ask Cooper for the Wi-Fi password and he doesn't seem to want to talk to me tonight.

I must have been really, really imagining some kind of connection between us.

My phone rings. To my complete lack of surprise, it's my mom. Best get it over with, maybe I can buy myself a couple days' peace.

"Hey, Mom," I say, with forced happiness. She starts right up, and I let her go, tossing in comments at the appropriate times.

I'm alive. Yes. I'm at Cooper's. No. No problems finding the place. Yes, he seems great, just like Uncle Troy said. No, I haven't given it to him yet. Because I haven't unpacked yet. I will. I promise.

I sense her slowing down and jump on the opening. "I'm kind of tired, Mom. Think I'm going to take a shower and go to bed early." It's not even nine yet, but maybe she'll buy it.

"That sounds like a good idea. I'm so excited for you, baby! It's going to be great. I miss you already. Grandma and Pop-pop and Gigi send their love."

"Tell them I love them back. I miss you, too. I'll call in a couple of days, after I get more settled, okay?"

"Okay." She doesn't sound thrilled.

"Try to keep the texting down to three a day, all right? And try not to panic if I don't answer right away." She won't, but it's worth a shot. Eventually, she's got to let me go. It's way past time.

"I'll try," she says. "I'm know I'm a pain. I just worry when I don't hear from you." Her voice trails off, full of things we don't talk about anymore.

"I know. I love you. Hug Gigi for me."

"Night, baby. Sleep tight. Don't let the bedbugs bite."

"Night, Mom." I toss the phone to the end of the bed with a sigh and rub my eyes with the heels of my hands. Then I let out a long breath. New start. New life. New Sean. It's going to be great. Really.

I stare at the ceiling for a minute or two, and then drag myself off to the shower. Be nice to be wet and warm instead of wet and cold for a minute.

———

The bathroom is stocked with a clean towel and washcloth. There are unopened bottles of shampoo and conditioner and a bar of soap in the shower, and on the sink, a brand-new toothbrush still in its box sits next to a full-sized tube of Crest toothpaste. I touch it as if it's gold-plated. Cooper bought me a toothbrush. And toothpaste. That's so sweet.

Sweet baby Jesus, I'm losing my mind.

Sure, Cooper is so hot I can barely speak around him. I didn't know I had a type, but apparently I do, and it's gruff burly men with biceps just begging to be touched, golden-brown scruff I need to feel with my lips, and eyes that bore into mine like I'm being interrogated. Damn. If he was interrogating me, I'd tell him whatever he wanted to hear.

And since he's gay, it's not *impossible* that he could want me. Just improbable. Those looks had to mean something, though, right? Why isn't there some kind of manual? *The Gay Man's Book of Looks: How to Read his Mind*.

I stare in the mirror at my reflection. Would I be into me if I weren't me? Maybe? I mean, I'm not hideous. I'm kind of scrawny. Troy says I'm *slender*. A little weird combination of tan skin and light eyes. My lips are kind of wide. I touch them tentatively. Springy. I've heard the term blow-job lips. Maybe this is them? God, I can't even imagine. Well, that's a lie. I can totally imagine giving Cooper a blow job. I had to stop myself imagining it when I was driving here from the vet. Not that I've done that, as such, but I have hours of theory and research into how to do it under my belt. So to speak.

I snort at myself. What do I think is going to happen? I'll lure Cooper into my bed with my nonexistent powers of seduction, and then he'll initiate me into the secret world of kinky gay sex and we'll live happily ever after?

Sure. More likely, I'll flirt awkwardly, make a fool of myself, and make things so uncomfortable here that Cooper kicks me out. Then, because I don't have enough money for rent, I'll end up sleeping in my truck and sneaking into the university gym to shower.

I haven't seen much that needs work in the house yet, beyond the floors in the downstairs living area. The original flooring had been ripped up and the subflooring was uneven and warped in some places. This bathroom is as old as the kitchen, but it's scrupulously clean, if empty. I'd put money that no one's been using it. There's nothing but dust and cleaning supplies and a plunger under the sink.

The tub/shower combo isn't fancy, but the hot water is abundant and the pressure is perfect. I take my time.

It's around ten by the time I get out of the shower. Rain beats against the dormer window. When I open the door to let the steam out, a breeze from the open window at the other end of the hall carries the scent of rain, wet dirt, and, if I'm not losing my mind, bacon.

All of a sudden, I'm starving.

Led by my nose, I wrap a towel around my hips and take a step into the hallway to see if that glorious scent is real or just a figment of my imagination.

Of course, the first thing I see is Cooper. He's standing on the bottom step, hand heavy on the banister, head down. The landing creaks as I step on it. Cooper looks up and our eyes meet. That same zing of desire I'd felt before zaps down my spine. Damn it. He gets this deer in the headlights look and his eyes slide down my body. I feel his gaze on my naked skin like the touch of the sun.

My hand tightens on the towel wrapped around my waist and I get the sudden urge to cover my nipples. I suppress the ridiculous giggles that bubble up in my chest.

Cooper's changed into sweat pants and an old T-shirt. His arms are covered with dark hair and more of it peeks from the stretched-out collar of his shirt. And that was definitely a tattoo I caught a glimpse of before. He looks solid and warm and a whole lot of grown-ass man and I bet his shirt smells like fabric softener. Cooper definitely uses fabric softener. He probably gives great hugs, too.

Yeah, the contrast between our bodies puts the final nail in the coffin of my inchoate dreams of seduction. *Slender, my ass, Uncle Troy.* Next to Cooper, I'm downright scrawny, my chest hairless and my arms and legs too long and gawky.

Cooper's body on the other hand. My mind searches for the words. *Strong, unyielding, capable.* I could write poems about his arms alone. No, I definitely *will* be writing poems about them.

His gaze snaps back to my face. Thank God, because this towel is not going to hide the effect he has on me for very much longer. Even with the dark circles under his eyes, and a pinched look to the edges of them that reminds me of my Gigi Jean when her arthritis is acting up, he's still one of the best-looking men I've ever seen in real life.

"I made some food," he says. His voice is a deep grumble that goes right to my stupidly hopeful cock.

"Yes, sir," I croak. "I'll just…" I look down at my towel and then tilt my head in the direction of my room.

Oh my God. Is that a blush? It's hard to tell behind the beard, but those cheekbones are pinker and I would swear his eyes dropped back down to my towel. That's flirting, right? I grin at him and raise my eyebrows, praying I look seductive and not like a cut-rate Joker.

He looks away first. "Yeah," he says. "Yes. And, you know, you don't have to eat. I just meant, if you're hungry. It's just eggs. And bacon. And pancakes."

Before I can say anything, my stomach growls loud enough for him to hear.

Cooper gives me a smile that makes him even more handsome

and touchable. "Guess you're hungry. C'mon down when you're ready."

"Give me forty seconds to make myself pretty," I say, giving him a wink. Then I turn and flee in terror at what I've done. *Oh, God.* Why did I wink? What the hell was that? *God, I'm an idiot.*

Hoping I didn't make as much of a fool of myself as I think, I force myself to go downstairs. He's sitting at a small kitchen table. A plate of scrambled eggs in front of him, one in front of the empty seat across from him, and a third piled with toast and bacon in between them. "I didn't know what you wanted to drink," he says. "There's milk and orange juice in the fridge. There's a glass in the dish drain." He's got a cup of black coffee.

"Thanks." I'll go with orange juice even though I just brushed my teeth. I'll feel like a six-year-old if I drink a glass of milk in front of him.

"This looks great. Thanks." I sit down and across from him and smile. He smiles back, puzzled, and I realize I'm waiting for him to say grace.

He points to the bacon. "Help yourself."

The salty bacony goodness makes me groan with pleasure. There's something different about it. Something sweet, I don't recognize. "This is so good," I say around a mouthful of eggs. Table manners be damned, I'm starved.

"It's just eggs and bacon. Nothing special," he says, but he's smiling as he does.

"No, the bacon is extra good. What's different about it?"

"It's maple glazed," he says.

"And these pancakes," I say, waving a forkful at him. "Amazing."

"It's the real maple syrup."

"I'm sensing a theme," I say, narrowing my eyes.

His chuckle warms my heart. "This is Vermont. By law, all meals must incorporate maple syrup in at least one dish."

"Really?"

"No, not really," he says, amusement at my gullibility in his eyes, and I get a glimpse of how we'll be when the awkwardness wears off. Oh, it could be dangerously good.

When he lifts his coffee mug for another sip, pain flashes briefly across his face, wiping away his smile.

"Everything okay?" I ask.

"I'm fine," he snaps. "You ready to start working tomorrow?"

Then again it could be terrible. I nod like a dashboard bobble-head on a bumpy road. "Yeah, sure. Of course. What are we doing first?"

He sits back, a tightening of his mouth and a narrowing of his eyes another sign of pain. What's bothering him? Headache, maybe?

"First priority is the flooring," he says. "I've stripped it but I need to even out the subflooring and put down something new."

"Are you thinking carpeting or wood?" I ask.

That surprises a laugh out of him. "Carpeting? What is this, 1988? I've been looking at some of that laminate that looks like wood planks."

"Yeah, that looks nice. My grandma put them in the kitchen. Well, mostly me and my pop-pop, my grandpa, did the work. She supervised."

"You're close with your grandparents?" he asks.

"Oh yeah. Ma and I lived with them a long time."

He's stopped eating, his fork tapping gently on the edge of his plate. The sound is loud in the quiet house. "And they're okay with you being gay?"

I shrug one shoulder. "They would probably prefer I wasn't." There's no probably about it. Some days I'd prefer I wasn't, but I was born this way, I guess. "But they're not gonna kick me and Uncle Troy out of the family. Plus my great-grandma, Gigi Jean, loves Troy's husband. That helps a lot."

He blinks quickly. "Great-grandmother? You have a great-grandmother still living?"

Where I'm from, lots of people do. It's not that uncommon. "Yeah. My mom's grandma. She lives with them."

"How old is she?"

"Oh, man. Let's see, my mom is forty this year, something she will not let me forget. Grandma is pert near sixty-three? Sixty-two? Somethin' like that. So Gigi's got to be older than that. Maybe eighty-four? Eighty-five? Pretty old. She's slowin' down."

"I can't even imagine," he says. "Do you have a big family? Cousins? Aunts, uncles?" Whatever was hurting him seems to have passed. He's relaxed against the back of the chair, coffee mug in hand.

"Eh, it's mid-sized I guess. Personally, I'm an only child. One of only two I knew growing up. But my mom is one of four, and there are a lot of relatives. Italian on my grandma's side, Irish on my grandpa's. Catholic on both, so it kind of comes with the territory."

"For some reason, I didn't picture Italians in West Virginia."

"Really? Where do you think pepperoni rolls came from?"

He's smiling at me. *Gah*, he's extra good-looking when he has that real smile. I should keep track of how often I see it.

"I've never even heard of a pepperoni roll," he says, raising his eyebrows.

I gasp, dropping my toast dramatically. "Never heard of them? You've never eaten a pepperoni roll?"

He shakes his head.

I mirror his headshake. "One day, we'll eat pepperoni rolls and I'll give you a little history of West Virginia and the railroads and the people who built them and worked the mines." I bet my mom would mail some rolls up to me.

"It's a date," he says and there's that flash of something between us as our eyes meet.

My heart is pounding. I swallow and lick my lips. "Cheap date," I say, mustering my courage.

His eyes drop to the plate and the moment is gone. I quickly eat the rest of my food. When I reach for his plate and offer to do the dishes, he waves me away. "I got it. Just go to bed. I'll see you in the morning, we'll start making a list."

Feeling like I've been sent to my room, I nod and leave. What else can I do? *It's only the first day, Cooper doesn't hate you*, I tell myself. *You didn't make a fool out of yourself. And look, you're out of West Virginia. You got a place to live, a job to do, someone who might turn out to be a friend. School starts in a few weeks.*

Clichés be dammed. Tomorrow truly is the first day of the rest of my life.

5

SEAN

As far as first days of the rest of my life go, this isn't a bad way to start.

It's a picture-perfect morning. It's still cool, but there's the promise of heat in the air. White fluffy clouds sail across a robin's-egg-blue sky, and there's a slight breeze coming off the lake rustling the dark green leaves. The lake is dotted with sailboats, kiteboards, paddleboards, and jet skis.

Lake Champlain is the biggest lake I've ever seen. Rolling green hills surround it, and it's dotted with islands. Off to the south, some kind of seawall stretches from the mainland to one of the islands. Squinting, I can just about make out movement on it, possibly pedestrians and bicyclists. How cool is that? I should buy a bike and check it out. Wonder if Cooper has a bike?

What Cooper does have is a private beach. Very nice. It's small, close to the house, and the yard is mostly dirt and scraggly grass. Coarse sand replaces the dirt the closer it gets to the shore. There are about fifteen feet of open beach, bracketed by low but steep bluffs on either side as if something took a giant bite out of the earth.

A speed boat zooms past me, dragging some kind of inflatable tube behind it. The kids on the tube are whooping with joy. Screw the bike. We need a boat. I bet we could row or boat over to some of those islands.

Man, I can see myself falling in love with this place. *Please let this whole arrangement work out. Cooper has to like me.* There's no way I can go back home, and without him letting me live here for free, I can't afford to stay.

I'm not completely broke. Between some scholarships, my savings, and an unexpectedly generous donation from my extended family that caught me and my mother by total surprise and made us both cry, if I live frugally, I should be able to get through the next two years without taking any loans. Which is awesome because I'm not counting on my bachelor's degree in English (emphasis on modern poetry, thank you very much) to get me a job with some impressive starting salary. Or any job, really.

So, Sean, what kind of job do you expect to get after college? What exactly are your plans? Fuck if I know. I reckon I'll get the degree and go from there. All I know is that if I want to be any kind of writer worth anything, I need a different life than the one I've had. My world is so small.

This view, now, it's pure poetry. Pulling my ever-present spiral notebook out of my pocket, I try to put down some phrases and thoughts about the beauty of the landscape and how it feels to be finally starting on my path.

Ten minutes later, all I have is twenty different ways to describe Cooper's eyes. Well, he is inspiring. I roll my eyes at myself and shove the notebook back in my pocket.

"Morning," the man himself calls from the door as if conjured by my thoughts, though if he had come from my thoughts, he'd be shirtless.

I swear I try not to ogle him, but with the way he's standing, it's almost impossible not to. His back is to the door, his strong legs stretched out in front him. His arms are crossed over his chest, and he holds a coffee cup in one hand. And there's that killer smile. It takes a few years off his age and makes him look softer and kinder.

My eyes slip down from his mouth, roam across his broad shoulders, and slip down over the curves of his bulging biceps. I detour across his wide chest and over to his other arm before slipping down his tight abs to where his T-shirt hangs loosely around his trim waist. Good Lord, he must work out all the time.

It's so hard to believe he's gay. Looking at him, I would never have guessed. He looks totally normal. Unlike me.

He clears his throat and my eyes snap back to his face.

Crap. That was neither subtle nor slow, Sean. Way to go. Sexually harass the man you need to impress.

Cooper doesn't appear to be offended though. His easy smile is gone, yeah, but that hot look is back in his eyes, and he's uncrossed his arms and is facing me directly.

Woah-kay. Licking my dry lips, I shove my hands into the back pockets of my shorts, stretching my neck side to side to mask the shiver running down my spine.

Taking a deep breath, I force myself to walk over to him. "Morning."

"Enjoying the view?" he asks with a quirk of his lips that might be a grin, might be him trying not to laugh at me checking him out.

My breath catches in my chest. What do I say? Is he flirting with me? Should I try to flirt back? What do I do? Make eye contact and be all like *yeah I am*? Lord take me now. Is this, like, normal joke flirting between two gay guys? Is he making fun of me?

His eyes soften, and his smile turns sweet. "The lake," he says, pointing with his coffee cup. "Is it everything you expected?"

The breath leaves my lungs and my shoulders unclench. "Oh, yes." I look back like it might have changed in the five seconds since I last saw it. "You weren't kidding. It's gorgeous."

"I love it," he says.

"I can see why. You wanna go down to the water? Have a swim before we start working?"

"Not a big fan of sand between my toes," he says.

"Maybe buying a house on the beach wasn't a brilliant idea then." I grin up at him to let him know it's a joke. Is this flirting? Oh my, God. What if I *am* flirting and he doesn't want me to? I mean, of course, he doesn't want me to.

"The plan is to put a low deck out here, connecting my bedroom and the living room, and build a walkway to the beach. I'd love to get it finished before winter, but I'm not sure I can."

"I bet we can together," I say.

"Maybe," he says with an appraising glance. "I'd like that." The lake catches his attention again. "You can go for a swim later, if you want. Let's make some plans first."

"Sounds good. Oh, hey, is that a bike trail going across the lake?" I ask, pointing at the seawall.

"Uh huh," he confirms, going into the house. "Used to be a railroad track. It connects with the greenway on this side, and you can follow it right into town. You can get to school that way."

"Wish I'd brought my bike. I didn't know if I'd have a place for it and it didn't really fit in the truck, so I left it."

"I bet you can get one off Craigslist or something," he says. "I'll ask around."

"Do you have one?" I ask, thinking of my plans to bike to the island.

"No. Not since I was a kid."

"You should get one. We could bike together."

His forehead wrinkles and he frowns. "Not sure I can. Maybe. Huh."

With that mysterious statement, he disappears back inside the house.

Breakfast is a cheese omelet and toast for me and a veggie egg-white omelet for him.

"I guess to get a body like that, you have to eat right, too," I say as I drink my coffee and watch him cook. "Not just work out. You must go to the gym like all the time."

He laughs. "Genetics plays a part, too. Everyone has their own body shape. You can maximize it, but you can't change your basic makeup."

"Too bad." I hold my arm out bent at the elbow, like a little kid making a muscle. "I'm scrawny."

"Slender," he corrects.

I scoff. "Six of one, half-dozen of the other. All I know is I could work out all day and all night and not have those muscles. I can't even gain weight if I try. Makes my sister nuts."

"You're fine," he says. "Grab some plates."

We work our way through the food in comfortable silence. Cooper is absorbed in the book he's reading. Judging by the cover, it's some kind of military thriller.

"Do you mind if I check my phone?" I ask.

Not looking up from his book, he shakes his head.

There are a couple of old texts from my mom and some from my best friend, Richie. I ignore the former and read the latter. He wants to know what the "old guy" is like.

I point my phone at Cooper. "Smile."

His brow furrows. "Why?" he asks suspiciously.

I snap the pic. Cooper with a glare feels more authentic than Cooper with a smile anyway. "My friend Richie wants to know what you look like," I tell him.

Cooper blinks at me, and goes back to his book.

Not so old, I text to Richie, not expecting a reply. He works with his dad and uncles building houses and they would have started pretty early this morning.

Surprisingly, he responds. *Dang. Not old at all. Kind of hot, right? I mean, for a dude. Looks kind of grumpy though.*

That's just his face, I reply with a smile emoji.

That's one of the reasons Richie's my best friend. He's okay with me being gay and treats me like any other normal guy. He's the only one I'd told. I'd waited until after graduation and then I did it on a Friday after work, so he had the weekend to think on it.

For two days, I worried that I'd lost a friend and a job.

But come Monday morning, he was pulling up to my house and picking me up like normal, so I figured we were all right.

Since he was the only one I told, I'd wondered briefly if he'd been how my dad found out, but I realized he'd never do that to me. I must have been running my mouth too much, not paying attention to who was listening.

Now we're good. He doesn't know everything, all the bullshit with my dad, just that I disappeared for a while. When I called him, he asked me if I was okay and told me I still had a job, when I was ready. I told him thank you and that I was fine and that was the end of it.

Yeah, he's hot. A total bear, I text back.

Bear? Is that a gay thing?

Look it up, I tell him.

Hell no. I'm still scarred from looking up gay daddy. Couldn't look my dad in the eye for two weeks.

I laugh out loud.

The n*ow what*? look Cooper shoots me is one I'm sure I'll get very familiar with.

"Just Richie being a joker."

"Boyfriend?" Cooper asks, stabbing at his eggs.

I snort imagining it. "Please. Even if Richie was gay, I wouldn't date him. He hasn't voluntarily read a book since first grade."

"And that matters?"

"To me it does," I say.

He lifts his book up. "Me, too." He looks more relaxed now. It's a good look on him. "So. Am I Richie approved?" he asks.

I nod.

"Glad to hear it." He drops his fork to his plate with a clatter. "You ready to make that list?"

I put the phone aside. "I am."

When he pulls a small spiral notebook from his pocket, I laugh.

"Now what?"

I show him my identical notebook and he nods approvingly. "They're very handy."

"They are," I agree.

"So. The floors," he says.

"And the baseboards. Does any of the drywall need repairs while we're there?"

He nods, making notes in his book. "I'm thinking about putting a set of French doors from the living room to the back-yard," he says. "Should be able to do that where the old door is. Or maybe sliding doors, I haven't decided. What do you think?"

Glancing up at the ceiling, I try to remember some of the jobs I've worked on with Richie. "Both are good," I say, picturing Cooper's living room. "Sliding's better if you don't have a lot of room."

"That's what I was thinking," he says.

"What else?" I ask. I'm itching to get working. The house is cute, and with some upgrades it could be awesome. The kitchen, for example, could use an overhaul. "Got any plans for the kitchen?"

"Gonna redo the cabinets, make some new drawers. But don't worry about it. We have enough work to keep you busy until school starts."

The way he says that gives me a cold feeling in my stomach. "Well, yeah, but I'll still have time to help you even when school starts. I was thinking after we do the floors, we tackle anything outside or things like replacing windows that'll require lettin' the outside in. That way, in the winter, we can do the inside stuff. Bring the kitchen into the twenty-first century. We can get fa-a-ancy."

My grin fades as I take in his expression. He's leaning back in his chair, arms crossed over his chest and my friend the glower is back. "Or not," I say. "Not fancy is fine."

"How long..." He stops and tries again. He drops his arms and his glower softens to a mere frown. "I don't think you'll want to make the trip from your place to here in the winter. The days are short and the roads are bad."

My place? Oh. Oh shit. I can feel the tops of my ears getting red. I hate that I blush so easily. It's the fucking stupidest reaction and I have zero control over it. If anyone tells you people with olive skin can't blush, they're liars.

"Oh, I thought..."

I stand up abruptly, startling him. "I need more coffee. You want some?"

"Sure," he says, draining the one he's holding and handing me his mug.

I refill our cups slowly, stirring sugar and milk into mine as if it will explode if I get it wrong. He doesn't say anything, but I can feel his eyes on me. Okay. Clearly, we're working under different assumptions. I thought I was staying through the school year. Which, now that I think of it, is pretty damn presumptuous. But he has to let me stay at least until the end of the semester, right?

God, this is embarrassing. But I can't stir my coffee forever. It's okay. I'll figure something out. I don't have enough of a budget for the dorms, but I bet I can rent a room somewhere that isn't too expensive. I'll get a job in town. There's got to be jobs. I force down my embarrassment and go to the table.

"I'm not kicking you out," Cooper says quickly. "You don't have an eviction date or anything. But why would you want to stay here longer than you have to?"

Besides being around your hotness? I don't say that.

"Don't you want to live somewhere better for you?" he continues.

"Better how?"

"Closer to school, with kids your own age. Roommates, friends. And I thought Troy said you were looking for a job. Someplace in town would make that way easier. Especially in the winter. I don't know what West Virginia is like, but it's no joke up here. And dating. Dating's going to be so much easier if you're in town."

"Dating?" I ask.

"I assume you're going to want to go on dates at some point. Do kids not date anymore?"

His genuine concern for my love life is almost enough to make me confess my complete and total lack of experience. *Almost* enough. I'm not ready for his pity.

Then again, should I ever get to the point where I did maybe want to have some alone time with someone else, it might be awkward bringing them here. Not that I can imagine wanting someone more than Cooper.

"Yeah, I guess you're right." My accent slips out the way it always does when I'm upset, the right coming out as "raht." Still feels like he's trying to get rid of me.

I drum my fingers on the table and frown at him. "You know I'll still help out here even if I live in town, right?"

"I'm not kicking you out," he repeats. "Just trying to make a realistic plan."

"No. I know. Really. I appreciate the heck outta you lettin' me stay here." I take a deep breath. "I'll start looking for a place."

"Shit," he says, running a hand through his hair. "Don't. I'm sorry I'm being a dick. This house is the only place I've ever lived in that's just mine. Hell, it's one of the first times I've had a bedroom to myself."

"Really?"

"I know, it sounds stupid. But it was either foster homes or group homes as a kid, and in the army, I lived in dorms or the barracks until I hit E-6. And that was right before I got…out."

"And here I am, crashing your space. I'm sorry."

He rubs his face and I wish I knew him better so I could read what he's thinking. "Look. You've been in town less than twenty-four hours. First time leaving home, right?"

My cheeks burn with embarrassment. "Yeah. It's pathetic. I know."

He reaches across the table and places his hand on mine. "Hey, no. It's not."

My mouth twists with the effort of not contradicting him.

"It's not." He squeezes my hand. "Everyone does things in their own time. And it's no bad thing to have a family that loves you and who you want to be with. I never had that. You should treasure it."

"Never?" I said.

His hand tightens over mine. "Never. Foster kid, remember?"

"Oh man, that sucks. You're on your own then?"

He barks a laugh and leans back in his chair, his hand slipping off mine. "Well, now I have you." The warmth in his look more than makes up for the loss of his body heat.

My heart flutters. If he only knew all the ways I want him to have me. "Looks like," I say. "That mean you're not gonna kick me out?"

He rolls his eyes. "I wasn't…"

A spot of hope blooms in my chest.

"Let's do this. You plan to stay here for the semester. That's end of December, right?"

I nod.

"That'll give you a long time to find something. You don't need to figure everything out today."

"Oh, thank God." I slump back in my chair.

He laughs. "I bet you find something sooner. I'll bet you'll be dying to get out of here in no time."

"Yeah?" I ask. "Put your money where your mouth is?"

The wide smile on his face makes him even more handsome, and I can't resist taking another photo.

"Stop taking pictures of me," he says crossly.

"Uh uh. I need proof that you actually can smile, so when I tell people they believe me." I send this one to Richie as well.

Now the frown is back. "I smile," he says. "I'm not grumpy, I swear. I just," he waves his hand around his face, "I just look like this. I can't help it."

I lean forward and stare at him, as if I'm searching for something. "You look just fine," I say. "Don't change a thing."

Now it's his turn to blush and the thought of it pushes me back into my chair. Was *that* flirting? Good lord, how does anyone ever know? I'm never going to get a boyfriend.

"Yes," he says.

"Yes, what?" I've lost the thread of the conversation.

"Yes, I'll put my money where my mouth is. Twenty bucks says you're out of here before Thanksgiving."

I hold my hand out over the table. "You're on."

He shakes my hand. "You better be good for it, Johnson."

"Cross my heart and hope to die, Hill," I say solemnly.

"Put some shoes on," he says, releasing my hand to my great sorrow. "We need to run a couple of errands."

"Want to take Rusty?" I offer. "She can hold a lot of stuff."

"No offense to you, Troy, or Rusty, but I'll feel better taking mine. It's twenty years newer."

"Hey," I say, reaching across the table and laying my hand over his, looking deep in his eyes. "I like old things. They've got class, style."

His eyes widen and his nostrils flare. He shuts that look down quickly, but not before I see it. That's good, right? Does that mean he's into me? He shakes his head with a grin like he's humoring me, but he slides his hand slowly out from under mine. I don't help, leaving my hand where it is until, with one last brush of our fingertips, we're not touching anymore.

"And sometimes they break down on the side of the road and leave you stranded," he says, smile tight. He pushes away from the table. "Come on, I'll give you the nickel tour."

6

COOPER

Sean stares out the window as we drive down route 127, the main road from my place to Burlington. It runs along with the Winooski River for a bit and through hills and fields. The greenway bike path comes near at points and crosses over it at others.

"It's beautiful here," Sean says. "Reminds me of home."

"I've never been to West Virginia. It always sounded beautiful."

Late summer and fall is my favorite time of year in the northeast. Ask me in February and I'll be ready for a trip to Mexico, but summer (after the black flies are gone) and fall are my favorite times of year. My problems with Vermont have nothing to do with the natural beauty of the place. I love the mountains and the lakes.

The Adirondacks across the lake and the Green Mountains behind me offer all the fun I can want and I plan on taking advantage of it. I hadn't done much camping or hiking as a kid, but as fate would have it, I got stationed four hours from here at Fort Drum. The guys and I went out for fun and training many times.

Burlington might feel like it's in the middle of nowhere, but there are plenty of great places close enough for day trips or for even a long weekend. Boston is three and a half hours away, depending on traffic. Montreal is two. I bet Sean would love

Montreal. I wonder if he has a passport. If we get caught up with the work, it would be fun to take him on some day trips.

Dr. Moore calls before we make it to the hardware store. I put the call on speaker.

"I've got good news and bad news," he says. "Which do you want first?"

"Good news," Sean says before I can say anything. "Always good news."

"Do you eat dessert first?" I ask him.

"As often as I can get away with it," he answers.

"Why am I not surprised?" I shake my head and bite my cheek to stop the smile.

He's already made me laugh more this morning than I have all month.

Because of him, I woke up this morning looking forward to the day. It's been a long time since I did that. Most days, it's more determination than anticipation that's gotten me out of bed in the morning. I'm honest enough to admit to myself that it's because of Sean. Because of the way he makes me feel. I know a young gorgeous guy like him isn't going to stick around, let alone sleep with me, but damn it feels good to even feel that ball-tightening surge of desire.

When I saw him on the stairs last night wearing nothing but that towel, I felt like someone had punched me in the gut. In a good way. Despite my dirty imaginings, I was not prepared for the reality of a half-naked Sean.

Elegant. He's elegant like a statue. Flawless golden skin over a hairless chest, his nipples small and dark. The small hollows above the wings of his collarbones beg to be touched, and my mouth would fit perfectly against the curve from neck to shoulder. I could circle his delicate wrist with my fingers.

And then he winked, blushing afterward as if he couldn't believe he'd done it. I'd almost laughed, not because he was ridiculous, but because he was adorable. He'll be beating the college boys off with a stick. Probably some of the professors, as well. I hate the idea of some older guy creeping on him, taking advantage of his youth and innocence. I wonder how pissed off he'll be if I try to talk to him about it. Probably very. Maybe I'll find a way to bring it up indirectly.

Of course, at the moment, I'm the only older guy creeping on him, even if it's only a fantasy.

No matter how I keep telling myself it's wrong to be lusting after Sean, I can't help thinking that it feels damn good just to feel this level of desire again.

For a long time after the accident, sex wasn't even in the top ten of things I worried about. Everything happened so fast. First thing I remember after the vehicle tipped over in what felt like slow-motion was waking up in a hospital in Germany wondering why I couldn't feel my legs.

Once the initial shock wore off, I was too busy healing to worry about my libido. Then there I was, in rehab in Boston, looking at a hideous stump where my lower leg used to be and completely dependent on the kindness of strangers to do even the most basic tasks of life.

Between the depression, the drugs I was taking to counter the depression, and dealing with the loss of a limb, it's not too surprising I wasn't interested in sex for a while. Honestly, despite the various physical and mental health therapists assuring me I could and would have a healthy sex drive again, I'd thought it was gone forever.

This morning, my dick assured me it was not.

I decided not to take care of it, choosing instead to enjoy the feeling of desire. Now that I'm closed into a truck cab with barely a foot between us, I'm thinking that might have not been the best decision. Sean smells amazing, and that connection between us buzzes stronger than ever.

I haven't been a virgin since I was sixteen. There have been plenty of men I've been attracted to. Even thought I was in love once. But I've never felt anything like this before.

Dr. Moore clears his throat pointedly.

"Sorry," I say into the phone. "How is she?"

"The good news is the dog is stable and in good shape for a stray. The bad news is that we couldn't save her leg," he says.

"What do you mean?" Sean asks.

From the way that leg had looked last night, I'm not surprised. "It means they had to amputate," I explain.

Sean flinches. "Oh, poor baby."

"It's not that bad," I say at the same time as Dr. Moore says, "She'll be fine. She won't even notice."

"What's going to happen to her?" I ask.

"She's not chipped, so we can't locate an owner that way" Dr. Moore says. "I'll ask around, put up some notices and see if anyone claims her. She's young, maybe seven, eight months, and if she goes unclaimed, we'll try to find her a home. Since she's going to need extra care for a while, one of the techs will foster her. Truthfully, it's harder to find permanent homes for dogs like her."

"How about me?" I say, surprising myself as much as anyone else.

"Seriously?" Sean asks, eyes lighting up.

"Why not? I love dogs. Never had one of my own." A three-legged dog for a one-legged man. It's meant to be.

"I never had a dog either," Sean says wistfully.

"Well," the vet says cautiously, "It's not recommended to have a dog with medical issues for your first dog."

"Oh, I have experience managing medical issues," I say.

"Amputations can have a lot of complications," he warns. "I'm not so sure."

The eyes Sean turn on me look remarkably like the puppy's, wide and pleading, and I'm a sucker for them both. It does feel a little like the universe brought them into my life at the exact same moment. Maybe they were meant to be together.

Shit. Bad enough that I already feel as if the dog was meant to be mine, now I'll have to live with Sean's disappointment if we don't get her. "I'm familiar with the situation," I say, hoping my tone conveys how much I don't want to expand on that right now.

"Come by tomorrow and we can discuss it," the vet suggests. "We can see how the dog gets along with you."

"I'm on my way into town now," I say. "Any chance we could stop by today?"

"No problem," he says. "She's still groggy from the pain meds and anesthesia."

"Okay, doc. Call me if anything changes. Thank you."

"Will do." I hang up.

"That's good news about the dog," Sean says. "You really going to take her?"

"Why not?" I ask. "Any reason not to?"

"No," he says slowly. "But if you're trying to convince me to move out, getting a puppy is not the way to do it."

"So you're just using me for my dog?" I ask, risking a glance over at him.

"And your big," his eyes drop to my arms, "beachfront access."

His grin is addicting and I can't help smiling back. He might not know he's doing it, but Sean is flirting with me. I've gone to bed with people with less encouragement.

"That's why I got it," I say fluttering my eyelashes. "My beach-front brings all the boys to my yard."

His jaw drops and he bursts out with a laugh that hangs in the air. His expression shifts from admiring to assessing.

"What?"

He shrugs. "I don't know. You're just different than I expected you to be."

"How so?"

He doesn't answer. After a few moments of silence, I hand him my notebook. "Make a list of things we're going to need for Stumpy."

"Stumpy?"

"The dog."

He looks offended, jaw dropping and hand going to his chest. "You can't call her that!"

I laugh. "Sure I can."

"It's calling attention to her…her…"

I brace for him to say handicap or disability.

"Her uniqueness. She might be sensitive."

"She'll get over it. Eventually." My fingers flex around the steering wheel. "She has no choice," I say under my breath.

"How about Honey?" he suggests.

"Boring. Generic."

"Delilah?"

"Now you're reaching. I'm still thinking Stumpy."

"That's just wrong!" he says, laughing. "I'll come up with something perfect. Just give me time."

We throw names back and forth until we reach the hardware store.

This trip is more a scouting expedition than a shopping trip. I like to see my options next to each other. We leave without any flooring, but with a load of wood for the subflooring, a picnic table made of recycled tires that was on clearance, a handful of new tools, and a rented self-leveling rotary laser level.

"Ooh, fancy," Sean says loading the level into the back of the truck.

"How much building experience do you have?" I ask him. "Not that I'm not grateful for an extra pair of hands no matter what."

Sean slides the toolbox into the back. I'd gotten a second set of tools for him so we didn't have to fight over a hammer. "I've worked with Richie and his family since high school. They're contractors," he says. "You can call them if you want."

"It's not a job interview. So you can do most things?"

"I'm not going to be building anything by myself, but I'm a

great assistant. Not a fan of electrical work and plumbing," he says. "Or roofing."

"Why roofing? Not that I blame you. It's not my favorite either."

"I'm afraid of heights," he says, not the least embarrassed by that fact. "Ferris wheels. Cliffs. Even some bridges."

We climb into the truck and I check the time. Eleven thirty. "What do you say to running by the vet and checking on Stumpy and then grabbing an early lunch before heading home?" I ask.

"Sounds good," he replies. "Can we stop by a grocery store? Or I can go later by myself."

"There's one on the way home. What do you need?"

"I wanna pick up some tea and a few snacks, and I was thinking of making a pot of sauce and some meatballs? Would that be good?"

"What kind of monster turns down homemade meatballs and sauce?" I ask as I'm pulling out the parking lot. "But don't feel like you have to cook."

"I like cooking," he says. "I'm not bad at it, according to my grandma. It might be an Italian stereotype, but she's a genius in the kitchen. So is my Gigi."

"That's your great-grandmother, right?"

He hummed in response, fingers swiping his phone screen. "So is that a yes to the meatballs? We can make extra and freeze them."

"Hell, yeah, that's a yes," I assure him.

He finishes his texting and slides the phone into his pocket.

"How did you learn construction?" he asks. "I thought you were in the army."

"I learned in the army," I say. "Though I had a bit of experience before I joined up."

"Really?"

He sounds like he doesn't believe me. I'm used to that reaction. Most people have no idea what is involved in keeping a military force running. "Do you think it's all living in tents and driving around in tanks shooting people? It takes all kinds of jobs to make the army run. There are people whose entire job is managing laundry. I started in construction and masonry. We built a lot."

"Overseas?"

"Overseas and CONUS, continental U.S. I've built in all kinds of conditions, mountains, blizzards, deserts. Someone has to build all those bases."

"Dang. Not sure you even need me. I'm gonna have to cook a lot to pay my way," he says.

"Not that I'll say no to cooking, but you know some jobs require two people. And every job is easier with two people. Plus, like you pointed out, we're running out of summer."

It might not seem like it on this hot, bright summer day, but I know how quickly the weather can change. It's mid-August now, and we could have our first snowfall by mid-October. In between, of course, we'll have a beautiful fall if the weather holds.

"Did you ever date or anything? Like have a boyfriend?" Sean asks.

"Ever?" I ask, not following the topic change.

"I was thinking about what it would be like to be in the army and thought that it would be hard to date in the military with all the moving around and everything."

I shake my head. "Of course, you can date. Lots of men and women in the military are married, have kids, have families. I even know a few gay married couples."

His eyes widen.

"The thing civilians don't realize is that if you're not on a deployment, being in the military can be almost a nine to five job. I had weekends off, vacation days."

"Wow. Were you out in the military?"

"I didn't hide it, but I didn't go around introducing myself as 'gay Cooper' or anything like that. It was on a need-to-know basis."

"But if someone asked?"

"I wouldn't lie."

"Did you ever get shit for it?"

"Sometimes. I mean, the army is just people and some people are assholes. But most of the people I worked with were fine."

I think he says "so weird" under his breath.

"Did you have a boyfriend? Sean asks. "I mean if you want to talk about it. You don't have to. I get it."

"Get what?"

"If you don't want to talk about it."

I'm starting to think there is a lot going on in this kid's head and not all of it is good.

"About what, exactly?"

"About being gay." His voice drops on the word as if he's afraid to say it out loud.

Oh yeah, he has issues. I'm not unfamiliar with internalized homophobia. It's a tough thing to work through. Being ashamed of who you are, is no way to go through life.

I pick my next words carefully. "Listen, if you were talking to a friend, say Richie, and you asked him what girlfriends he'd had or if he was dating, would you consider that being him talking about being straight?"

"No. I mean, that's just...living. You don't have to talk about being straight. It just is."

"That's my point."

Sean contemplates my words, a faint understanding shimmering in his eyes.

I take pity on him. "In answer to your question, I dated a couple of people. Had a few relationships, but nothing too serious. Fort Drum isn't exactly a hot spot for singles. Most of the population is families. But Syracuse was an hour away and had a decent gay scene. I had a good time."

"Anybody now?"

I'm only half paying attention. It's a gorgeous Saturday in Burlington and parking spots are hard to come by. The streets are full of cars and pedestrians and I decide to try my luck at a parking garage a few blocks away. Slowly, I make my way through the crowded streets.

"No. Not in the market now," I answer as I brake sharply to avoid a pair of teenagers who have stepped out between two parked cars. "I have a house to fix up. Not interested in dating right now." That's the truth.

"So, no dating," Sean says. "Grindr, then? Perfect for all your no-strings attached hookup needs. I mean, I hear that's what most guys like to do."

There's a weird tone to his voice. Granted, I barely know the man, but I know what false bravado sounds like. The way he's twisting his phone in his hands betrays his nerves. I park the truck before answering. Turning to face him, I ask, "Is that what *you* like to do?"

Man, do I get a deer in the headlights look in return. Yeah, I didn't think so.

SEAN

I open my mouth and the most embarrassing sound I ever remember making comes out. Somewhere between a squawk and a bray. Sexy. "No. God no." I can feel my blush. Fuck. Why am I so awkward? "No. I mean I just got here."

"Back home?"

"God no. What if someone recognized me? No. I never..." I swear my face is going to be stuck on perma-blush.

My desire to have Cooper respect me, and keep looking at me like I'm someone worth looking at, is as strong as, yet sadly diametrically opposed to, my need to get some answers to the questions that have been building in my very soul since I first realized I liked boys the way I was supposed to like girls.

All my knowledge is theoretical. Information I've gleaned from the few and Reddit threads and articles on the internet I was brave enough to read. Before everything, I was too scared to look up anything much online. I couldn't chance leaving something incriminating on my phone or my computer at home, and I certainly wasn't going to use the computers at the public library or, God forbid, the school. After everything, I couldn't bring myself to look.

I'm twenty-three and I've never even been to a gay bar or a

Pride parade. Until I met Cooper, there's never been anyone I felt safe asking.

I need him to teach me everything. The things about dating and relationships that straight people seem to know from birth.

Like, how do you know if someone's interested in you? What do I do if they are and I'm interested in them, too? What if I'm not interested? How do you let someone know you like them? How do you ask someone on a date? When do you try to kiss them?

Then there are the questions specific to dating while gay. How am I supposed to treat another guy if we're dating? Who does the asking? Who pays? Do guys expect sex on the first date? How am I supposed to know who it's safe to talk to? Is there some secret handshake? Some kind of sign to look for, or do I just have to risk an ass-kicking every time I try to get a date? Is it hard to be out? Does being gay make him feel different? Would he change it if he could?

Is it worth it?

I gather my courage. "Can I ask you a question? Well, a bunch of questions to be honest."

"Of course," he says. "I don't promise to answer though, if it's personal."

"It's not personal. It's more general. About being gay and," I clear my suddenly thick throat and look down at my hands, "how to do it."

"How to be gay?" he asks with a puzzled expression.

I nod.

He opens and closes his mouth a few times as if he's second-guessing his answer before saying, "That's like asking how do you be human."

Sometimes I think I'm not sure I know how to do that, either.

I let my head drop against the window, not quite banging it, but close. God, I must sound like the biggest idiot on the planet. Some kind of poet I'll be if I can't say what I mean even in simple words. "I mean with like dating. And meeting people. Guys.

Men." No. I can't do this. My breath fogs the glass and I trace a spiral in the condensation with my fingertip.

Cooper makes a *go on* motion.

"Give me a second," I snap. "Please," I add when he gives me a level stare. "Sorry."

He raises his eyebrows but nods and turns his attention back to the road.

I take a deep breath. I *can* do this. If I don't figure out how to live as an out gay man, I let *them* win. I let my father win and I will die before I do that. *C'mon, Sean, no one has ever actually died of embarrassment, and did you actually think you had a shot with Cooper anyway?*

The leather seat creaks as I shift to face Cooper, my arm thrown over the seat back. "Okay. So. In, um, popular media…"

"Always a good source of information," he says, voice as dry as a desert.

"Please don't make this harder for me than it already is," I ask, proud of how steady my voice is. "I'm trying not to sound like an idiot. I know I'm ignorant about a lot of things. It's not like I have a lot of real life examples."

He flinches as if I'd hit him. "I'm sorry, Sean." We're at a stoplight, so he turns to face me, laying his hand on top of mine. "And not knowing something doesn't make you an idiot. How do we learn things if not by asking?"

The light turns green. Thank God. Talking to him is so much easier when he's not looking at me. "Gay men…" What's the least offensive way to ask this?

"On TV," Cooper prompts.

"You've been to clubs, right? Like gay clubs?" I try not to whisper the question as if my mother can somehow hear me.

"Yes," he says, not giving me anything.

"So, do people, guys, men, do they, like, actually hook up in the bathroom? Like, do things with strangers?" Now that I'm asking I can't remember how, exactly, I came to this assumption. Too much *Queer as Folk*? I had pirated both the US and UK versions as an oversexed, confused teen, watching them on my laptop the precious few times I had total privacy and ending up even more confused and sexually frustrated.

"It's been known to happen," he says, trying to hold back a grin at my naiveté.

Oh wow. Part of me had assumed that was something that only happened on television. I've been okay with fantasizing because it wasn't real, wasn't ever going to be real. Now that I know it's something that I might could do one night, it feels dirty. As much as it turns me on, it's equally embarrassing. Even thinking about it makes me feel like I'm the worst stereotype of a gay man. We're slutty, spread diseases, do drugs, and are doomed to die young and alone.

"Have you," I suck up my courage, "have you ever done that?"

A weighted silence builds while he considers his answer. I can almost feel him getting lost in his memories. I hate asking. It's embarrassing for both of us. But for some reason I can't quite articulate, knowing if he did or not feels like a matter of life or death.

"I have," he finally says, running his palm over the bumps of the steering wheel. "Not often. And not in, God, ten years?"

Wow. Okay. Something inside me relaxes as my brain does some moral recalculating. Cooper is a good man, I know he is. Troy trusts him. He had anonymous sex with someone in a bathroom, therefore, sex with anonymous people in a bathroom is something a good person could do. If it were the kind of thing this theoretical person might want to do.

This theoretical person might possibly even do that kind of thing with Cooper himself.

Every drop of moisture leaves my mouth, as I get an immediate vision of Cooper slamming me against the door of a toilet stall in some club. The floor beneath our feet vibrates with the bass from the music. A mere half-inch of steel is the only thing separating us from the other men in the bathroom. They can't see us, but they can hear us, and they know *exactly* what we're doing.

Shit. I cross my legs and shift away from Cooper. That's something I'll be revisiting alone in my room tonight. Maybe more than once.

"Did you like it?" I croak through a dry throat. Oh, God. I can't believe I had the nerve to ask him that. I can't even look at him.

To my surprise, he laughs. I risk a glance. He's got a small smile on his face and his expression is distant, like he's remembering something very good. "Yeah, I did. I liked it a lot sometimes." His eyes cut to mine. "Is that a problem?"

"No. God. No." I clear my throat. "How…what does it…how does it…" I can't even begin to form a coherent sentence.

Somehow, he understands what I can't ask. There's a heat in his eyes as he slides his gaze down my body before turning back to face the road.

Can he tell I'm hard? I hope not. Or maybe I hope he can?

"You know how it is. Some nights it's exactly what you need," he says, his voice dropping into something deep and rough, like he's turned on just remembering. "You're young, dressed to kill, and three drinks into the night."

The way his tongue darts out to wet his lips doesn't help my growing erection situation. I can't look away from him.

"The whole place smells like sweat and sex and you're feeling free and wild. The music beats through you like a heartbeat." He gently touches his fist to his chest, and I'm mesmerized. "Then the guy who's been eye-fucking you all night drags you to the packed dance floor."

Though I'm so hard it hurts, my dick trapped behind the inseam of my jeans and my thigh, I don't move. I don't even breathe, afraid the slightest noise will stop him. I might die if he does. I might come if he doesn't.

"You don't even know his name, but you've got him by the hips, and he's grinding up against you." His fingers flex around the steering wheel one at a time like he's got some anonymous man's body beneath his hands. "Then someone else presses against your back, or maybe sandwiches the first guy between you, staring right in your eyes as he slides his hands over your ass."

A pathetic whimper escapes from between my clenched teeth.

The truck engine revs as it surges forward, Cooper's foot heavy on the accelerator. My shoulder hits the back of the seat and I catch myself with a hand on the dashboard as he hits the brakes equally hard. My cock jumps at the sudden shifts of pressure and I squeeze my thighs together not sure if it's helping or making it worse.

Cooper clears his throat as he turns off the engine. "So. Yeah. That's how. That's how you end up hooking up in the bathroom of a club."

8

COOPER

Well, that was completely inappropriate. *Fuck.* Discussing the pros and cons of casual sex with a young guy trying to get a feel for the scene is one thing. Giving Sean a borderline pornographic play-by-play of what it can feel like is another, totally different, thing.

What was I thinking?

I turn into the parking garage. The machine at the gate spits out a ticket. Automatically, I take it, sticking it to the paperclip on my visor I keep just for that purpose. Now comes the slow winding hunt up the levels for a parking spot. If I'm lucky, I'll catch someone as they're pulling out.

Stop lying to yourself, you know damn well what you were thinking.

What I was thinking was how good it would feel to have Sean pressed up against a wall. Going by the bulge in his jeans, Sean was having similar thoughts. As hard as he tried to hide, that's how hard I tried to ignore it. Neither of us was very successful.

If there's a patron saint of poor decisions, and there really should be, maybe they'll intercede and Sean will let the topic die.

"Isn't that kind of, well, slutty?" he asks.

Guess there isn't.

What the fuck? While I struggle to formulate a response that isn't *fuck you*, the reverse lights of a minivan a few spots up the aisle turn on. Putting the truck in park, I hit my turn signal to keep assholes from trying to jump my spot and wait for it to pull out.

"Not that I'm calling you a slut. Or, or, that there is anything wrong with… being slutty?" His words tumble over each other in his rush to get them out.

The worst part is I think he means it. Sean thinks hooking up is something to be ashamed of. Something I, specifically, should be ashamed of. The van backs out of the spot, and I pull in.

"Cooper, I—"

"Come on," I bark, not checking to see if he is following.

I hear his footsteps as he jogs to catch up to me. He grabs my arm. "Hey."

I stop walking and turn to face him, looking pointedly at where his hand rests on my arm.

He drops it in a flash. "I'm sorry," he says, desperation clear in his voice. "Really sorry. Everything's coming out all wrong. It's just…gah." He runs his hands through his hair, making the thick waves stick up in all directions. "I didn't mean it like that." He winces as he tugs his own hair hard enough to hurt.

Jesus. What am I going to do with this kid? He's giving me emotional whiplash. One second he's half-naked and winking at me, the next he's calling me a slut. His remorse seems genuine, though, distress clear in his face.

His hair is soft and sleek when I reach up and untangle his fingers from his hair. "Don't hurt yourself." My thumb brushes around the curve of his ear as I tug his hand down.

Our bodies, our mouths, are inches apart, our fingers tangled together. The pink flush in the hollow of his throat spreads slowly up his neck as I stare at him, trying to get a read on him. He's almost as tall as I am. If either one of us leans forward even an inch, we'll be kissing.

A car creeps slowly past us, trailing an upbeat pop song in its wake.

In Sean's eyes, I see the same pain that was there last night. He's not trying to hurt me. Somewhere deep inside, he's hurt and he's trying to figure out how to make it stop. My heart aches for him.

I blink, breaking the connection between us and he looks away. "I'm getting the feeling there's a lot you want to know."

"So much." His voice wobbles between laughter and tears. "I really am sorry. I'm not judging you, I swear. I don't even know what I'm trying to say. I'm supposed to be better than this with words."

"It's okay." And it is. I'm not angry with him.

"We're good? For now, at least?"

"We're good," I assure him. "I think I see where you're coming from, but let's talk somewhere we're less likely to get hit by a car, okay?"

The side-grin doesn't chase all the darkness away, but it's a start. I start walking, jerking my head for him to follow.

"Where are we going?" he asks.

"Vet first. Then a snack and a drink, if you want. You are old enough to drink, right? We could get milkshakes instead."

That pulls a laugh out of him. He shoves my back. "Shut up. You know I am, old man. I could use a drink. Or two. Be my DD?"

"Just this once," I answer. Maybe a drink will help him figure out what it is he actually wants to ask me.

The vet's office is a few blocks down from the parking garage, and a few minutes of sunshine on my skin chases away the last of my bad mood.

Beside me, Sean quietly soaks up the scene.

On a beautiful summer weekend, Burlington is like something out of a storybook. Closed to vehicle traffic, Church Street is lined with one quaint store after another. Families and groups of teens stroll down the street and fill the café tables set up outside the many restaurants and cafes.

We stop at the Cherry Street Veterinary Clinic and Groom Room first. The strikingly handsome man at the front desk smiles as we come in. "Boys, so nice to see you again!"

"We're here to check on the dog," I tell him. "Dr. Moore said it was okay."

"Sure. Have a seat and I'll let him know you're here and see if we can find someone to take you back."

"Thank you."

Sean leans in close to me. "The guy at the desk, he's the one from last night, right? Do you think he and the vet are a couple?"

"He did kiss him and call him babe, so they aren't strangers."

"Cool."

After a few minutes of flipping through *Cat Fancy* magazine and discussing the merits of various cat breeds based solely on the photographs, Tai calls for us to follow him.

The puppy sleeps on a soft pad in a crate that looks large enough for her to stand up in, but not much more. Cleaned up and dry, her thick wavy fur is almost the same mahogany color as Sean's hair. She's been shaved at the back and where her damaged back leg used to be is nothing but a thick wrap of bandages.

"She's so cute," Sean says, leaning down to stick his fingers into the waist-level cage. "Oh. Is this okay?"

"Sure, just for a second though," he cautions. "She's still pretty out of it. We just finished the surgery an hour ago."

"Hi girl," Sean says, gently stroking a fingertip down her muzzle. One eyelid flutters open.

From the look in her eyes, I can tell she's on the good painkillers. Her tail thumps twice softly and she licks Sean's fingers before closing her eyes again.

"Poor baby," Sean says in that soft accent of his.

"She's going to be just fine," Dr. Moore assures us as he comes over. "Are you still interested in taking her home?"

"I am." There's no way I can leave her.

"He wants to call her Stumpy!" Sean says, straightening up and glaring at me in mock offense.

Dr. Moore laughs. "I think it's a perfect name." He hands me the Dew-Over T-shirt Dewey had given me. "If you leave me your email, I'll send you some information on what to expect. And we'll go over it in person before you pick her up. It's going to be a rough first few weeks," he cautions.

"Oh, I know," I say. Before I follow him, I reach into the crate and stroke her fur. "It'll be okay. How long does she have to stay here until we can pick her up?"

"A day or so," Dr. Moore answers. "I'll call the day before we release her, give you a heads-up."

"Thank you for taking care of her," Sean says. "I felt awful, seeing her lying there. And thinking, well, you know. The worst."

"Are you sure we can't pay?" I ask, mentally checking my bank balance.

"No it's covered, but should you want to make a donation to the emergency fund, I won't say no."

"I will."

"Where to next?" Sean asks when we go back outside.

"Snack and a drink?"

"Sounds like a plan. Do you have any place in particular in mind?"

"I do. Follow me."

9

SEAN

Cooper walks slowly down the sidewalk in front of me. I can't help but notice he has a slight limp. I wonder if it's service-related. For all I know, he twisted his ankle last week.

The scent from a bakery called the Maple Factory draws me like a moth to a flame. Breakfast seems a long time ago. My steps slow and I must make some kind of sound because Cooper laughs. "Hungry?"

"It smells so good," I say. "Can we stop?" I give him what Mom calls my puppy eyes.

"Don't give me those eyes," he says. "I'm immune."

I clasp my hands together at my chest and bat my eyelashes. "Please, Cooper? Please can we get some maple-flavored deliciousness? It's my first full day in Vermont."

"You know you don't have to ask me, right?" Cooper says with a warm smile that makes my heart flutter. "You can just tell me you're going to get some."

"But where's the fun in that?" I ask, putting a hand on his arm and drawing him gently toward the door. "I'll buy you a donut."

"Whoopie pie," he says.

"What?"

Inside, the smell is even more heavenly.

"Whoopie pie," Cooper says, pointing at the display case.

"Oh, a gob. My favorite."

"His, too," the girl behind the counter says tilting her head at Cooper. "Hi, Mr. Hill. The usual?"

"Oh, the usual?" I ask.

"I got them twice," he says. "Maybe three times," he admits. "And how do you know my name?"

"I have an excellent memory, and that's the name on your debit card. So unless that's not your card..." She gives him a pointed look.

"It's my card, I promise!" he says.

"And you've been in three weeks in a row, same time, same day of the week," the girl says. "Around here, that makes you a regular with a usual. Coffee today, too?"

"Busted," I say.

He rolls his eyes. "Fine. Yes, the usual, please, Jinn. And no on the coffee. We're headed to V and V."

"Make it two of the usual," I say. "And put it on my debit card."

"You don't even know what it is."

I give an exaggerated look around the store. "I'm sure I won't hate whatever it is."

It turns out to be maple-flavored whoopie pies, which taste as amazing as they sound. I take a bite as soon as Jinn hands me the bag.

"Wait two seconds," Cooper says. "You can eat it next door."

Next door turns out to be a combination bookstore and wine bar. A neon sign on the red brick building reads Vino and Veritas. I'm impressed by the rainbow flags in the windows on both sides.

"Ooh, bookstore," I say, shoving the whoopie pie back in the bag. "Can we?" I lick the sticky mapley sugar residue off my fingers

"Don't have to ask," Cooper reminds me, eyes locked on my fingers.

My heart speeds up as I pull my finger slowly out of my mouth like I know what I'm doing. God, I almost fucked up everything back there in the truck. I'd called him a slut. I'm lucky he's still speaking to me. I can't barely tell up from down when I'm around him. How am I supposed to figure out what that look means?

It hits me again how we're going to be around each other almost twenty-four-seven for the next few weeks. Good Lord. I'm not sure I'll survive. The revelation stops me with a hand on the door. Cooper's light touch on the small of my back jolts me into action.

Inside the small vestibule, a door to the right leads into the bookstore, the one on the left opens to the bar. "I can meet you on the other side if you want."

"I could use a new book or two," he says.

There's a window display of more books about chickens and chicken husbandry than I knew existed. "Ever think of keeping chickens?" I ask Cooper as we go in, the bell over the door ringing to announce us.

"I've considered it," he says to my surprise. "Be nice to have the eggs, but I don't know where to start. Do they needed heated coops in the winter?"

"Hey, chicken Coop. Cooper. Is there a connection?" I ask.

"Nope," someone says from behind me. The voice sounds like it belongs to an older woman. What I don't expect to see when I turn around is the oldest and shortest person I've ever seen in real life. From the top of her dandelion-fluff hair to the tip of her checkered Vans, she can't be more than five foot tall. She's wearing baggy jeans rolled at the cuff and a red plaid shirt buttoned from top to bottom. Pale blue eyes sparkle from a network of wrinkles. Even her hands are wrinkled.

"Hello," I say to her, with a surreptitious glance at Cooper in case this is someone he knows. His small shrug says it's not.

"Cooper comes from the word for a person who makes barrels and buckets and the like," she tells me. "It comes from the middle Dutch or middle low German *kūper* and from *kūpe*, cask, which in turn comes from the Latin *cupa 'tun*, or barrel."

Cooper and I exchange glances. "I didn't know that."

She points a finger at Cooper. "Now coop, as in where a chicken lives, come from the old English word *cype*, meaning a small structure for confining birds."

"Good to know," I say.

"Impressive," Cooper says.

"I used to be a linguistics professor," she says. "Now if you boys need any chicken info, young Harrison's husband Finn over at Puddlebrook Farms is the man to ask. Good-looking man, too," she adds.

"Who's Harrison?" I ask.

"The man who owns this whole place," she says, her completely white eyebrows rising to her forehead.

"I'm new in town," I explain. "Just got here yesterday."

She gives me a big smile. "Well, welcome to Burlington. You're starting off right." She nods at the bakery bag clutched in my hand.

The bookstore is warm and welcoming, with dark wood and soft music. The lighting is bright enough to see by but not garish. There are people sitting on the couches and the children's section is obviously popular.

"I'm going to check out the mysteries," Cooper says.

"Pick something good so I can borrow it," I tell him.

On the way to the register, a display of books stops me in my tracks. Holy shi…crap. Is that two guys? Two guys wrapped up in each other and almost kissing?

Wild horses can't keep me away. Oh, it definitely is. I shove my hands in my pockets and try to look casual as I sneak looks at the covers, which I'm sure makes me look like I'm casing the joint. *Damn.* There certainly is a wide variety of main characters to choose from. Firefighters and spies and tattoo artists, oh my. The titles aren't subtle either. *How to Bang a Billionaire*? Okay.

Jesus. Shouldn't these be behind a curtain or something? There are kids in this store.

One book cover is a man by himself. He's wearing a snazzy suit and he's looking directly at me. Those are some intense eyes. His smile makes him look like he has a good secret he's dying to tell me. I can see myself hanging out with him.

As I'm reaching for the book, a real live guy about my age catches my eye and smiles. I shove my hand back in my pocket and try to pretend like I wasn't just ogling the half-naked men on the covers. He seems to take that as an invitation to come over.

"Hi, I'm Briar," he says. "Can I help you find something?" Briar has pretty hazel eyes, dirty blond hair under a beanie despite the heat, something I've seen more than once today, and a nice dusting of scruff that I'm instantly jealous of. I can go five days without shaving and still have less facial hair then some twelve-year-olds.

Somehow he hones in on the book that's caught my eye. "Oh, do you like Alyssa Samuel? This one," he scans the display and picks up a different book with a much racier cover, "is one of my favorites."

I take it, because what else do you do when someone shoves a book at you? I take a quick look, registering the title, *Lost Key*, and the hot shirtless guys on the cover before hiding it against my chest. "I don't...I never read...her. Any..."

The gleam of excitement on his handsome face is killing me. He wants me to look at the book and like it and talk to him about it. I feel like if I don't, I'll be letting him down. And I can't do that to Briar. *Look at him. He's cute.*

Once again cursing my propensity for blushing, I force myself to read the back copy and then flip through the pages. The word cock practically leaps off the page and smacks me in the face. What the actual hell? I read closer. *When his mouth sank down the length of my cock without*...holy shit. I slam the book shut before my own cock can get any more ideas. They really keep these books right out in the open?

"Are you local?" he asks.

I nod.

"If you like romances, you should check out the Booklover Club. We meet every other Saturday at eleven."

"Do you go?" I ask him.

He smiles, which makes him even cuter. "It was my idea."

"And you read books like this?" In public. And discuss them.

"Sometimes. We read anything as long as it fits the definition of romance."

"Which is?" I can't help asking, even though I'm getting antsy standing here. I feel like there's a spotlight on me and a look on my face that screams I'm holding a book with graphic gay sex scenes.

"Has to have a happy ever after ending. Or at least happy for now."

I snort.

"Don't believe in happy ever after?" Briar asks.

"I want to," I admit.

"Don't we all? You should come." He leans in closer. "I met my boyfriend there."

"Lucky," I say.

Briar puts his hands in his pockets and smiles. "I can't promise the same results, but it's a good group."

Cooper comes up and looks over my shoulder. "What did you find?" he asks, glancing at the book in my hand before I can hide it. "Pretty sure that's not poetry," he says with a grin.

"No. Uh, Briar here suggested it. Says they have a book club."

Cooper flips through the pages. "Looks good." His eyebrows flick up and back down. "Hot. Can I borrow it when you're done?"

"Sure," I say. *Toto, I have a feeling we're not in Kansas anymore.*

"Ready for that drink and to finish our conversation?" Cooper asks.

"Sure." Which is only half of a lie. I'm not looking forward to the conversation but I could definitely use a drink or six.

"See you later?" Briar asks. "Maybe at book club?"

"Book club? Sounds perfect. He'll be back," Cooper promises for me.

Feeling more awkward than usual, I wave goodbye to Briar as I follow Cooper to the register.

The Vino part of Vino and Veritas is even more welcoming and comforting than the bookstore, with dark wood and leather. The music is loud enough to be heard but not intrusive. There's a curved bar to the right of the entrance, and booths along the wall with windows that look out onto Church Street. There's a small stage in the far corner and tables in the middle of the room. I don't recognize the music, but it's smooth and comforting. The whole place looks like what drinking a glass of whiskey feels like.

"Booth or table?" Cooper asks. "Or do you want to sit at the bar?"

"Booth, please. It feels weird to be sitting in the middle of the room."

"Plus it's fun to people watch out the windows," he says.

"Exactly."

The bartender introduces himself as Auden and tells us to sit anywhere.

A minute later, a curly-haired woman around my age wearing a Vino and Veritas apron comes to take our orders. "Hi boys," she says, handing us menus. "Can I start you with something to drink? Oh, hey, it's you," she says to Cooper before I can answer. "You're the guy who plays the twelve-string at open mic nights."

"That's me. Cooper," he says. "And you're Molly. The one with the beautiful voice."

"You're not so bad yourself," she says. "And those songs you play with no vocals, do you write them?" she asks.

"I do," he admits, and I add another item to my list of *Things Cooper Does That Turn Me On*. (Yes, it's an actual list in my notebook. The first two items on it are *Existing* and *Looking at Me Like That*, respectively.)

"We should totally team up one night," she says, clapping her hands. "I can play, but you know how some people need their hands to talk? I need mine to sing. I'm so much better handsfree!"

"Really?" Cooper asks.

"Really. I'll show you one night."

"No, I mean you'd want me to play while you sing?"

"Totally! You're so good." She turns to me. "Tell him how good he is."

"I didn't even know he played the guitar," I tell her.

"I play at open mic nights," Cooper explains. "I love writing songs. My music is never going to be on the radio, but I write it for me and whoever wants to listen to it."

"It's a gift," I tell him. "It's a gift from you to the world."

"Wow," Molly says. "That was beautiful."

"Yes, it was," Cooper says, looking directly at me in a way that makes my heart flutter.

Molly's eyes open wide. "Oh my God. Is this your first date?" Her voice drops. "Is this a blind date?"

Cooper looks a little stunned and I laugh. At him, at her question, at this whole situation. The last two days have gone nothing like I expected. Later I'll mourn for the time I wasted back home when this whole world was sitting here, waiting for me to grab it, but right now, I'm going to enjoy the hell out of finally being someplace where I can be myself.

"Kind of," I say. "My uncle is a friend of Cooper's. He set us up. My name is Sean Johnson. I'm going to school here and I needed a place to stay. Cooper needed some help on the fixerupper he bought, so it was a win-win."

"Perfect!" Molly claps her hands. "Do you play guitar, too?"

"No, ma'am. I have no musical ability, much to my dismay. I

do write poetry, though," I tell her with a shy smile. I have a feeling that is not going to get me laughed at the way it did back home either.

"Poetry?" Cooper asks. "I can see it," he says when I nod.

"Oh, your accent is so cute," she says. "Not as sexy as Jax's but he's British, so, you know." She shrugs at the universal truth that British accents are at the top of the sexy pyramid. "We do poetry at open mic nights, too. You should check the sign-up sheet."

I can see the bar is getting busier and am going to suggest we order when Molly barges ahead again. "Are you single?" she asks.

"Which one of us?"

"Both of you."

"Single and ready to mingle," I say. Cooper looks skeptical. Smart man. I don't believe me either. But I have to start somewhere and I'm tired of being scared.

"You should date each other," Molly says.

"I'm too old for him," Cooper tells her.

Molly and I make simultaneous scoffing noises. She looks me over and raises one eyebrow as if to ask my opinion on the age gap.

I shrug, hoping it conveys that it's Cooper's problem, not mine.

She nods and then says extra perkily, "Well, if that's the case, I'm sure I know someone I can set you up with. What are you looking for? Guy? Girl? Neither? Either?"

"Wow, this really is a full-service bar," I say. "And I'd love to meet a nice guy."

"I'll see what I can do," she says.

Cooper's grumpy face makes a return appearance, and I'm going to pretend it's because he's not a fan of the idea. "Open mic same day, same time, as usual, Molly?" he asks like a man desperate to change the topic.

Pretending to scratch her forehead, Molly shields her face from Cooper and gives me a wink. Oh, yeah. She got my message.

"Same time," she assures Cooper. "So. Boys. What can I start you off with?"

"I'll have a cider and an order of the maple-glazed sausages," Cooper says.

"Excellent choice," she says. "And you?"

"Cider? Is this local hard apple cider?" I ask. She nods. "Then I'll have that, too. I'm doing the Burlington immersion experience today."

"You want some fries with that?" she asks. "They're hand-cut."

"Sure, why not?" Fries and whoopie pies for lunch. Just what the doctor ordered.

COOPER

Sean collapses against the bench after Molly leaves. "Did I sound okay?" He glances around the bar to make sure no one is paying any attention to us and he leans forward conspiratorially, "Or did I sound like this was my first time in a gay bar?"

This is part of the Sean Johnson whiplash experience.

Sometimes he sounds like a grown man and sometimes he sounds like a kid who laughs nervously every time he hears the word breasts.

"First of all, it's not a gay bar. It's just a bar that makes a point of being welcoming and inclusive to people of all races, sexes, genders, and gender expressions. Got it?"

He nods quickly. "I wasn't trying to be offensive, I swear."

"I know. And everybody has their first time doing everything. No one's going to mock you for it. No strangers anyway," I add with a smile. "I reserve the right to gently poke fun at you for certain things."

I can already tell Sean walks through the world imaging everyone's eyes on him. Judging him on what he says, how he says it, how he looks, and what he does. It must be exhausting.

Hell, I know it's exhausting. Maybe I can help him with that, help him get more comfortable in his own skin.

"Are you going to take Molly up on her offer?" I ask as if I don't care. He should let Molly fix him up. She's close to his age, I bet they'll get along great.

"Her offer to set me up with someone or to sign up for open mic night?"

"Both, actually."

"Blind dates, no. Open mic night..." His nose wrinkles adorably as he considers it. I resist the urge to run my finger down it. "I'm not so sure I'm ready for that, either."

"I didn't know you were a poet," I say. Why is that so sexy?

"What? You don't know everything about me after our," he mimes checking a watch he isn't wearing, "less than twenty-four hours together?"

I could remind him that he knows some damn personal information about me if only to see that sweet pink blush on his cheeks again, but I refrain. Because I am an adult. An adult who hasn't thought about sex in the last few months as often as I have in these less than twenty-four hours.

"I'm not," he says. "Well. Kind of," he amends quickly. "Someday, I hope to be. I write some, but it's not very good. I'll get better though."

"I bet you will. I bet you can do anything you set your mind to."

He frowns, running his finger across the tabletop. "Not anything."

I take the opening. "Does this have something to do with those questions you were wanting to ask me?" There's obviously so much he doesn't know about living as a gay man. Is it wrong that I want to be the one to show him how it can be?

"Oh, sweet baby Jesus," he whispers. "I was hoping you'd forget. Sure you don't want something harder than cider? Tequila? Whiskey? How much would you have to drink to forget what I said? I can drive home."

"More than I feel like drinking today, and not in your dreams," I tell him. I shift in the booth until my back is against the wall and rest my left leg on the seat. I know it's rude, but it's hot today and between the jeans, the socks, and the protective sleeve, my stump is sweating like crazy. The prosthesis is feeling a little loose. I'll have to adjust it before we leave.

"Seriously, you don't have to," I assure Sean. "But it would make me happy to help you with something that's bothering you."

"Last night, I was worried I wouldn't be able to recognize you at the diner, and now I'm asking personal questions about your sex life." He covers his face with his hand, elbow on the table.

"Some things are easier to talk about with a stranger."

Sean shakes his head. "You don't feel like a stranger. Feels like I've known you for a long time. Is that weird?"

"If it is, I'm weird, too, because I feel the same way. Maybe we were friends in a previous life," I say.

Sean rubs his chest with his fist. "It's like I have a million questions inside me that never had an outlet before. And now, now that I know about you. That you're gay, I kind of want to vomit them all out at once."

"Nice image," I say with a quirk of my mouth.

"Maybe it's stupid," he continues as if I hadn't interrupted, "but I already trust you. I know you won't laugh at me. In a mean way."

"I would never," I promise. "Even if you were a total stranger I knew I'd never see again. But you're not, Sean. You're family of a man I like very much, and someone I would like to be friends with."

I swear his smile lights up the bar. "Yeah? Really? You want to be my friend?"

I roll my eyes. "You make it sound like we just met on the playground."

He reaches over and hooks our pinkies together. "Cooper, do you wanna be friends? Best friends?" He bats his eyes at me. "Please? Can we be BFFs?"

"I changed my mind," I say.

"Changed your mind about what?" Molly says. "Do you want something instead of the cider?" She's carrying a tray with two bottles and two frosted mugs on it.

"About being my BFF," Sean says.

"I doubt that," she says, serving us our drinks. "I have a feeling he's dying to be your friend." She places my mug and bottle on the table in front of me with a heavy thud. "Besides, you're a babe, with those eyes and that hair. I don't think you'll be *friendless* for very long if you don't want to be."

Got it. Message received, Molly.

"Fine. I'll take it under consideration," I tell Sean. "It depends on what you think of the cider."

He takes a sip, nods, and then takes another. Molly and I watch for his reaction.

"Oh, that's good," he says, taking another long pull. "Delicious. I'm going to need another one of those."

"I guess we can be friends," I say.

"I'll bring you another with your food," Molly tells him.

Sean nibbles on his whoopie pie as he drinks his cider. I can tell he's trying to organize his thoughts so I give him space. We're in no hurry. I wasn't expecting to get any repair work done today and I can think of much worse ways to kill time than sitting in a cozy, air-conditioned bar, sipping cider with Sean. That sounds like a song. Sipping cider with Sean.

"What?" Sean asks.

"What what?"

"You snorted," he says.

"Just laughing at some accidental alliteration going on in my head."

"Don't you hate it when that happens? Share with the class?"

"Sipping cider with Sean," I confess.

He nods approvingly. "I am so down with that." He finishes the last drop of his cider and sets the mug down firmly on the table. "Okay. I think I've managed to get a little handle on what's been going on in my head."

Now he sounds like adult Sean again. "What is it? Wait." I stop him before he can answer. "One second. You don't get a pass on the slutty comment."

"I know. I'm sorry. That was thoughtless and rude." There's a look of genuine remorse on his face. "As soon as I said it, I regretted it. I sounded like…well, let's just say I sounded like some people that I do not like very much and hope never to sound like again."

"Thank you. But just to be clear, judging people, men or women, gay or straight, by how many sexual partners they have or haven't had is meaningless. The important thing about a date, partner, or even bathroom hookup, is how they treat you and if you're both on the same page regarding what you're getting out of the relationship."

"No matter how fleeting," he says, fighting a grin.

"No matter how fleeting," I echo, fighting my own grin. "That said, hooking up is not mandatory. You don't have to do anything you don't want to."

"Feels that way."

"I guarantee you there are many guys who hook up indiscriminately. There are lots of men in long-term, committed relationships. Look at Troy and Dmitri."

"There has to be something between bathroom blowjobs and marriage," he sighs.

"Yes. It's called dating. What we were just talking about, remember? People do it all the time."

"But not you?"

"Not me *right now*," I clarify. "But I'd like to. In the future."

"Good to know," he says, picking up his mug and frowning when he finds it empty. "Do you want to get married? Have kids?"

"Why, Sean. This is so sudden. We've just met."

His eyes widen in surprise before he laughs loudly. "Jerk. You know what I mean. Do you want to get married and have kids with someone? Eventually."

"Yes. Eventually," I tell him. "I wouldn't mind a few kids."

My answer catches him by surprise. Is the idea of me being a father so unbelievable?

"I want that, too," he says with surprising certainty. He points his finger at me, cutting off the stupid question I was going to ask. "Yes, I'm sure. And no, I'm not too young to know. Half the kids I graduated high school with are already married with kids and no one says boo to them about being too young."

I hold up my hands in surrender. "You're right. I know. A lot of soldiers get married young, too."

He goes quiet again, rolling the empty glass between his palms. Sighing softly, he shifts in his seat, resting one elbow on the table and covering his mouth with his hand. There's a wary, yearning expression in his eyes, as if he wants something he isn't sure he can have.

"What?" I ask gently.

"People told me…I was taught, I couldn't have that if I kept on being gay," he says quietly. "Couldn't have a family of my own."

My heart breaks for him even as I'm flooded with an anger with no outlet. If I could, I'd track down those nameless people and beat the crap out of them. How dare they make him, and God knows how many other queer kids, think they deserve less than everything in life? How dare they make people believe the love they feel is only a hollow imitation of "real" heterosexual love?

The tragedy is that it's never just one person, one institution, no matter how homophobic. It's a thousand faceless voices. It's constant unfunny gay jokes from friends who don't see how an uttered "fag" or "queer" cuts deep into your soul and a little more joy seeps out through the wound.

It's the death of your very being by a million papercuts.

My leg drops to the ground with a thud as I turn to face him. Reaching across the table, I take both of his hands in mine and squeeze as if I can force my words through his skin. "You can one hundred percent be gay and have that."

He squeezes back, nodding silently.

When his grip loosens, I slide my hands off his and smile at him. "But maybe you should start with dating before you go shopping for cribs."

The laugh I surprise out of him is loud and long. A few smiling heads turn in our direction wanting to see what caused that joyous sound.

"Hold on, let me write that down." He pulls his notebook out of his pocket and writes HOW TO BE GAY across the top in block letters clear enough for me to read from across the table. Below that he writes #1 – Start with dating a man.

"That's a good place to start," Molly says from behind me. I didn't even hear her come up.

"Thanks," he tells her, both for the comment and the plate of pork deliciousness she sets on the table in front of him. "I'm a fast learner."

She puts the large plate of thick-cut fries in front of me. "I hear it's easier when you love what you're studying." She gives Sean a wink and another bottle of cider.

I wait until we're out of her line of sight to swap our plates.

"Those look good." Sean's gaze lingers longingly on the sumptuous sausages moving farther away from him. He turns his big baby blues on me, silently begging me to share my bounty.

"Immune, remember?" I shove an entire sausage into my mouth.

He gasps. Changing tactics, he leans forward, clasping his hands in front of his chest and batting his long, dark eyelashes. His eyes should be registered as weapons of my destruction. "Pretty please with sugar on top? Can I try your sausage, Cooper?"

A piece of bacon goes down the wrong pipe, and I cover my mouth as I try not to choke to death.

He blinks his bright blue eyes. "I'm talking about your delicious maple-bacon wrapped sausages, of course."

"Unbelievable," I mutter when I can breathe again. He smiles when I spear two sausages and drag his plate toward me. "Does that work every time?"

"I don't know what you're talking about," he says with a bright smile. "See? I knew you were my friend."

Keeping my expression blank, I slide a portion of his fries onto my plate in exchange. "You're welcome."

The moan he gives at his first bite of sausage, and the expression of bliss on his face goes directly to my groin.

"Oh my God." His expression is near orgasmic.

What I wouldn't give to see that look and hear that sound while I was giving him an actual orgasm.

"Those things are so freaking delicious they should be illegal." His second bite is accompanied by a second, less pornographic, moan. "I am seriously in love with all things maple-flavored."

"Welcome to Vermont. What do you think of it?"

There's pure happiness in his eyes when he smiles at me. "I love it."

I am in so much trouble.

COOPER

Later that night, Sean and I christen the picnic table with a meal of meatballs and beer while watching the sunset over the lake. The food is delicious, the sunset gorgeous, and the company completely captivating. "This is exactly what I imagined doing when I bought this place," I say.

"Eating meatballs with a stranger?" Sean asks.

"Having dinner with friends and watching the sunset from my own backyard."

"We're friends?" he asks.

"Best friends, remember?"

The grin he gives me is worth the price of the table, chairs, and the beer.

It's getting dark, so we carry everything back into the kitchen. Sean starts to fill the sink with soapy water and I wave him away.

"You cooked, I clean. That's an immutable law of the universe."

"Immutable, eh? Big word."

"I got a word of the day calendar in a Secret Santa a few years ago."

"For real?" he asks, scraping our bowls into the garbage can.

"Cross my heart. It was supposed to be a joke, I think, but it turned out to be pretty cool." I take the bowls from him.

Sean leans against the counter next to me. "Ooh, talk big words to me," he says. "It's so sexy."

"Flippant. Not showing a serious or respectful attitude." I elbow him in the side.

Sean touches his fingertips to his chest. "Is that a dig at me? Should I be hurt?"

"You should go play video games with Richie. Didn't I hear you talking about that earlier?"

"You did." He doesn't seem in a rush to leave. "But I was thinking we could watch a movie. Unless you're sick of me?" he asks, cheeks pink with embarrassment.

If only that was the problem. Today was the best day I've had in a long time. Ending it on the sofa with Sean leaning against my chest as we watch a movie sounds perfect. Which is why I need him to go upstairs. I have to get myself under control. I'm sure this is simply a combination of my long stretch of celibacy and the forced proximity with an adorable man. Eventually, it will cool off if we get some space.

"I'm not sick of you even a little bit," I reassure him. "I have some things to do and I bet Richie misses you."

"You can play with us if you want," he offers.

"I'm good," I say. "I'm really bad at video games."

"I could teach you," he says.

"No, thank you. Go play. I have some work to do anyway."

He sighs heavily and pushes off from the counter. "Okay, I can take a hint. I'll go to my room."

He sounds put out, but when I look over at him, I see the grin he's trying to hide. I flick some soap bubbles at him. "Go."

Laughter trails behind him as he leaves. I have to fight the impulse to tell him I've changed my mind.

———

After everything is cleaned up, I sit on the couch and turn on the television and queue up the next episode of *Grey's Anatomy*. My roomie at rehab had suckered me into watching on nights when we were too tired and in too much pain to deal with anything serious and needed something to take our minds off everything. We'd made it through nine seasons before I'd been kicked out. Since she was dealing with a double amputation, she still had a couple of months left. She made me promise to stay in touch and to keep watching.

Not hard to do since there were a dozen and a half seasons and the damn show was still being produced. Five months later, I was still watching the show and texting her stupid comments to make her laugh. Every now and then we'd watch at the same time, video chatting so it almost felt like we were hanging out together again.

Tonight it's just me and my trusty notebook. As the theme plays, I dig my notebook out of my pocket. I'm a couple of pages into it before I realize it's not my notebook, it's Sean's. I must have grabbed it off the table at V and V.

Before I can stop myself, I'm flipping through the pages. His handwriting is large, looping, and enthusiastic. Some pages hold numbered lists with a neat title at the top. There's a shopping list with items crossed off. A packing list with the word socks circled multiple times.

Some of the pages have snippets of sentences, random phrases, scrawled recklessly across them. Variations on a theme, a word or two changed each time. It reminds me of my failed attempt at writing lyrics, and I realize I'm looking at Sean's writing.

Lines blurring beneath my wheels, leading me away (taking?)

Pickup trucks outnumber Subarus.

Seagulls screaming out my confusion. Blood red drinks and blood red lips. My heart aches for something I don't have a name for.

The past trails behind me and the road unspools into the future. Baby steps. Baby miles. Baby milestones I should have reached by now.

Destiny desired.

Destined desire.

A dance of destined desire. A dance of destiny, desired. Sired. Tired. I'm so tired.

I flip quickly through the pages as only glancing at the words makes me less of a voyeur. The notebook feels like a window into Sean's soul, mundane lists of tasks and appointments alternate with more phrases and half-written poems full of yearning and desire, poems about the uncertainty of youth and the future. Hopes and dreams and wishes interspersed with the minutiae of everyday life.

On one page, "Places to Visit" is underlined with a list of cities written below it. Rome. Paris. Stockholm. Buenos Aires. London. New York. California. Venice. Sydney. The names are written in blue ink or black ink, pencil and markers, as if he adds to the list with whatever pen is nearest each time a new destination calls to him.

With Sean's words of *desire* and *destiny* haunting me, I let myself imagine taking Sean to these places, showing him the world.

I fall a little bit in love with him.

When I'd agreed to letting Sean stay here, I'd been expecting a college freshman, interested in girls, parties, his friends. College kids weren't a demographic I had a lot of experience interacting with.

Sean is so much more than I'd expected. He's already something special, and when he busts out of his cocoon, he's going to be amazing. He deserves to see the world, to experience everything it has to offer, and the world needs to see him.

The ceiling above me squeaks as Sean walks down the upstairs hall and I shove the notebook back into my pocket. Heart pounding, I pat my other pockets, searching for my notebook. It's there, in a pocket on my left leg where I couldn't feel it.

I've found out things about Sean he might not want me to have known yet. I have the urge to confess, but I can picture his embarrassment if I do that. No, better to keep it to myself. I can't unsee what I saw, but if I want to have any kind of chance of something real with Sean, and I can't deny that I do, I have to tell him about my leg. Though I've only known him for such a short time, I trust him.

I text him. *Hey, if you get a chance, come down before you turn in for the night.*

Not two minutes later, he's running down the stairs. "Coop, what's up? Everything okay?"

"Everything's fine. There's just something I wanted to share with you. Come over here."

He walks slowly toward me. "You're kind of freaking me out, man." He looks at the TV. "And not just because you're watching *Grey's Anatomy.*"

"Don't judge me for my taste in television," I protest, even as I'm shutting it off.

"Oh, I'm totally judging you," he says with a grin. He's dressed for bed, in a soft T-shirt and a pair of cotton boxer shorts with cartoon characters on them, and there's sweat at his hairline and under his arms. "Shit," I say. "Is it too hot up there? I forgot about it." The house is old and doesn't have air-conditioning.

He shrugs. "It's not too bad."

"You can have the fan from my room. I'll get a window air conditioner tomorrow." Pulling out my notebook, I add "window a/c" to the list of supplies.

"You don't have to do that," he says as he sits next to me on the couch. His cheeks are pink and I feel the heat coming off his body. He smells like clean sweat and laundry detergent. "Now what did you want to tell me? I'm dying."

"It's nothing bad, I promise." I shake my head at myself. "I'm making more of a deal of it than it is, actually."

"What? Tell me already."

I reach down and unzip the bottom part of my pants. I slide it down and pull it off over my sneaker. As part of my plan for not drawing attention to myself, I wear a cosmetic foam cover that goes from the top of my foot to my knee to fill out the leg of my pants, but it doesn't pass for a real leg.

"Here," I say, reaching out for his hand and guiding it to my leg. "Feel."

He touches it gently and his eyes widen. "Holy crap," he says, and then he pokes it and knocks on it. "I knew something was up!" He's grinning triumphantly.

"No, you didn't," I respond.

"I totally did. You were limping. Kind of walking funny. I wasn't going to ask."

"Well, now you can ask away," I tell him.

"Can I see the whole thing?" He pokes at it again. "It's spongey. I thought they were metal."

"It's a cover. I don't necessarily have to use it but the legs of my pants hang funny if I don't."

He kneels down to get a closer look. "Is this okay?"

"Go ahead."

"There are so many parts," he says. "I don't think I realized that. Can you put on different feet?"

"Yep. Different feet and foot shells. This is the one I use the most, though. It works well with pants and it's a little bit flexible at the ankle. Take the sneaker off and you can see better."

"You don't mind?"

Mind? I'm having trouble keeping my mind out of the gutter with him kneeling in front of me like that. Watching him undressing me, even if it's only taking off my sneakers, it a little bit of delicious torture. "Go ahead."

He gently lifts my leg, his hand around the back of my calf. I wish I could feel him touching me. Sometimes I forget how many layers I'm wearing. First the sneaker comes off. Then the normal sock I wear over the foot shell. The foot shell goes over another sock that protects the shell from the metal foot.

"If you want, I can take it off and you can see all the parts."

"You don't mind?" he asks from his spot on the floor. "You really don't have to. I don't want to be rude."

I shrug. "If you're living here, you're going to see everything anyway. I put it on and take it off at least once a day. I wasn't trying to hide it because I'm embarrassed, it's because I'm vain," I say with a shake of my head. "I'll need you to get my crutches from the bedroom."

"No problem," he says. "I always wondered how they attach."

"This is a suction-based prosthesis. It has a one-way valve that forces the air out with each step." I point out all the parts, starting from the foot and moving up. "Foot sleeve. Foot. Post that connects the foot to the socket. Socket sleeve." The sleeve comes far up my thigh. I roll the rubber sleeve down below the top of the socket. "Socket." I knock on it. "Ready?" I ask. He nods and I lift my leg out of the socket and set it aside. "You can put the sneaker back on."

"Now the rest." I name the parts for him. "Socks. These I can add or take off during the day if my stump swells." Today I'm only wearing one. I take it off and toss it on the couch. "Liner. You might want to back up a bit. There can be some sweat buildup."

"Gross," he says and then immediately blushes.

I laugh. "Yeah, it can be." I roll the liner off, turning it inside out as it goes. "That's why we have the liner liner. To soak up the sweat." I leave the liner liner on, buying myself a little extra time before he has to see my naked stump.

"You must have been dying today with the long pants."

"I sweat all the time," I confess. "I've never been much of a shorts guy, anyway, but now, if I'm out with the leg showing everybody looks at me. It's hard to disappear into a crowd and everybody wants to know what happened. Even the ones that don't ask directly."

"That would be annoying," he says. "I can see why it's easier to hide it."

"People see that I'm an amputee and they make all kinds of assumptions about what I can and can't do. It feels like they either think I need help going to the bathroom and are amazed I can function or they treat me like some kind of inspirational speaker and tell me how brave I am for...for I don't know what exactly. Not sitting in a corner and crying? They tell me how they 'couldn't handle it,' as if what I am now is so awful they'd kill themselves if it happened to them." I can hear my voice getting more strident as I speak. Sometimes I forget how much anger I still have. It comes out at random times and can be triggered by the most random things.

Sean surges up and hugs me, a full-on chest-to-chest, arms-around-my-shoulders hug. Caught by surprise, I freeze for a long few seconds, but Sean holds on, and eventually, I relax and hug him back. It feels unexpectedly wonderful. I can't remember the last time someone hugged me. Maybe it was when my buddy Eddie visited me in the hospital almost a year ago.

"What was that for?" I ask when he breaks the hug. I miss his touch immediately.

"Seemed like you needed a hug," he says. His cheeks are faintly pink but he looks me right in the eye.

"Thanks," I say gruffly. "It felt good."

"You feel good," he says under his breath, then he smiles at me. "Maybe I'll do it again," he says, looking pleased with himself. "When you least expect it. Sneak attack hugs."

"Just be careful," I warn. "I tip over a lot easier now than I used to."

"I'll make sure to only tackle hug you near soft surfaces."

"Thanks, that's swell."

"I can't imagine anyone looking at you and thinking you're helpless," he says. "You're built like a tank." Emboldened by the hug, he reaches out and squeezes my bicep. "I mean, damn."

Okay. I can't lie. Hearing him say that makes me puff out my chest a little more, maybe flex my arms. "The stronger you are, the easier it is to use the prosthesis and the crutches. Core strength is important. I do a lot of yoga for balance, too."

"I guess you are balancing on top of that thing. You must have abs of steel." His eyes drop to my stomach as if he can see through my shirt.

I'm half-tempted to take it off and show him my six-pack. I'm in better shape now than I was right out of boot camp.

"So, can I ask what happened? Was it an IED or an attack? Is this why you retired?" he asks. "Oh shit. Sorry. You don't have to answer if it's too painful or whatever."

"I told you you could ask. There was no bomb or attack. Believe it or not, it was a vehicle rollover. We were going from base to a construction site in the mountains of somewhere I can't tell you, and the guy driving was new. He took a turn on a muddy curve a little too fast, we hit a pothole and he lost control of the truck. Flipped a couple of times going down the hill."

"Dang that sounds terrifying."

"It was. One kid, new guy, nineteen years old. He died."

Sean covers his mouth with his hands, his eyes wide and stricken. "Oh no. I'm so sorry."

I shake my head. That is something I don't want to talk about. Stupid waste of a life. "Anyway, my leg was crushed."

"Was it just the leg?" he asks.

"The leg was the worst hurt. But my left shoulder got fucked up, I had a concussion, and my spine got knocked around good. It's not so bad yet, but the doctors are keeping an eye on it."

"Wow," Sean says. "I would have never known. And you did all of this construction by yourself?"

"No. I paid contractors to do the big stuff. Making a master bed and bath downstairs. Making a shower that I can use easily. I did pull up all the flooring and replace a few of the outlets."

"You're amazing."

"Nah. Lots of people had it worse. As far as losing a limb, this is pretty mild. I still have the knee joint and it's my left leg. I don't even need special accommodations for the truck."

"I mean, if I had to pick a partial limb to lose…" he says with a grin.

"Exactly."

"So do you wear that prosthesis all day, every day?"

My grimace gives me away.

"You're not supposed to, are you?" he asks.

"I can. It's up to me to pay attention to my body, to see if I'm overdoing it. With the suction suspension system on this leg, my stump shrinks during the day and the prosthesis can get loose. I have to adjust it, add socks or take them off, which is a pain in the ass when I'm wearing long pants."

"Is there anything you can do about that?" he asks.

"Not much, but I'm trying to get approved for one with a vacuum suspension which should help minimize the swelling. We'll see. It would be cool to have a new one, then I can use this one as a backup for swimming in the lake."

"Do they make swim fin feet? Can you get a cool cover? Like I've seen legs that look like they're carved. Or cyberpunk. Ooh, that would be awesome. Or the bouncy running ones?"

"I can get whatever I can pay for over and above what the VA will pay."

"We did so much walking around today! Does it hurt?"

"Not hurt so much as it's uncomfortable and sweaty," I confess. "Speaking of, I need to wash these pieces out. Can you get my crutches for me? They're next to the bed." I hadn't planned on taking the leg off, otherwise I would have gotten them beforehand.

"No problem. Want me to bring this into the room, too?" he asks, pointing at the prosthesis.

"Please."

He's there and back in seconds with the crutches.

"Thanks." I slip my forearms into the crutches.

"You'll wait while I rinse the liner off?" I ask, not ready to let Richie have him back quite yet.

"Of course. You want me to make some tea? A snack?"

"Tea sounds great. I'll be back in a few minutes."

Taking off the leg is a relief. We had done more walking than I was used to. Which reminds me that I really need to get back to my workouts. A quick check with a hand mirror shows me my stump looks fine. No redness or bruising. Sometimes I can see the skin breaking down before I feel it. The earlier I catch a problem, the easier it is to fix.

I wash the sweat of the day off and change into my favorite pair of gym shorts and an old T-shirt. Taking a deep breath to chase away a stupid flutter of nerves, I head back into the living room.

Sean turns to watch me over the back of the couch. Except for a glance at the crutches, he keeps his eyes on my face. For the most part. Every few seconds, his eyes drop to my arms and chest. I'm not complaining.

When he meets my eyes again, I grin. Caught, he blushes, exactly like I hoped he would. There's something so sweet and innocent about his blushes. I sit on the couch, leaning my crutches against the arm. "You can look," I assure him. "It's okay."

He does, head tilting as he examines what's left of my leg. I flex my knee, making the stump move and he jumps.

"That's weird," he says almost accusingly. "Not, like, in general, but just when you move it. Why is that weird?"

"How many leg amputations have you seen in your life?"

"Counting yours? One."

"Takes a while to get used to." I should know. Damn thing still catches me by surprise, especially in the mornings when I've been walking around with two legs in my dreams.

"It's not ugly or anything. It's just part of you. But somehow that flexing it felt like a Muppet waving at me. Like I should glue googly eyes to your knee."

"Sean!" It would be easier to pull off being offended if I could stop laughing. "I can honestly say I have never had that reaction before."

He's facing me, sitting sideways on the sofa with one leg tucked under him, and he's running his palm gently over my knee. I'm not sure if he's quite aware of it and I'm not about to tell him just in case he stops.

"Definitely googly eyes. And I'll call it Stumpy. Oh shit!" His eyes open wide and he yanks his hand away. "Stumpy. The dog! Now I get it!"

"You…you're…" I trail off, shaking my head. I can't look away from him. First, he cooks me dinner, and then there's that damn notebook, and now this completely unexpected reaction.

Whatever Sean reads in my expression, makes his eyelashes flutter and his cheeks flush. He looks down at the floor and then back up at me. "I'm what?" he asks like a challenge.

"You're something special, Sean Johnson."

Blue eyes sparkling, he gives me a smile that stretches slowly across his face. "You ain't so bad yourself, Cooper Hill."

"I was afraid you'd think it was ugly," I confess. "I like the way you look at me, and I didn't want that to change."

"I like looking at you. I can't imagine thinking any part of you is ugly. And I like the way you look at me, too."

The moment stretches and the air between us practically crackles with electricity. Something has to break. Heart pounding, I'm a half a second away from leaning forward, wrapping my hand around the back of his head and pulling him in for a hard kiss, when he shifts away from me. His leg drops to the ground and he picks up his mug of tea off the coffee table with both hands, staring into it.

I barely manage to keep my breathing normal. More of Sean's emotional whiplash. I mirror his position, taking the cup of tea he made for me. "Thanks for the tea," I say.

"No problem."

Maybe I pushed too hard. We could both use a breather. "I'm kind of tired," I say. "I think I'll take my tea—"

"Wait," he says, laying a hand on my arm. "Don't go."

I settle back against the sofa. "Okay."

He takes a deep breath. "Since you shared something personal with me, I wanted to share something with you."

"Okay," I say. "I'm listening."

He spins the mug between his palms. "You won't laugh?"

"I promise I would never laugh at anything personal you trust me with. I would never do that."

He tilts his head to give me an appraising stare. "No," he says slowly. "I don't think you would. Okay. It's just…I know what you mean about not wanting people to look at you differently, or treat you different because of something about you."

"Yeah?"

"Yeah." He takes a deep breath then looks me in the eye. "I'm a virgin."

"A virgin," I echo as if I've never heard the word before.

He nods, face bright red. "Completely. I've never even been kissed." He runs out of the room before I can respond.

SEAN

"You told him?" Richie says. I called him first thing in the morning. I haven't even gone down to the bathroom yet.

"Yeah, I told him. And then I high-tailed it out of the room. Like a…"

"Like a virgin," Richie says with a laugh. "Touched for the very first time."

"Screw you, Richie. This is serious."

"Dude, it's not that big a deal. He's totally into you. He showed you his stump! You're living together, you watch movies together. Eat meals together and he says he likes the way you look at him. Which I kind of picture like those cartoons with the wolf with his tongue hanging out and little hearts floating around his head."

"I repeat, screw you."

"Tell me I'm wrong." He waits a few seconds before saying, "That's what I thought. Just kiss him already. Grab his dick or something."

"I'm not going to do that," I say, even though I kind of want to. It would certainly be an unambiguous action. "Hey, Richie, are you really okay with me being gay? It don't bother you?"

"C'mon Sean. You really think I would care?"

"No. Not really."

"Frankly if I were you, I'd be way more embarrassed about being a twenty-three-year-old virgin," he says.

"I am embarrassed about it! That's why I called you, though I'm rethinking that life choice. You're supposed to tell me it's okay."

"All joking aside, it is okay." His voice gets deeper, more serious. "There's nothing wrong with you."

Richie is the only one who knows everything about what happened to me. Even my mom doesn't know more than the broad details. "I'm not telling him about that," I say. "He already probably thinks I'm a freak."

Richie sighs heavily. "He doesn't think you're a freak. He probably thinks it's hot. Lots of guys like virgins. This way he gets to be the first one to show you all the pleasures of the flesh."

"Pleasures of the flesh? Are you reading your sister's romance novels again?"

"Hey, they're hot, don't hate."

"I'm not hating. And thank you."

"Kiss him. Seriously. Just plant one on him, get it over with."

God, how I want to do that. I almost did it last night, but I'm a coward. I pace the length of my bedroom, stopping to look out the window at the small sliver of the lake I can see. "What if he doesn't want it? What if I make a fool of myself? It's going to make living together slightly fucking awkward, don't you think?"

"He's a guy. You're young and hot. He's going to like it." He sighs deeply again at my patheticness. "Johnson, I swear to God if you don't kiss that man and lose your virginity in the next, ummm, forty-eight hours, I am going to fly up to Vermont and kiss you myself just to end this torture."

"You will not!" I say emphatically. "You're not gay."

"You don't know that," he says airily as if it's no big deal. "I could be. Maybe I'm bi. There's this new guy on the crew, I don't know, man. There's something about him."

"You're serious," I say. I can't believe it. Richie never even hinted about something like that before.

"I think I am," he says quietly as if even he can't quite believe it.

By the time Richie and I are done analyzing his feelings and dissecting every conversation he and this new guy have had and I head downstairs, Cooper is gone. A note on the table and a text on my phone I hadn't noticed let me know he's headed into town for some supplies and can I get started on the subflooring.

No problem, I text back. *See you when you get back.* It feels good to know he trusts me to work on my own. Still, I can't decide if I'm more disappointed I can't take Richie's advice right away or relieved I can put off the awkwardness a little while longer.

After Cooper gets back, we spend the day working on the floor. Working together isn't as awkward as I feared. We alternate control of the music, sharing our favorites with each other. He teases me about my love of nineties alternative music, though I catch him singing along to more than one song, and I give him crap for knowing the lyrics to a lot of country music. I love hearing him sing, though. His voice gives me chills.

Now that I know he wears a prosthesis, I'm aware of small hesitations in his movement, especially when he kneels and stands up. He tells me no when I ask if it hurts to kneel.

Cooper takes pity on me, I guess, and doesn't bring up my confession from the night before. But that almost kiss on the couch hangs in the air. Truthfully, it's kept me so horny all day, I'm lucky I don't put a nail through my foot.

When we're done for the day, I head upstairs for a quick shower that ends up being a long shower due to me having to take care of the results of fantasizing about the kiss that wasn't and what might follow if we ever do kiss. Whistling under my breath, I hurry down the stairs, hoping my face doesn't broadcast what I've been doing.

"Hey, Coop," I call before I'm even all the way down. "Want to get a bite to eat at the diner? I'm too tired to cook."

There's no answer, and the living room is empty. The sound of someone playing the guitar floats in through the open window. When I look out the window, I see Cooper sitting on the picnic table with his back to the door, a campfire flickering in the sand. A waterfall of music like nothing I've ever heard before flows from the guitar slung around over his shoulder.

Moving as quietly as possible so I won't disturb him, I slip out the back door and into something magical. The sun is going down, setting the sky on fire. Dark purple clouds float in a neon orange sky and a cool breeze is blowing off the lake. And in the center of it all, limned in dancing firelight, is Cooper, a man I didn't know two days ago but who has somehow become the center of my world.

The music flowing from his guitar fills me with a yearning for something I can't quite name. It's like a poem I can see the shape of but one for which I don't quite yet have the words.

I lose track of time listening to him play the same piece of music over and over again. Eventually, he stops playing and pushes the guitar behind his back. He reaches for his notebook and a pencil and makes some notes. Pulling the guitar back around, he plays a few notes, stares into the distance, plays them again, and then writes down something else.

He's writing a song. I standing there watching Cooper create music out of nothing. How am I not supposed to fall in love with him right this second?

Humming under his breath, he tries a new arrangement, and I step forward before I can stop myself. "No, the first one. Play that one again."

Cooper turns to look at me over his shoulder and he smiles, the laugh lines around his eyes crinkling. Even though we've spent the last eight hours in the same room, he still looks so happy to see me. I know how he feels.

"So you like this one?" He plays the first arrangement again. "Or this one better?" He plays the second one.

"Definitely the first one." I straddle the bench by his fake leg, resting my elbow on the table.

Cooper looks down at me. "Why?"

"They're both beautiful," I say and it's true. "But the first one, it's more poignant. It's sad, but it makes me feel like the sadness won't stay. The second one sounds like the sadness is all there is."

He stares at me for a long second and then nods. "Poignant. Yes. That's exactly the feeling I was searching for. Maybe a little sad, but with a realization that the loss was, in the long run, necessary." Cooper looks contemplative and quietly plays both tunes again. He's humming along, listening hard, and he smiles like he's pleased with what he's hearing. "The first one it is," and he bends down and makes some more notations in his notebook.

"What kind of guitar is that?"

"It's a twelve-string," Cooper says, strumming the strings. "Have you ever seen one before?"

"Never."

"Here." Cooper lifts the strap over his head and hands me the guitar.

I hold my arms up, afraid to touch it.

"It's okay, you won't hurt her. She's survived a long time, I think she can survive a few minutes with Sean Johnson."

I don't pretend I know what I'm doing. I turn on the bench, so that the table presses into my back, and lay the instrument across my lap. It looks like someone took a regular guitar and doubled each string. I hover my fingertip over the strings and look at Cooper for permission.

"Just be gentle with her."

The strings are rougher against my fingertips than I expected. I love the cascade of sound that results from the simplest touch.

Smiling, I hand the guitar back up to Cooper. "Play me some more?"

"I think that could be arranged." He pulls the strap back over his head, fingers dancing lightly on the strings, starting and stopping a few songs. Then he smiles to himself, strums a few chords, and picks at the strings at the same time, filling the air with more sound than I thought a guitar could make.

For some reason, Cooper deliberately avoids looking at me. I don't mind, it gives me more time to look at him, to catalog all the little things that make this moment so special. Later, when I've had time to process everything, to turn the memory over in my head and examine it from every angle, I'll write about it. Right now, I soak it all in.

The campfire, the spectacular sunset, and the graceful dance of his fingers on the strings. The way his foot taps in time with the music, the secretive smile on his face, and the way he hums the song under his breath. It slowly dawns on me that I know this song. I know it very well.

"Hey!" I say, sitting up straighter, and pointing at him.

Cooper chuckles.

" 'Take Me Home Country Roads?' Are you kidding me? Unbelievable." Talk about poignant. That song hits different when I'm the farthest away I've ever been from my home in West Virginia.

"Do you miss it?" he asks, still strumming the tune.

"It's only been three days. Well, five if you count travel time. You can't miss nothing in three days."

He laughs and then he starts singing. His voice is warm and smooth. Higher than his speaking voice. Halfway through the song, Cooper smiles at me. "You have a lovely voice," he says and I realize I've been singing. *Dang it*. How'm I not supposed to sing along with that song?

"Keep going," he urges when I stop. He replays the intro into the verse, encouraging me to keep singing with his eyes.

When I find the tune again best as I can—Lord knows I'm no

singer—Cooper comes in with the harmony. His voice adds a depth to the tune that a solo voice can't capture. I try hard to stay on tune, to not let the notes Cooper is singing throw me off. It's harder than I thought, but Cooper picks out the melody clear and strong and his eyes never leave mine.

The music floats over the fire and into the water. The last note seems to hang in the night sky.

"That was amazing," I say breathlessly.

Cooper stares at me like he can't see anything else. The fire cracks and pops in the silence, sending sparks floating into the deep purple sky.

"Beautiful," he says, laying the guitar on the table next to him.

I can't look away. The air between us feels charged, thicker somehow, and I swear I'm almost trembling. I stand up, Cooper's eyes following my movement. He spreads his knees and I step between them.

We're almost the same height, but with him sitting, I'm taller and he tilts his head to look at me.

Once again, a kiss hangs in the air between us.

This is it. It's up to me. Cooper won't make the first move, especially after the bombshell I dropped on him last night. I thought I'd be more nervous when this moment finally arrived. I thought it would be something less deliberate, more rushed and desperate. I imagined some faceless man shoving me against a wall and laying one on me.

This feels worlds better.

Bracing my hands on Cooper's knees, I lean down, closing the distance between our faces. "I really want to kiss you."

Heat flares in his eyes. "I'd very much appreciate it if you would."

Heart pounding and hands trembling, I do. And for the first time in my life, another man's lips are on mine, and it's good. So good. His mouth is soft and warm. How can something so gentle make me tremble so hard?

Cooper reaches for my hips, and I break the kiss. Before he can feel rejected, I come in at a slightly different angle and kiss him again.

He makes a pleased sound in his throat.

Feeling brave, I dart my tongue out, licking at the seam of his lips. *Oh, that's nice.*

Cooper exhales through his nose and wraps one of his hands around the back of my neck. His calluses scraping across my skin make me shiver. "May I?" he asks against my mouth.

I lean my forehead on his. "Oh, God, please. I have no idea what I'm doing." My heart is pounding so hard with these simple kisses, I wonder briefly if I'll survive anything else.

"You're doing great," Cooper assures me. "Now less talking. More kissing." He fists a hand in my shirt and pulls me in until his hand is trapped between our bodies. I brace a knee up on the bench for balance, my hands land on the table on either side of him. With a hand on the back of my head, he tugs me down, tilting my head sideways until our mouths slot together like two puzzle pieces.

Cooper's lips are plush and insistent. He cups my head with both hands, thumbs caressing the hinge of my jaw. "Open up, baby."

Baby. Should I like that so much? With a whimper, I do.

His tongue pushes in, flicking against mine, dragging along the length of it, and mapping the shape of my mouth. The entire time, Cooper's hands keep my head exactly where he wants it.

It's a revelation. An epiphany. Twenty-three years I waited for this. And I tell you what, it was worth the wait. Cooper is a kissing virtuoso.

When his tongue withdraws, mine follows his into the warm, wet cavern of his mouth.

When he sucks on my tongue, it feels like it's directly connected to my cock. Holy crap. There's more whimpering and some moaning. Most of which is from me, but Cooper's also making happy sounds. *Closer.* I have to get closer to him.

The world narrows down to only the places where our bodies

touch. Years of suppressed desire roar through me, knocking my feet out from underneath me, drowning me in want, and the only thing that can save me is Cooper's mouth. I climb onto the bench, my arms slipping around him to hold us together.

I had no idea kissing could be like this. None. My brain shuts off. I shove my hands under Cooper's shirt, desperate for skin. My fingers slip, nails scratching in the sweat on his back. Can people have an orgasm just from kissing? I'm about one second away from finding out. My dick is so hard that Cooper has to feel it pressing into his stomach. His very firm, muscled stomach.

Cooper shudders once strongly and pulls away. Breathing heavily, he places his hand flat on my chest. "Wait."

"Oh, God." I step back until I'm no longer kneeling on the bench. "Did I do something wrong? Was that bad?"

Cooper grabs my arms before I can get too far away.

13

COOPER

Was that *bad*? Is he insane? That was a hell of a first kiss. That was a hell of a kiss, period. Way better than my barely remembered first kiss. "No. You're perfect. Dazzling."

"Good," he says with a shy smile. Between the burn from my beard and the flush of his arousal, his skin is beautifully pink. "Because I don't want you to kick me out because I'm bad at kissing."

I reel him in for another quick kiss. "Never. Though if you leave wet laundry in the washing machine and it gets that awful smell, we might have to have words."

"I won't do that. Cross my heart."

"And if you were somehow bad at kissing, which you are most definitely not, I would teach you." God, there are so many things I want to teach him.

"Oh, yeah? Are you a good teacher?" he asks, coyly looking up through his lashes at me.

"I am," I say. "I have a confession."

Sean looks suspiciously at me. "Oh? What?"

"I've wanted to kiss you since the first second I saw you standing in the pouring rain."

"It was such a romantic moment. I think you had me at 'Can't you fucking drive?'" He bats his long eyelashes at me.

I laugh loudly and wrap my hands loosely around his hips. "For me, it was when you asked me if I was always a dick or only on special occasions."

"Imagine how thrilled I was to find out it was only on special occasions," he says through a grin.

Time to move this party somewhere more comfortable. "Let me up," I tell him, laughing at the expression on his face. He looks like a kicked puppy. "I would like to continue this somewhere softer. I've been sitting on this picnic table for an hour. My butt is sore."

"Aww, you want me to rub it for you?" he asks, fluttering his eyelashes. Given how long and dark they are and how gorgeous his eyes are, it's a very effective trick. Between that and the blushing, if we ever do become a couple, I'll be putty in his hands.

I cup his face again, running my thumb along his plush lower lip. "I want you to rub everything. And I'd love to return the favor."

There's the blush. God, he's unbelievably pretty. How stupid are the men of West Virginia to let him get away? Oh, well. Their loss is my gain.

"Okay," he says, and he holds his hand out. He drags me, laughing, behind him into the house.

As soon as we cross the threshold, I crowd him against the wall for another scorching kiss. His dick is rock hard under the thin basketball shorts he's wearing. I'm almost in the same state. I can't remember the last time something as simple as kissing got me so hard.

"Jeez...and crackers," he says through panting breaths, when we break for oxygen.

God, he's adorable. "What do I have to do to get you to curse?"

He puts a trembling finger on my lips and shakes his head.

"There's a difference between cursing and taking the Lord's name in vain. One I can do, as long as my momma's not around, the other, uh-huh. I can't help feeling my grandma will know somehow."

"Hmm. And we don't want her knowing about this," I agree.

He shakes his head slowly. "No sir. We do not."

I pull him back to me, plastering my body to his. "Let's see if we can find out what makes you say things that neither of them would approve of." Pulling out all the stops, I kiss my way up his long neck to nip at his earlobe. He tastes like salt and soap.

My hands are under his shirt, fingers pressing into the sexy as fuck dimples on either side of the base of his spine. He's a live wire, shivering under my every touch. His fingers dig into my hips and I'm not one-hundred percent sure it's all arousal. Time for a check-in.

I lift my head from the soft curve of his jaw. "You still good?" I ask. "Do you want to stop?"

"Oh God, please don't stop." Sliding his fingers through my hair, he grasps the short strands and guides my mouth back to his neck. "Kiss me."

We make out like teenagers, my mouth leaving marks on his beautiful olive skin, my thigh between his legs putting the slightest pressure against his balls. His gasps and moans are music to my ears, but there's a tension in him. Acting on a gut feeling, I grab his shoulders and flip us around, so it's my back against the wall.

"Touch me," I beg. "I need your hands on me."

Sean instantly relaxes, collapsing against me and riding my thigh as he seals our mouths together. "Oh, God. I'm gonna come. I'm so close." He shoves his hand under my shirt. "Can you—"

Before he can finish asking, I reach behind my head with one hand and yank the offending garment off. I toss it over his shoulder.

"That was…very impressive. Nice…" He lays his hands flat against my chest. "Nice. Oh, God, very nice. Can I…?" He slides his hands up a millimeter, his long, graceful fingers tracing my collarbones.

"Baby, you can do anything you want." The *baby* slips out but he's not objecting. Maybe he didn't hear it. He is a tad distracted, all his attention focused on touching as much of my body as he can.

His gentle exploration of my chest and shoulders and arms drives me slowly wild. Hands on his hips, I keep our lower bodies pressed together. I want him to feel how hard he makes me, how much I want him.

He leans in and kisses the curve of my neck, one of my favorite places to be kissed. His tongue darts out, tasting the skin. "God, you taste good," he mutters quietly. "How do you taste so good?"

With a hand on the back of his head, I hold him in place. "More," I growl. "Harder."

He presses harder against me, sucking on the skin. I tilt my head to give him better access, breathing heavily. His mouth slides up my neck and suddenly I feel a sharp pain as he bites down on the tendon with the perfect amount of force.

My knees buckle. "Fuck," we both say.

"God, Sean." I reach around and grab the pert globes of his perfect ass, squeezing them as I pull him into me, grinding our erections together.

The sound that comes out of his mouth is a garbled mess of consonants and vowels, and his hands dig into my shoulders as he shudders. "Holy shit," he says, pulling away from me and pressing his against his erection.

"Too much, too fast?" I ask.

"Maybe a bit," he says apologetically, biting his lower lip. "I don't want to come so fast."

"Wanna slow down a little?" My hand is on his hip, my thumb gently rubbing the soft skin near his waist.

"Is that okay? You won't be mad?"

I shake my head. "Never, baby. I love that you said something. I can't read your mind, and I need to know you're still enjoying this. It's always okay to stop anytime, no matter what we are doing. Now and in the future. You just say the word. Okay?"

"Okay." He closes his eyes and takes a few deep breaths. "It's just…it's a lot, you know? Overwhelming." He inhales and exhales heavily. "I never…I didn't know it would feel like all that."

Brushing his soft thick hair away from his eyes, I knock our foreheads together. "Can I tell you a secret?"

He nods.

"I never knew it could feel like this either," I whisper in his ear. "But I always wanted it to."

He shivers under my hands. "God, Cooper," he whispers. "You cain't say things like that."

"No?" I tuck a curl of hair behind his ear, caressing the shell of it as I do. "Why not?"

"Because you're making me crazy. I cain't even think." His hands are all over me again, running from the waistband of my pants to my shoulders, then down my arms where his fingers tighten around my biceps with a muttered curse. "Damn."

The urge to grab him, put his back to the wall, and rut against him until we both come in our pants is almost overwhelming, but I get the feeling he doesn't like feeling caged in, so I tuck my hands behind my back.

When Sean sees, he sucks a breath in through his teeth. *Oh, he likes that*, something I'll have to remember for later.

He slides fingers through the dark hair on my chest. When his palms glide across my nipples, almost by accident, I shudder and my head drops back, hitting the wall with a dull thud. With a soft *huh* of discovery, he does it again, deliberately this time, his palm pressing firmly against the hard points of my nipples.

I grunt, and barely resist thrusting against him.

"You like that?" he asks breathlessly, eyes huge and dark.

"Yeah," I say with a shaky laugh. "A lot."

He nods absently, staring at his hands on my chest. The contrast of his darker skin against my white skin is so pretty.

Glancing up as if asking permission, he reaches out with one fingertip, hovering a hair's breadth away from my nipple.

"Please," I ask quietly.

He drags a fingertip over both nipples at the same time, smiling as they tighten under his touch. "Can I pinch them?"

Holy shit, this man is going to be the death of me and we've barely started. "Please, God, yes. Hard."

Sean takes me at my word, pinching and rolling them between his fingers, a little harder than I'm used to, but the burn goes right to my cock. I moan loudly as my back arches off the wall and my cock jumps hard enough in my pants that he has to have felt it against his leg.

"Jesus Christ," he says, awed.

Grabbing his wrists, I laugh weakly. "So that's what it takes to make you break? Me almost coming in my pants."

"You...did you?" His eyes drop to the giant tent in my pants. "Really?"

"Really."

"That's so fucking hot." He looks back at my hard, red nipples and groans, grabbing his cock tightly as if he's holding back his orgasm.

"Can we...can we maybe go to the couch?" he asks between panting breaths. "I ain't sure how much longer my knees are gonna work for."

It's so hot the way he forgets to hide his accent when he's turned on.

Taking his mouth in a bruising kiss, I walk us backward through the minefield of loose boards and tools boxes on the floor until his knees hit the couch. Not breaking the kiss, I flip us and drop on the couch, grabbing two handfuls of his shirt and tugging him down with me until he's straddling my lap.

When his ass lands on my hard cock, we both groan.

"Shirt off, please" I beg, not really up to full sentences right now.

His chest is as lovely as I remember from that first night,

smoothly muscled, dark nipples and a trim waist. When I lay my hand on his chest and spread my fingers, I can touch both his nipples at the same time, the sound of his gasp like a caress. "You're okay?" I ask, checking in. "This isn't too much? Remember we can always stop."

"No. It's good, great. Fine. Don't stop."

"Fine?"

"Amazing, stupendous, incredible, stupendous. For fuck's sake, Cooper. I got at least a decade of sexual repression to make up for and if you stop I might spontaneously combust. And all that would be left of me is my legs from the shins down and a big ole pile of ash." He grinds down on my cock.

Despite how close I am, I can't help laughing. "That's very specific. And vivid."

"And really hard to explain," he says seriously, looking down at me with wide innocent eyes and a grin he's trying to hold back. "You'll probably get arrested for murder."

"Hmm. We don't want that."

"No, we do not."

"So we'd better get back to the kissing."

"And gropin'," he says. "Big fan of the gropin'." He reaches down and takes my hands, pulling them around his back to his ass. "Please."

"You're not going to regret this tomorrow and make it awkward, are you?" I ask. I know I should shut up, but this moment feels big. Important. Sean was a virgin before this. And no matter how much virginity is a social construct, the first time you share orgasms with someone is a big deal.

"Cross my heart," he says. "Are you?"

"Never. But I know from experience things are often a lot less clear after the orgasms. You might have second thoughts."

"Are there going to be orgasms?" His fingers are back on my nipples. They're going to be sore tomorrow but it feels so fucking good I can't ask him to stop.

"There's going to be at least one if you don't stop doing that," I promise.

"Can you come from just this?" he asks, eyes wide.

"Keep doing it and grinding down on my lap and you'll find out."

"Shit. God, Cooper. I'm so hard it hurts."

"Let me make you feel good?"

He nods wildly. "Yes. God. Please."

"Trust me?"

"Implicitly."

I shake my head. "I can barely speak and you can still use words like 'implicitly.' I'm going to have to up my game."

"Big words," he says with a grin, draping his arms over my shoulders.

Raising my eyebrows at the challenge in his tone, I drag my hand down his chest and touch his cock for the first time. He whines and shudders.

"Good?" I ask.

He nods rapidly.

I hook my finger over the elastic waistband of his shorts. "Can I?"

Holding his breath, he nods again.

Part of me wants to grin at his enthusiasm, but I'm as affected as he is. Both of us stare at the space between us as I gently lift his shorts over his cock and tug them down as far as I can.

His cock is as pretty as he is. Long and gracefully curved over a thatch of silky, dark hair. The tip is shiny with his arousal and my mouth waters at the thought of taking him between my lips. But not right now. He feels too good on my lap. Wrapping my fingers around that gorgeous cock, I drag my hand down slowly but not too tightly, mindful of the friction of my callused hands on his sensitive skin.

"Fuuuuuck," he moans loudly, hips arching toward me as he rises to his knees for a second before collapsing back down when I reach the root. "Oh, God, Cooper. Oh, fuck."

One touch, and he's throbbing in my grasp.

His nostrils flare as he pants heavily, trying to make it last.

Slow, I drag my hand back up, running a gentle finger over the tip to spread that silky fluid around. That gets me another full-body shudder and the whimpering sound I'm already addicted to.

His shorts roll up, snapping against his cock and trapping it on his body. With a sound of frustration, he stands up. Before I can protest, he rips the shorts off his body, tosses them behind him, and climbs back on top of me, gifting me with a lap full of a completely naked Sean.

"Fuck, yes," I say, dragging my hands from the tops of his shoulders, down his back, and under the curve of his ass. "God, your skin is so soft."

"Oh." His eyes fly to mine as if he only this second realizes he's nude, and I learn that his blush goes all the way down to his collarbones. "Oh, jeez." His eyes lock on the erection pressing painfully against my zipper. Then he bites his bottom lip. "Fuck it." He yanks the button of my shorts open with one hand. He shoves his hands into my underwear, forcing the zipper of my shorts down as he grips my cock with a shaking hand.

I barely dare to breathe as he strokes me, wrist bent at an angle that has to be painful. I put a hand on his arm, and he freezes, eyes darting to mine. "Am I doing it wrong?"

I thrust my hips against his hand so he can see how hard he's gotten me. "God, no. I just want to make it better for both of us. Trust me?"

He nods.

I tap his hip. "Up." He goes up on his knees and I lift my hips, shoving my pants down as far as I can, and then pull him back down. "Kiss me," I say, wrapping my arms around him.

Our cocks brush together as we kiss. The pressure is just light enough to be frustrating, so I reach between us, trying to hold us against one another. The feel of him rubbing against me is as maddening as his mouth on mine. I can't get enough of his kissing. Maybe it's because he's so inexperienced or maybe he just likes it, too, but he doesn't kiss like it's something to be checked off the list before we get to the good stuff. He kisses like it's his favorite thing in the world, like he wants to do it all day.

"More," he says. "I need more."

"Me, too. I need to feel you." I tip sideways, pulling him down on top of me. Then it's some completely undignified wiggling and some close calls with elbows and knees, before we're both naked and he's sprawled out on top of me, bracketed by my legs. It would help if we could stop kissing, but we can't.

Sean's arms are wrapped around my neck. I've got one of mine around his sleek, slender body right at the sweet dip of his spine, pulling him as tightly against me as I can. My other hand is welded to his ass, gripping hard enough to bruise as I encourage him to thrust against me.

Every roll of his hips makes our cocks slide against each other. I feel the give of his stomach and the tip of my cock slips across the dip of his navel, drawing a curse out of me.

His hips slap against me like he's fucking me, an animalistic grunt forced out with each thrust. The thought of him fucking me for real almost pushes me over the edge and I clench every muscle in my body to hold my orgasm back. Christ. Which one of us is the virgin here? I can't come before he does.

"God, God," he pants, breath hot against my mouth. "Your muscles...I can feel 'em."

I thrust up hard, circling my hips at the same time, and he yells. The friction is almost too much, sweat and precum no substitute for lube, but at least it keeps me from going off in under ten seconds.

The room is full of the sounds and musky scents of sex. Groans and grunts, the slap of body against body, and the wet smack of lips meeting and separating. Sean drops his head into the curve of my neck, panting into my skin. He's grabbed on to the arm of the couch for more leverage, the muscles in his arms straining as he pulls himself forward.

My hands slip on the sweat of his back, my nails scoring his sides as I grab for him.

"Fuck, fuck," he says, thrusts growing faster and more erratic. I love the way his cock punches into my stomach and the drag of his balls over mine. It's almost enough.

Licking my fingers and palm, I get them as wet as I have the patience for, and I wedge my hand between our bodies. He lifts his hips, giving me room to work as I grope blindly for our cocks. We groan in unison as I get my hand around both of our cocks. With my free hand, I hold him as tightly against me as I can.

The sounds he is making in my ear are enough to get me off. Sweet high-pitched whimpers, deep groans that sound like they come from the depth of his being, low muffled curses, and, best of all, my name accompanying all of them. I wish I could record it and play it back on the lonely nights after he leaves.

"Come on, baby," I say into his ear. "I wanna feel you come for me. Come on."

"Cooper," he says like he's dying. "God, jeez, Cooper."

Despite being on the edge of orgasm, I laugh. "Jeez," I echo.

"Shut up," he says, shoulders shaking with laugher and arousal.

I squeeze my hand tighter around us and turn my head to kiss wherever I can reach. "You're killing me. Come on. I need to feel you lose it all over me."

With a desperate, inelegant grunt he ruts against me. I reach as far back over his ass as I can, fingers barely brushing his balls before I drag them up between his cheeks, ghosting over his hole.

He comes with a shout, body gone as rigid as steel as his cock throbs and shoots in my hand. I stroke us hard and fast until I come, too, hot pulses of cum slicking our way.

Sean collapses against me, shuddering and gasping for air. I give one last stroke, dragging another yell and one last pulse of orgasm out of him, before pulling my hand out from between us.

I hold my cum-covered hand awkwardly away from both his body and the back of the couch. My heart is pounding in the aftermath of the best orgasm I've had in recent memory. *Best ever*, a little voice says in my head, but I'm not ready to face that.

COOPER

Sean's head rolls boneless against my chest. "Holy fucking cheese-balls," he says. "I think you killed me. I'm near dead."

I kiss the top of his head. "Well, at least you died with a smile on your face."

"Died doin' what I love."

"This was your first time," I point out.

He lifts his head, propping it up with his hand. His fingers tickle the hairs on my chest. "Yeah, and I loved it," he says with a big smile. He wiggles his hips, grimacing at the feel of sticky, rapidly-cooling spunk trapped between our stomachs. "Kind of messy now, though."

"Ah, yeah," I say with a pointed look at my hand.

He snorts a laugh. Hanging his head off the side of my body, he scans for something to wipe us off with. "Aha." He reaches out, grunts, shifts, and reaches further. I hold on to his hips to keep him from falling and he gives it one last try. "Got it!" he says triumphantly, holding up my boxer briefs.

"Good enough for now."

It is. Barely. But the couch is wide, and we end up with Sean on his side, pressed between me and the back of the sofa, his head on my shoulder and my arm around him. One of his legs is draped over my body, and his arm is across my chest. His fingers trail lightly through the hair there. "You like my chest hair?"

"Umm-hmm. It's sexy," he says. "You're sexy."

"You're…incredible," I say. I want to ask him if he's okay. We went right from his first kiss to mutual orgasms, and even I'm shaken by the intensity of our connection. It's miles away from anything I've experienced before. We just met. I must be losing my mind. Or maybe I'm lonelier than I want to admit.

Sean cups my cheek. "Thank you."

The contrast between the sweetness of this kiss and the way he looked and sounded when he came makes my head and heart spin. "Thank you for what?"

"Thank you for making my first kisses, my first everything, so wonderful. I can't imagine anyone better for it."

My heart aches with this gift he has given me; with the trust he's placed in me. Everything has happened so fast, I can't see past this moment to even try and imagine how it's going to go. But I know that I'll hold onto him as long as I can.

The thought of someone else's hands on him, of someone else showing him how good sex can feel, fills me with a burning, green jealousy the likes of which I've never before experienced. It's not like me. I'm not possessive.

Except, I guess, when it comes to Sean. I pull him in for a hot kiss. "Thank you for trusting me and picking me to give that first kiss to."

"Yeah? It felt good for you, too?" he asks shyly, as if he didn't just rock my world, but then again, he has nothing to compare it to. He might think sex is like this every time.

"Good? It was amazing, stupendous, outstanding. Best ever."

His grin is blinding. "Really?" He sinks back down on top of me. "Man, I feel so good."

"You'll feel better after a shower," I say. A not-so-subtle hint.

"And dinner," he says. "I'm starvin'. Feed me?"

"How 'bout we both shower and let Dewey feed us?"

"Excellent plan," he says.

"We have to get off the couch to shower."

Eyes still closed, he hums in agreement and kisses my shoulder but doesn't move.

"Sean." I shake him gently.

"Five minutes," he mumbles.

Who am I to argue? I card my fingers through his hair until he falls asleep, his body relaxed and warm. I tug the throw blanket from the back of the couch over both of us. If you can't beat 'em, join 'em.

Sean's twitching pulls me from my light sleep. Sweat coats his back and his hands scrabble across my chest, nails catching on skin. Man, I was out. I hadn't expected to go down so hard. "Hey," I say softly, dropping a kiss on the top of his head. The arm I had around his back is numb.

He mutters something, flinching in his sleep.

I gently shake his shoulder. "Sean, baby. Wake up."

"No!" His eyes spring open. There's no recognition in them though he's looking directly at me.

"Sean. It's okay." I reach for his face and he scrambles back away from me. His hand sinks into my stomach, all his weight behind it, as his knee hits me in the balls. "Fuuuck," I wheeze with what little air remains in my lungs.

Sean gets tangled in the blanket and falls off the couch, his head and chest hitting the floor first. Grabbing the blanket, he scuttles backward again until he hits the wall.

He's apologizing by the time I can sit up.

"Sorry! Sorry. I don't know what happened." He's holding his head in his hands, elbows on his knees. "I think I was having a nightmare."

"I think so, too." Trying not to wince, I rub some feeling back into my numb arm. "I hope it wasn't about me." I grin to let him know I'm joking. "What time is it?"

"Uh." He looks out the window at the dark. "I have no idea." When he looks back at me, his eyes widen like he'd forgotten I was completely naked. "Oh, wow."

"Good wow or bad wow?" I ask, stretching my shoulders out.

"Good. Gah." Rubbing a hand across his face, he shakes his head like he's clearing out the cobwebs. "Can't even remember what I was dreaming about." The look he gives me is full of heat, and he's grinning. "But I know what I'll be dreaming about a lot later." His stomach growls loudly. "After that dinner you promised me."

"Quick clean up and go?" I'm too hungry myself to wait for a shower. I'd have to take off the leg and it's too much work.

"Absolutely." He jumps up from the floor in a graceful move I envy. Wrapping the blanket around himself, he walks back to the couch and gives me a quick kiss. "I'll be back down in five minutes."

———

Dewey's behind the counter at the diner, like he is every night, and after Debbie takes our order, he comes over to chat and ask about the dog. He's glad we're taking her in, and I promise them both to bring the puppy to the diner for a visit when she's strong enough.

"Dr. Moore says she's about nine months old, and part Bernese Mountain Dog," I tell them.

Dewey whistles. "Those are some big dogs," he says. "Can't wait to meet her."

"Big puppy recuperating from major surgery? She's going to keep you busy," Debbie warns. "I hope you boys have a lot of pee-pee pads and don't need much sleep."

Sean and I exchange glances and then laugh. I don't know why I'm laughing. It just seems to want to come out.

After the dinner comes, pork chops for me, steak and a baked potato for Sean, we eat mostly in silence. I sense Sean with-drawing with each minute that goes by.

"Are you okay?" I ask after watching him push a piece of fat around his plate. "Are *we* okay?"

He frowns, a tiny wrinkle appearing between his eyebrows. "Yeah. Yes. I mean. That was okay, right?"

"It was perfect," I say, keeping my voice low.

"I just...all this, it just happened really, really fast and maybe that's business as usual with you, what with the bathroom hooking up and all...but I don't want you to think I'm..."

Oh, I see where this is going. "Slutty?" I ask, leaning back in the booth. "Sean," I say warningly. "Are you really comparing what we did with a bathroom hookup?"

Sean sighs and rolls his eyes. He tosses his fork down. "God." He rubs his eyes with both hands. "I'm so bad at this. No. Not really. Sorry. And I promised not to be awkward. Fuck." He stares at his plate, pushing the potato skin and limp green beans around it.

Part of me almost relaxes. Unconsciously, I think I've been expecting something like this. "Sean, look at me."

He lifts his eyes but not his head.

"Repeat after me, there is no such thing as slutty behavior. It's a meaningless word."

I can see in his eyes that he wants to believe me, but he's not convinced. "I think there's lotsa people would disagree with you, there."

"Luckily for me, they're not invited to this party," I say with a smile. I lean forward and he mirrors me, our heads as close across the table as we can get them. "Did we go too fast? Did we do anything you didn't want to do?"

"No. Lord, no. I loved it. But," he looks around to make sure no one is paying any attention to us, "I went from kissin' you on the beach to sitting naked on your lap in 'bout six point seven seconds. Some might see that as a mite—"

"Hot," I say, cutting him off. "It was one of the hottest things I've ever seen."

"Yeah?" he asks, a smile lighting up his face. "You thought it was hot?"

"Couldn't you tell?"

"Well, you did seem mighty appreciative," he says.

"Next time, I'll try to make my *appreciation* clearer," I promise.

"'About that next time," he says slowly. "I'm kind of, well, trying to figure out what the rules are. What the boundaries are? I know it's ridiculously early for this kind of conversation, but I guess I'm just an old-fashioned boy. Are we friends? Friends with benefits?" He looks down and then up at me from below those killer eyelashes. "More?"

He is an old-fashioned boy and to my surprise, I love it. I'm tired of hookups, commitment-phobes, friends with benefits who disappear just as I start thinking maybe we could be more, and ambiguous relationships where it doesn't become evident until it's too late that you're both working under different assumptions. It's refreshing to be with someone who wants a relationship.

"Well, we're friends yet, with or without benefits."

He rears back, hurt in his eyes.

"Shit. That came out wrong." I reach for his hand.

Debbie is headed our way, but when she sees me reach for Sean, she stops, gives me a thumbs-up, and detours to another table. "I only meant we aren't friends with benefits. We can be more. I want to take the time to get to know you. To discover what you like, what you don't, and all that."

"Considering we're living together, that won't take too long," he says. "So what are we calling this?"

"Remember when I said dating was the step between bathroom blowjobs and marriage?"

He nods. "I do. You're saying you want to date me?"

"I am."

He looks thoughtful. "Can you date someone when you're technically already living together?"

"I guess we'll find out."

He smiles. "Does that mean you're going to take me on a date? A real date?"

"Does this not count?" I ask, indicating the diner.

"You buyin'?" he asks.

"Sure. You can even have dessert."

"Wow," he says with a smile. "You're spoiling me already."

I smile back. Sean doesn't know it, but I am romantic as fuck and I've been waiting a long time to be able to show it. "Don't worry," I tell him. "We'll go on some real dates, and I promise to do it right."

"I can't hardly wait," he says. He cranes his neck to look around the diner, smiling when he catching Debbie's eye.

"What can I get you, honey?" she asks, reaching for our plates.

"Bring me your finest pie and a cup of coffee, decaf, if you don't mind."

"I don't mind at all. Are you celebrating something?"

"I guess we are."

"Good for you," Debbie says. "You should always celebrate whenever you can. Cooper, you want anything?"

"Just coffee, please. Decaf, too."

"You got it. Two coffees and a dealer's choice piece of pie coming right up."

"I can't wait to see what happens," Sean says as she walks away.

Neither can I.

15

SEAN

"You believe in reincarnation?" I ask Cooper, slack-jawed. I hadn't seen that coming.

"I'm not saying I'm a hundred percent convinced, but there is a body of evidence in support of it."

"Get out," I say.

"He's right," Oz says. Oz is this giant of a man who works at V and V. He's got to be six-four, six-five, and seriously muscled with an almost-shaved head. Luckily, he's one of the most laid-back guys I know.

"You, too?" I ask.

Cooper wasn't joking about dating. It's been a coupla weeks since that first kiss and things just keep getting better. September is here and the leaves are starting to turn. One of my favorite things to do on these glorious autumn days is going for long drives around the lake or up into the hills. He wants to take me to Montreal, and I want to go badly, but we have to wait until I get my passport.

After the drives, we often find ourselves walking down Church Street and hanging out at V and V, browsing the bookstore and trying out whatever new local drink Tanner has on offer.

There aren't words for how it feels for me to be in a place like this where people feel safe being who they are, loving who they want. Seeing gay couples being casually affectionate in public is not something I ever expected to see.

I love it.

We also end up talking about the oddest things.

Case in point, this conversation we're having with Molly and Oz.

Oz shrugs. "I heard a story on NPR about it. The guy was pretty convincing."

Cooper nods in agreement. "One of my buddies, his youngest kid, it was the creepiest thing."

He takes a long pull of his beer. I've never been a huge beer fan, but I don't mind the taste of it in his mouth when we kiss.

Yeah. Kissing. Big fan. If there was a kissing Olympics, Cooper would definitely get a gold medal. In the three weeks or so since that first kiss, it's become a daily, and nightly, and afternoon-ly, event. I love kissing him, love making out on the couch while we pretend to watch a movie. We let the feelings grow, hands exploring, mouths traveling. Sometimes that's as far as it goes. We slow down, and one of us lays his head on the other's lap, and we cuddle and watch TV.

Sometimes we don't stop. Oh, the things I have learned. Frottage is a new word for me, but it's rocketed to the top of charts. Sure, the first time Cooper blew me was a life-changing experience. Big fan of the blow job. But there's something about feeling his whole body against mine while we kiss that I love more than anything.

"Well?" Molly asks when he doesn't say anything else. "What was creepy about him? Besides the normal creepiness of kids."

Turns out Molly was serious about having Cooper back her up

on open mic night. They've practiced together a few times. She's seriously become one of my favorite people in this town.

"Kids aren't creepy," I tell her.

"Yeah, they are. Always looking at you. Always sticky with mysterious substances."

"They are often sticky," Oz agrees.

"Don't you two have jobs?" I ask.

"I'm on a break," Molly says.

Oz looks over to Tanner, who's behind the bar tonight. He gives Tanner a thumbs up followed by a thumbs down. Tanner shakes his head but dismisses Oz with a wave of his bar towel. Oz smiles and gives him a thumbs up. "We're good," he says.

Cooper shrugs. "So, I'm over at my buddy's house, and we're watching some documentary on the Titanic. I'm not really paying attention, but his kid is staring at the television. Out of nowhere, the kid goes, 'That's wrong. Daddy, they got the picture wrong.'"

"Picture of the boat?" Oz asks.

Cooper shakes his head. "Kid makes Wash rewind and stop on schematics of the boiler room."

"Get out," Molly says.

"Cross my heart," Cooper replies. "Then the kid points at the TV and says, 'The boilers were on the other side. I was right there.' He's pointing at this space in the corner. 'I drowned there, that's why I don't like water.' So Wash and I have to check it out, and sure enough, the kid is completely right."

Molly gasps.

"How does a four-year-old know what a boiler is?" I ask.

"That's your takeaway?" Cooper asks. "I'm disappointed, Johnson. I wouldn't have taken you for a skeptic."

I smile at him over the edge of my glass. These are some of my favorite nights.

"The thing I find so fascinating about reincarnation," Oz says, "is that it implies the existence of some kind of essence separate from the physical body that is what makes me 'I' rather than someone else that exists after this body dies. An immortal soul, you could say."

"Where does it go after death?" Molly asks. "Is there some kind of cosmic waiting room?"

"Or is time not actually linear?" Oz asks. "Maybe it just appears that way to us. Because of how we interact with the quantum realm."

"Quantum consciousness," Cooper says with an emphatic smack to the tabletop. "Exactly."

I can't resist. I grab his T-shirt and pull him in for a kiss that goes on long enough, Molly tells us to get a room.

"What was that for?" he asks.

Not able to put words to what I'm feeling, I shake my head. "You're just so…wonderful. So you weren't joking when you said maybe we were friends in a previous life?"

"It would explain a lot," he says seriously. "And you can't laugh. Only poke gentle fun, remember? We had a deal."

"I'm not laughing," I say, and give him another quick kiss.

The smile on his face is worth the lingering discomfort I feel at public displays of affection.

After that, the conversation continues in the same vein. I find out that Cooper and Oz believe that ghosts are possible. Molly and I are pro-alien. We all agree that while time travel might be theoretically possible, it's probably not a good idea.

"Food's ready," Tanner calls from the bar.

Molly checks the time on her phone. "Oops, my break is over."

"It was over twenty minutes ago," Oz tells her as he knocks their shoulders together.

"See you later, boys," Molly says.

"I'm out, too. Be cool," Oz says.

"I got you something," Cooper says after they leave.

"More books?" I ask. As was our usual M.O., we'd stopped at the bookstore before hitting the wine bar. The living room book-shelf is already in danger of overflowing.

"You know," I say, as he puts a bag from the bookstore on the table, "there's this place called a library that will let you read all the books you want for *free*."

He gives me the look and pulls the bag toward him slowly. "If you don't want your present, I can return it," he says.

"No! I want it! Here, have a sausage." I slide the plate over to him, willing to make the sacrifice. I've never gotten a gift from anybody but family before.

He pulls a rectangular package out of the bag. "Here you go. Oh, and this, too." There's a second, smaller box. They're both wrapped like real presents.

"For me? Why?" I ask, not giving him time to answer.

"I saw it and it made me think of you, so I got it," he says as if it's something people do all the time. "I thought you'd like it."

"Really?"

"It's just a little something," he says, but he's smiling at me.

Pushing down the urge to rip the paper off what is obviously a book, I slide my fingers carefully across the seams of the paper to pull the tape off.

It's a beautiful brown leather-covered journal with a brass lock keeping it closed and a real fountain pen. All I can do is stare at it. Cooper nudges it closer to me. "Open it."

Hands shaking, I do, ripping off the paper and opening the black clamshell to reveal a beautiful fountain pen the color of the sky.

"I thought it would be perfect for your poems."

I shake my head, not trusting my voice. I blink back tears.

"Do you not like them?" Cooper asks. "We can exchange it if you want. Either one. I kept the receipts."

I hug the book and pen to my chest as if he's going to rip them out of my hands. "No. It's perfect. Beautiful. It's too good for my terrible poems."

"I seriously doubt your poems are terrible," he says, reaching for a sausage.

"You don't know, you've never read them," I say.

He shrugs. "You've never asked me to."

He's right. He's shared his music and his injury with me, and I haven't let him in at all. It's so unfair. But still. "No, trust me," I assure him. "They're terrible."

"Did you get a bad grade on something?" Cooper asks.

"Not yet," I say automatically. "It's fine."

Cooper stares at me.

I drop my head into my arms. "You're right. It's not fine. I'm terrible at this. School is harder than I thought it would be. When I'm in class, everything makes sense, and I think I understand everything my Modern Poetry professor is saying, but she's not happy with my first assignment and I don't know why."

"Did you ask her?"

I shake my head. "I don't wanna bother her. I should be able to figure this out myself."

"That's not how life works, Sean. Trust me, I was a staff sergeant, which meant I had men working under me. I'd much rather they asked me if they weren't sure what to do instead of trying to guess what I meant. I'm pretty sure professors are the same way. That's why they have office hours, Sean. Go talk to her."

"She already thinks I'm an idiot. Last thing I need to do is talk to her and prove it."

"There is no way in the world she thinks you're an idiot."

"You don't know that."

"And neither do you. Go, or I'll make you watch nothing but musicals for the next week."

"You wouldn't dare." There are movies and genres we agree on, action movies, heists, and fast cars. And things we don't agree on. For some unimaginable reason, Cooper loves musicals. And I'm not talking about Disney films like *The Lion King*. No, he loves vintage movies from the fifties starring actors who died before I was born, and songs I've never heard before. We have a deal, he gets to watch a musical, and then I get to watch a foreign film with subtitles.

"Try me," he says with a smile.

"Fine," I say grudgingly. "She has office hours on Tuesday when I'm on campus. I'll go then."

And he brightens up, eyes twinkling with promises I know he can keep. "Hey," he says, holding out his hand across the table.

I take it.

"Everything is going to be fine at school. You're brilliant and I love the way your mind works."

"But you—"

"I may not have read what you've written, but I listen to you speak every day. You're a born storyteller," he says. "You'll figure out a way to get the voice down in a way that will make you and your professor happy. You're going to dazzle them, just the way you dazzle me."

Holy Mother Mary. What did I ever do to have anyone, let alone this kind, generous, loving man, look at me like that? To have that much faith in me? He has more faith in me than I have in myself, that's for sure. "Thank you. You make me believe it."

"Good," he says.

I laugh. "You're mighty feisty today."

"I liked seeing you on my beach this morning, playing with our–the dog. You looked beautiful. Like you belonged there."

"Cooper." It's all I say. My heart seems to have gotten stuck in my throat, blocking my words. Which is a blessing because I'm pretty sure there's no falling left to do. I'm almost positively, definitely in love with Cooper Hill.

It's terrifying. But the scariest thing is that I might be the only one.

Before I'd met Cooper, I hadn't realized how alone someone could be in the world. Cooper has no family. No close friends anywhere, and though he'd been born and raised in Burlington, there wasn't anyone he considered a friend here, either.

All he has is me, and I'm kind of a mess. What if I do something stupid? What if I hurt him? Then who will he have to love him? Outside of Stumpy, of course.

I'm going to be the best boyfriend for him. I'm going to do everything right.

All the way home from the bar, I hadn't been able to take my hands off him. He threatened to make me walk if I didn't stop distracting him. I had my first orgasm of the evening while I was leaning against the kitchen sink fully-dressed.

Number two comes on the couch that has seen many of them since we started. "I have something for you," I say to Cooper after we get our breath back.

"Yeah?" he says. "Do I have to move to get it? Do either of us have to move?" I'm lying on top of him, our bodies in real danger of sticking together. He's petting my hair, seemingly content to stay like this as long as I'll let him. I'll let him do it forever.

"Yes," I say.

"Then I don't want it."

"It's a notebook of my poems."

He lifts my head up by the hair and cranes his neck to meet my eyes. "You want me to read them?"

"I do." I drop my head back down on my chest. "But not until I'm in my room, okay? And if you hate them, don't tell me."

"Thank you," he says. "For trusting me."

"I'd trust you with a lot more than that," I say.

For that, I get a kiss that leads to orgasm number three.

After that, I barely have the energy to walk upstairs on wobbly legs and grab my notebook. "Cooper," I call from the stairs. "I'm too tired, come get it."

"Are you still naked?" he calls from his bedroom.

"Naked and sticky," I reassure him. "I'm too tired to shower. Don't judge."

When he comes to the staircase, he's naked as well, and on his crutches. The sex-drunk smile on his face is adorable. I'm sure I look even more in love. "If there was any way I could get it up again, I would jump you right now," I confess, leaning over the banister.

Crutch dangling from his forearm, Cooper puts his hand over mine. "I appreciate the sentiment, but think I would actually pass out." He tilts his head up, and I lean over the railing, stretching as far as I can, and kiss him. Then I hand him the notebook. "Good night," I say.

"Good night," he says with a smile.

He doesn't have to ask me if I want to sleep in his bed with him, it's a standing offer. I will. One day soon.

16
SEAN

Pulling down the driveway a few days later, I mentally replay my day, trying to decide if my cranky mood is a reasonable response to a day full of small annoyances or the result of not eating lunch.

Probably a little of both, I decide. I'm also exhausted. Lately, I'm tired all the time. And sometimes it feels like my brain is trying to think through a deep fog.

Dropping my backpack on the kitchen table, I follow the sound of music to the workshop in the back. Cooper's doing something loud with the router, and sawdust covers him from head to toe. Stumpy is curled up on her dog bed in the corner. She lifts her head when she sees me and stands up to stretch. With a cute doggy yawn, she shakes her head and hops over to me.

Cooper turns his head to check on her and see me in the doorway. "Hey," he says breaking into a smile. "You're home early."

"Class was canceled," I say. "Professor was a no-show."

"Why do you sound annoyed about it?" he asks.

Stumpy jumps up, trying to lick my face, though she's way too small to reach yet. It's a habit we've been trying to break her of. "Down, Stumpy. Down," I say sternly, putting a gentle hand on her shoulder.

"I had an hour break before class. If I'd known it was canceled I woulda just come home."

When Stumpy finally settles, I scratch behind her ears. "Good girl." I give her more pets before going over to Cooper and kissing him hello.

"I see where I stand," he says. "Dog first, then me."

"Maybe you should run over and try to lick me when I come home," I suggest. "Then I'd deal with you first."

"Would you tell me I was a good boy if I did?" he asks, using his sex voice, the one he knows gives me the chills.

"I might," I say a little breathlessly. "Depending on where you licked me."

His eyes flash hot and his smile turns wicked. I step back before he can grab me.

"Not now. You're all sweaty and gross and covered in sawdust."

He looks down at his chest as if he hadn't noticed until I mentioned it. "I thought you were supposed to like my manly sweat."

"That was your other boyfriend," I say with a laugh.

"Be that way," he says.

"I will. You good in here?" I ask.

He nods. "Just finishing up some boards for the siding. What are you going to do?"

"That last wall in the living room needs painted. Though I'd start on that."

"Good idea. Did you eat anything?" he asks.

"Yes, Mom," I say, rolling my eyes. "I swear you're trying to fatten me up."

"I like to feed you. Sue me."

"I like when you feed me," I admit. Giving him a quick kiss, careful not to touch him, I head to the house to start painting.

I'm up on Cooper's rickety wooden deathtrap pretending to be a ladder when the patio doors we'd installed a week ago slide open and he comes in.

He's still sweaty and sawdust clings to his leg, but now he's shirtless, something I greatly appreciate. He's taken off the cosmetic cover he wears to protect his prosthesis from the dust. He'll leave it outside until he can clean it off. Call me strange, but I kind of like his leg without the cover. It's got a Terminator-esque feel that I dig. I haven't talked him into buying any cool covers for it yet, but I've worn him down enough to at least look at some with me. I've got my eye on this cool steampunk one. Give me time. I'll convince him.

He stops at the base of the ladder and looks up. "Looking good," he said.

"Thanks. I'm just cutting in around the ceiling and door-frame." I twist around to look at him, and the ladder sways. I grab onto the top.

He puts a hand on my calf and smiles. "I wasn't talking about the paint. Nice outfit."

Since it's hot and I'm painting, no point in wearing a lot of clothes. All I've got on is some ancient gray sweatpants I cut down into shorts. "This old thing?" I say, batting my eyelashes. "It's nothing."

He slides his hand up the back of my thigh, fingertips flirting with the leg opening of my shorts. "I don't think those flip-flops are OSHA-approved, though."

I snort. "I don't think this ladder is OSHA-approved. And I'm not about to get splinters from it."

"Hmm," he says, hand slipping under my shorts to cup my ass.

"Hey," I say. "No hanky panky until you shower."

"Hanky panky?" he says with a laugh and a squeeze. "But you're at such a convenient height."

"Convenient for what?" I say, my brain as usual lagging behind my dick in getting with the program.

"Turn around and I'll show you."

Who would say no to that? Not me. I turn around, carefully, because flip-flops really aren't the best footwear for climbing ladders. This, unsurprisingly, puts me cock to mouth with Cooper. "I think I see where you're going here," I say, already breathless.

"I knew you were a smart boy," he says, and then he kisses the skin right below my belly button. He takes a step back to look at me. "Those shorts are..." He shakes his head as if words have failed him. "Pornographic. You're not wearing anything under them, are you?"

I shake my head, grinning when he growls. I love when I get him to make that sound. I don't know if he does it consciously, but it's all kinds of sexy to me. Very caveman.

He reaches for my hips and then stops himself. "Okay?" he asks.

My heart and my cock jump. The way he asks permission before doing anything makes me feel cared for and safe. I point to the tent growing in my shorts. "I think we're all in agreement here."

He catches me by surprise when instead of pulling down my shorts, he slides his hand up the leg opening, fingers caressing my very sensitive balls. I suck in a lungful of oxygen and jolt at the unexpected touch. The stupid ladder sways like it's in a storm.

Cooper laughs but doesn't move his hand. "That," I say, voice shaking as I wag my finger at him, "that is definitely not an OSHA-approved use of a ladder."

"I won't tell them if you won't." He shoves his hand in further, sliding it around my cock, his thumb rubbing over the head and my eyes roll back in my head. "Fu-u-u-dge," I moan.

He laughs at me again.

"I hate you," I lie, thrusting my hips forward, trying to make him get with the program already.

"I know. And you don't want me to touch you because I'm sweaty and gross," he says, all fake sorry.

And then the bastard actually *pulls his hand out* of my shorts.

"I'm sorry," I say quickly. "You're perfect and you smell like roses and the sawdust is quite fetching. Now would you please touch me again?"

"Since you asked so nicely," he says, finally, *finally* pulling my shorts down. Since they really are old, they slip right down to my feet.

"That's definitely a safety hazard," Cooper says. He taps my shin to get me to lift my leg, and pulls them off, tossing them to the side.

Realizing that I'm now completely naked (except for the flip-flops, which I'm not taking off because splinters), he steps back to get a good look. I lean back, resting my elbows on the top step, knowing it will make my back curve and display my now-very-hard cock to great advantage.

He gets this look in his eye that makes my stomach do a flip. "The way you look," he says softly.

"Cooper, please." Suddenly, I don't just want him, I need him. I need to know he wants me.

With a wicked grin, he licks a stripe up it and then swirls his tongue around the head in a move that makes me weak in the knees. My hands land on his shoulders for support.

The way his mouth feels on mine drives me insane. Someday, I'm going to get the nerve up to reciprocate. Despite Cooper's assurances that there's no bad way to give a blow job, I'm still worried I'm going to be terrible at it.

I'm going to do it very soon, though. I want to make Cooper feel as good as he makes me feel. Which is very, very good.

"Oh, good. So good," I babble. "Don't stop."

He laughs evilly and then proceeds to drive any remnant of a bad mood out of my mind, body, and heart.

After, I take Stumpy outside to pee and get some exercise.

I hold the toy in front of her face. "Look, Stumpy. A toy!" I'm trying to sound like this stuffed animal is the best thing since wet dog food.

She looks at me as if I'm insane but she loves me enough to give whatever I am asking her to do a try.

"It's fetch. I throw Krakey, and you bring it back. It's great fun. All the doggies love it." I gave her beloved stuffed kraken a gentle toss onto the scrubby grass.

Balancing on three legs, she wags her tail and looks at me with her big brown eyes. I toss the ball a short distance. She follows it with her eyes and then looks back at me. I can almost hear her thoughts. *You threw Krakey away! Krakey is my friend! How could you betray me like that?*

Having her around has turned out to be better than I imagined. She's full of life, always happy to see me, and has a way of knowing when I need something to cuddle. Something about the feel of her fur under my palms, and her soft weight pressed against my legs, makes the vague anxiety and anger that comes over me every now and then go away.

We were able to take her home sooner than I'd expected. The vet was right. Her care is a lot. But Cooper is an expert, and sooner than I'd expected, she was up and moving. Now you would never know she'd ever walked on four legs.

The vet says it's not unusual and because she is young it's easier for her to recuperate. Cooper and I of course think it's because she's special and more brilliant than most dogs, despite her inability to eat without spreading kibble all over the floor or drink without getting her entire face and front paws wet.

Doc Moore has also impressed on us that she is probably going to be big, and if bored, destructive. So we have to work on manners and obedience training as early as possible.

She'll be better off with something to do, he told us.

Hence, the rather unsuccessful attempts to teach her to fetch.

"I don't think she's a fetching breed," Cooper says from the doorway.

"I read both breeds like to herd," I say. "Maybe we should get some chickens. Give her something to do."

"I'm not sure chickens like being herded," he says.

"We'll ask Finn."

Cooper sits down on the bench of the picnic table, smiling at me as he absently pets Stumpy's head. She's resting it on his knee and gazing up at him in adoration. Much like I do, I suspect.

We should put a deck out here with a walkway down to the water. A dock of some kind would be good, so Cooper would have a place to leave his crutches and where he could get in and out of the lake easily. He's told me he misses swimming but he doesn't have a leg he can swim in, and there is no graceful way in or out of the water on one leg. He'd have to scooch down on his butt until the water was high enough to hold him up.

Down on the beach, the gulls are circling, coming closer and closer to the ground. Must be something dead down there.

"What do you want for dinner?" he asks.

"What are my options?"

"Hamburgers or something delivered."

"You just want to use the grill," I say.

We'd bought one last week. A giant, multi-leveled thing that gleamed like a beetle carapace in the sun. I'd given him a lot of crap about performative masculinity and his caveman-like need to cook slabs of meat over fire. But I sure did like the food he cooked on it.

"Guilty."

"Burgers it is then. You get down with your inner suburban dad."

He raises one eyebrow. "I thought dad bods were in now?"

I walk over to him and slide my hands under his shirt. "I don't know any dads that look like this."

He laughs at the happy sound I make and the way I press against him as I run my fingertips over the speedbumps of his abs and through the silky hair on his chest.

I'm not even a little bit embarrassed. I love his body. He spent his adult life keeping it fit and now post-surgery and injury, it's even more important that he stays strong. The result is a visible six pack, biceps I can't reach my hand around, and an ass you can bounce a quarter off.

Lucky me.

The squabbling of the gulls pierces my ears. Ugh, those stupid birds. "I think something died down by the water," I say with a quick kiss to his mouth. "I'll go get rid of it."

"Leave it," he says. "The birds will take care of it."

"I can't stand the way they scream," I tell him. "Grates on my nerves." Stumpy whines and presses against my leg, sad that the attention isn't on her for a change. "It will just take two seconds. Keep hold of Stumpy for me? I don't want her getting all wet and muddy."

"Sure."

I chase the gulls away from the fish carcass they were fighting over. And by chase I mean I wave my arms and yell at them until they hop a few feet away, eying me warily. These birds are the size of cats and not afraid of me at all.

I lift the remains up by the tail and toss it back into the lake. Maybe some other, bigger fish will eat it and the gulls will leave me alone.

Job done, I head back to the house to wash up and help Cooper with dinner.

17

SEAN

As a reward for Cooper's hard work and his truly stellar blow job, I make dinner and tackle the cleanup. I'm wrist-deep in soapy water, humming along with the music from my phone when he wraps his arms around me from behind. He kisses softly up my neck to the curve of my jaw, giving me goosebumps. I can't bat him away without splashing water, and slippery floors and three-legged dogs are a bad combination, so all I can do is squirm. "Gah, get off!"

He laughs and pinches my ass, so I flick some soap bubbles at his face. "Did you want something? Some of us are trying to work here."

He sticks a finger in the soapy water. "You know it's easier to get them clean in hot water, right?" Reaching around me, he turns on the hot tap and lets it run a bit.

Taking advantage of his proximity, I kiss his neck right where the short beard turns to stubble, and it's his turn to shiver. "I'm almost finished. What are we watching tonight?"

"I was thinking *In Bruges*. You haven't seen it, right?"

"Nope." I shut the hot water off.

"It's surprisingly funny. You'll like it," he says, giving my ass another squeeze and some light caresses. With this kind of incentive, I'll do the dishes all the time.

"Bring it on. So, what did you want? Besides to feel me up, not that I'm objecting."

"I'm making a shopping list. Need anything? I already have the fabric softener and apples you mentioned."

A few days after I moved in, I found that I was right in my suspicions. Cooper does use fabric softener and he always smells great, even when he's hot and sweaty. Sometimes I think he smells better that way, but I may be biased.

"How about some chicken wings? I had a craving. Oh, and more Frosted Mini-Wheats." Cereal is my late-night snack of choice. Nothing hits like a bowl of crunchy sugar and icy cold milk at midnight.

"You have a problem," Cooper says. "Is there a Frosted Mini-Wheats twelve-step program?"

"I can quit anytime I want," I protest. "I just don't want to."

"Keep telling yourself that." With one last kiss, he extricates his crutch from between my body and the sink and swings over to the fridge for a quick inventory. "Fine. I'll enable your sugar addiction, but only because you taste good when you eat that crap."

"The wages of sin," I say sorrowfully. "Or something like that."

"Worth four dollars for a box of cereal." The fridge door closes with a dull thud. "I'm going to run to the store quick. Then movie?"

"It's a date."

He gives me a fly-by kiss on his way out of the kitchen.

I go back to the dishes, and the view outside the window catches my attention. The screen is dirty and hard to see through, and the shrubs could use a trimming, but the breeze is nice and I can catch a small glimpse of the lake and the sun sparkling on its surface.

My thoughts drift to the various things I need to take care of. I have some reading to do for my culture, imperialism, and globalization class. Before school started, I was dreading that course, but it's turned into one of my favorite classes. It's making me take a look at a lot of my assumptions about what "real" literature is and why I feel that way.

My savings are getting low, and I should probably look for a part-time job.

And I found some interesting crown molding ideas, I'll run them by Cooper later. Turns out I've got a knack with the table router and we've been experimenting with some fancy cuts.

The lead singer of the Dreamers sings about how the night feels brand new and how he only has bad things on his mind, and I remember hearing the song last night when Cooper and I were watching some movie I can't remember.

I'm underneath Cooper, back flat against the soft couch cushions. Forearms braced on either side of my head, Cooper's hands are buried in my hair. His body is heavy, and his chest hair scrapes across my nipples. His strong thighs forcing my legs apart as he thrust slowly, so slowly, against me. I claw at his back, leaving pink lines on his skin.

Heat scalds my hands, and I leap back, yanking my hands out of the dirty water. Heart pounding, I take deep breaths, trying to get my head under control. The water isn't hot. It's barely lukewarm.

Back when I was away, they used to stick our hands into boiling water while they made us watch porn.

Water splashes on my face. The greasy yellow foam sponge is crushed in my fist. *Sorry sponge.*

Back to shopping. Lube. We've taken to stashing lube under the couch. Do we need a refill?

The plate in my hand squeaks under the force of my sponge and I set it in the drying rack. Squeezing some dish soap onto the sponge, I fish another glass out from under the water. It's the one I used this morning for my orange juice.

We finished the orange juice. I wonder if Cooper put that on the list.

Orange light from the setting sun squeezes its way through the dirty openings in the window screen. Surely it's not that late already? I check the clock to see it's been almost forty minutes since Cooper left. Wow, time flies when you're doing the dishes, I guess.

The sun was setting last night by the time Cooper and I gave up even pretending to watch the movie. Some nights are like that. The movie he wants to watch tonight sounds good. *In Brussels*? Belgium? Something with a B.

Cooper's kissing me deep and perfect, his tongue brushing mine in rhythm with the drag of his cock. Torturously slow. His hands in my hair control the kiss. He's on top of me, covering my entire body. My fingers dig into the muscles of his ass, urging him on. My thighs clamp against him. My foot slips into emptiness where I expect a furred calf and I jolt, groaning when that pushes me into Cooper. I'm begging him. Faster. More. Please. But he's bigger and stronger. In control. And I can't move him.

I shove the sponge into the glass, twisting it around. My hand is too big to fit inside the cup. Why the hell do they make the openings so small? It's so fucking stupid.

Cooper's hands are big. Wrapped around my cock and pulling it to his lap. Holding it against his, his knuckles pressing into my stomach.

A gull screams outside the window and it sounds like a kid sobbing in the distance. When I was away, I hated hearing the other kids cry. Some of them were so young, only thirteen or fourteen, and I couldn't help them. Couldn't even help myself.

It's just another wild Friday night at Casa Hill. This is it? This is the gay lifestyle that everybody warned me against? This is my life of sin and debauchery? Dishes and laundry and arguing about who changed the toilet paper last? Fuck that. Fuck everyone. It's so stupid.

If some rando is going to hate me simply because I'm gay,

maybe I should go out and slut it up. Why not? I've already been found guilty, might as well do the crime.

Stupid. Unfair. It's all so stupid. A loud crash followed by the sound of breaking glass splits the air. "It's so fucking stupid!" My throat hurts from yelling. Across the kitchen, right beside the side door, there's a dent and a new stain. Water drips down the wall, pointing the way to the shattered glass on the floor.

Holy fuck. Stupid. It's all so stupid.

Stumpy races in, nails scratching on the linoleum tiles. "Stop!" I yell, holding out my hand as if that might work. She doesn't listen. She's just a baby. She doesn't understand.

I drop to my knees and grab her as she hops her way toward me. "There's glass, baby. You have to stay out." She wiggles onto my lap. Pretty soon she'll be too big for it, but it works for now. I cradle her face in my hands, shaking it back and forth to make her ears flap. "I know," I croon. "It's not fair. No, it's not."

My hands are shaking, so I hold her a little tighter. Water drips from my soaking wet shirt to the floor.

The kitchen door opens. Stumpy yips in greeting, wiggling in desperation to run to Cooper. "No! Stop." My voice is hoarse.

Even with my back to the door, I can tell Cooper's stopped. The cool night air slips down the neck of my shirt and gives me goosebumps.

"Sean?" Plastic bags rattle. "What's going on? Are you all right?"

I don't look at him. "Yeah, I just, uh, dropped a glass." I turn and smile at him as if that will help sell the obvious lie. *Please believe me. Please don't ask me more.*

"Dropped with extreme prejudice, looks like." He looks from the mess to the sink, to the clock on the wall, and then back at me. "Why don't you take Stumpy outside for some air while I get this cleaned up?"

"No," I snap. Does he think I can't clean up after myself? Like I'm a child? "It was my acc-accident. I made the mess. I'll clean it up."

He steps further into the kitchen, letting the door close behind him. Shifting the grocery bags to one hand, he reaches down to pick up the largest shards of glass. "School got you that upset?" he asks without looking at me.

"Stop. I said I'd take care of it."

"You're barefoot," he says in a calm, rational tone that makes me want to hurl another glass at him. "And you're holding the dog."

"And you have groceries to get out of the truck." I struggle to my feet, not letting go of Stumpy as I do. I don't want her to get glass in her paws. "I'll put her in her crate, put shoes on, and then I'll clean it up." The kitchen is a mess. There's water everywhere and half the dishes are still dirty. Great. Just great.

You know what I don't need? This bullshit starting again. Goddamn it, why won't it just go away? How long am I going to have the deal with this?

Cooper walks over to the table, keeping distance between us. I follow him with my eyes. He puts the bags down. "The groceries will keep," he says with a smile meant to placate me. "We still had plenty of ice cream, so I didn't get any new. How about I take the puppy and crate her while you get your shoes?"

He holds out his arms and the puppy almost wiggles herself out of my grasp and onto the floor. "Jesus, dog. Cut it the fuck out already!"

Cooper's standing next to me now, like he teleported here. "Sean. Give me the dog." His voice is stern.

I do.

"And put some shoes on. Please," he adds softly. "I don't want you to get glass in your foot."

Dropping my gaze to the floor, I shove my hands in my pockets and nod. "Yeah. Fine. I'll—" I motion to the door. Not waiting for him to move, I scurry around him to go find my sneakers.

Cooper brings the rest of the groceries in through the back door while I mop the floor. After putting away the temperature-sensitive food like milk and sour cream, he sits at the kitchen table.

When I'm done mopping, I head back to the goddamn dishes. "Are you just going to sit there and watch?" I ask him.

"Yep," he says. "Do you want to talk about it?"

"There's nothing to talk about. I just dropped the glass."

"You dropped it horizontally across the kitchen?"

My sigh makes ripples on the water, and I grip the edge of the sink so hard my knuckles turn white. "I'm fine. Just a little stressed."

Cooper drums his fingers on the table, nails clicking on the surface. "Have you been stressed like this before?"

I carefully place a clean plate in the dish rack. "No. Yes. It's… fine. It's just stress. School. Money. Old shit I should have let go of a long time ago. You know how it is."

He looks so freaking concerned, and he's sitting so still. Like he's afraid I'm going to break, or maybe explode if he says or does the wrong thing. I'm so goddamn tired of people treating me like I'm fragile. How far away do I have to run to leave everything behind me?

I drop a mug I was cleaning back into the sink. Screw the dishes. They can sit. "I'm pretty tired," I say with my back still toward Cooper. "And I have some reading to do. I'm going to go to bed early. Raincheck on the movie?"

"Sean."

I turn and face him, crossing my arms. "Cooper."

He's looking at me like he's trying to read my mind. Good luck with that. I match him, stare for stare. *Look all you want. You're not going to see anything.*

Trying another tactic, he smiles at me and holds out his arms for me to come to him, a move that usually works. "Are you sure you don't want to sit and watch with me? I'll give you a neck massage, make some tea, help you destress?"

Enough. I pull the stopper out of the sink and let the water swirl away. "I just need some time alone. Is that too much to ask? God, we're together almost every waking minute. Can I just have one night to myself?" I'm not quite yelling at the end, but I am speaking louder than I normally do.

"Of course," Cooper says, annoyingly calm. "Go. I'll see you in the morning."

I storm out without a good night.

God, I'm being such a dick. I know it. But I can't seem to stop. I do need to be alone. Maybe take a shower, do some reading and homework. Put away the folded laundry that's been sitting on the floor for a week. Or maybe I'll see if Richie wants to play some Halo so I can shoot things.

Yeah. Shooting things sounds perfect.

SEAN

As soon as I think that, my phone beeps with a text from Richie. *Johnson, get off ur bf dick and get in the damn game.* Perfect timing.

I should never have told him about me and Cooper hooking up. He's more interested in the details than I would have predicted. But who else was I going to talk about it with? Also, the cute guy on the construction site now has a name that pops up with increasing frequency in his conversations. Joel. One day soon, I'll call him on it.

It takes me no time at all to turn on the computer and log in. I quickly lose myself in the fake violence and trash talk.

"If you fuckers tunnel any harder we're going to reach the Earth's core," CkMstr26 yells over the team chat.

I've got Richie on speaker over the phone so we can talk privately. I just have to remember to mute my mic when I don't want the group to hear what I'm saying. We do it so often, I'm an expert in paying attention to both conversations. I'm only about fifty-fifty in remembering to mute my mic though.

"Yeah, I can't fucking believe my little sister is talking about getting married," Richie is saying. "She's seventeen! And she's known this asshole like, what, three months?"

"What kind of loser would marry into your inbred family?"

someone on the team chat asks. Oops. Richie's even worse than I am about remembering to mute his mic.

"Ask your mom," Richie answers. Any version of "your mom" is a time-honored insult.

I mute my mic. "Three months is longer than I've known Cooper," I point out.

"Are you engaged?"

"No. Shit." I unmute. "Over there, over there!" I twist my body as if that will get my teammate to move. Wish I had an Xbox, playing on the PC isn't as much fun.

"It's not like Missy's in love," Richie continues between bouts of yelling at our teammates and hooting over kills. "Rafi, you fucking trash."

"How do you know?" I ask.

"How do I know Rafi's trash?" Richie replies. "His mom told me."

"Mute, damn it," I tell him. I wait until his group chat icon shows he's muted to ask, "How do you know Missy's not in love?"

He scoffs as if the very idea is ridiculous. "She's a kid and the guy is some jock. She's not in love, she just wants the D."

"How do you know she isn't?" I press. "Like, what could she say that would make you believe it? How did you know you were in love with Liza?"

Liza was Richie's girlfriend all through high school. We all thought for sure they'd be one of those couples who got hitched a week after graduation. Instead, she dumped him at our graduation party and headed to California for college.

"Dude. Seriously? Bite me, Crash, you asshole." That last part is directed at Crash, not me. "Are you tellin' me you are in love with this guy I haven't even met?"

"Who's in love with a guy?" Crash asks.

"Your mom," someone with a very young-sounding voice says. Richie's always inviting new people to run with us without doing any kind of check on who they might be. I hate playing with kids. Besides the fact that they suck at trash talking, gaming makes me curse and every time I do or talk trash, I feel like I'm contributing to the delinquency of a minor.

And God forbid it comes out that I'm gay. I don't want to be accused of being a pedo because I was playing Halo with some anonymous thirteen-year-old.

Mute your mike you fucking idiot, I text to Richie. He does.

"I am not *telling* you anything," I say. I'm a little distracted trying to snipe the asshole that's been spawn camping my team for the past ten minutes

"Oh, pardon me, your highness," he says in a fake snooty accent. "Please continue."

"Shut up." Richie has been giving me shit for trying to hide my accent, but he's never left Clarksburg, let alone the state. He hasn't seen the way people look at you like you're stupid when they hear it. I'm just trying to sound normal. "Never mind. I don't know what I was thinkin' askin' your sorry ass anyway."

Richie sighs. "Look. Beats the fuck outta me how you know. I don't know if I was in love with Liza."

"You said you were."

"I was seventeen, eighteen. I was thinking with my dick. She was hot and fun to hang out with. She let me have sex with her, and my ma and sisters liked her. Prob'ly more than they like me, I'm bein' honest."

"That doesn't help me at all." Not that I'd expected Richie to be a font of insight, but he has more first-hand knowledge with relationships than I do, that's for sure. "God damn it, Jazzy, you fucking leech," I yell into my headset mic. "Get in there and fight."

"Well, some of us ain't got your way with words, college boy." Richie sighs. "I might think I loved her. I couldn't imagine living without her. And I'll punch you if you repeat this, but I still miss her. I didn't realize how much I needed her. Problem was, she obviously didn't need me."

"Aw, poor Gonzo, dumped by his hot girlfriend," Crash says. Gonzo is Richie's handle on most games.

"Least I had one," Richie says. "Maybe when your balls drop, you can have one, too." Crash is sixteen and sounds like he's twelve.

I'd let the subject drop, but I need to know if I'm in love with Cooper. It matters. *Mute for five minutes?* I text. *I need to talk.*

It takes until we've killed a few bad guys for Richie to see my text. "Oh shit, sorry," he says. "What's up?" he asks over the phone.

"I think I might be in love with Cooper."

Richie gives a low whistle. "That was quick."

I sigh. "That's why I think that maybe I'm not? So, how do I know?"

"Jeez, dude. I don't know. With Liza, I felt like these sparks, you know? Every time I saw her. You got sparks with this guy? Do you want to jump his bones?"

"So many sparks, man. That is not the problem." I know for a fact that I'm in lust with Cooper. That's a much simpler emotion.

"Sean, dude, I'm not seeing what the problem is here."

"I want to do stuff with him. Like all the time." Cooper makes me want to do things I feel like I should go to confession for just thinking about.

"Good for you. You need it, man."

"It can't be normal to want sex this much." Despite having shoved a pillow behind my back, I can't get comfortable on the bed. If I'm going to stay here longer, I need to get some kind of desk and chair and a real mattress.

"First of all, that's totally normal. And secondly, fuck normal. What does that even mean? Liking sex is, like, nature. It's supposed to feel good and we're supposed to want to do it. Gotta maintain the species, right? Is your guy telling you that? Making you feel like a freak?"

"No. God no. He prob'ly wishes we'd do more." He's probably dying of blue balls. I know I am.

"Awesome. Green light. Go for it."

"You don't think it's kind of slutty, especially if I'm not in love with him?"

"I'm not following," Richie says. Which makes sense because I'm not even sure where I'm going with this. "Are you asking me if it's slutty for you to have the hots for your buff live-in boyfriend who wants to do what I imagine are disgustingly sexy things to you all day, every day?"

"Guess I am. D'you think that's stupid?" Of course, he does.

"Hell, yes, I think that's stupid. It's not like you're fifteen years old, for God's sake. You're a grown-ass man. So is he. Go for it. Grab him. Get naked. Get freaky on every surface. That's what's normal. Whatever you got going on in your head is what's fucked up."

Well, shit. Is it? I need to think about this a bit. Cooper's not some random guy. I'm near in love with him, far as I can tell. It's okay to want to have sex with someone you're in love with, even if you're gay, right?

"Besides," Richie says, interrupting my very important musing. "Who cares what you and Cooper are doing and how much you're doing it. Ain't nobody's business and how they gonna find out anyway, 'less you do it in public? Not like you're gonna text your momma every time you fuck, right?"

"You're right," I say, leaving out the fact that we haven't actually done that yet.

"Always am, dude. Now you gonna get your head in the game or what?"

"It's in. It's in."

I wake up God knows how much later, heart pounding with fear, echoes of far-away screams ringing in my ears, lungs choked by the stifling heat and humidity of a long-ago Alabama summer.

The stench of too many scared kids crammed into windowless, airless rooms clings to my nose.

The sheets are twisted around my legs, trapping me against the mattress. All my muscles are stiff and aching. My eyes are crusty and burning from sweat and tears of rage and helplessness. There's a lingering smell of drying seaweed and industrial cleaner and fear.

Fuck. Not again. *Get it together, Johnson.*

My eyes strain to see through the darkness. It's not real. It can't be real. Nightmare. It's nothing but a nightmare.

Yanking and kicking the sheet off, I struggle to get out of the damn air mattress. According to my phone, it's almost one a.m., less than two hours after I said goodbye to Richie. Dawn is a long way away.

Well, that sucks. I feel the nightmare lingering, waiting for me to drop my guard so it can ambush me again. There'll be no more sleep for me tonight.

I take deep breaths, shake my arms out, and pace around the room, trying to talk the fear away.

You're not there anymore. You're at Cooper's house. You're fine. Safe.

I walk to the bathroom, squinting my eyes against the bright light. Washing my face helps bring me back all the way to the present. So does taking a long drink directly from the faucet. Hands curled around the cool porcelain of the old sink, I stare at myself in the mirror. Unsurprisingly, I look like shit. Makes sense, it's been a shitty day.

All I want right now is Cooper. I was a dick to him earlier, and I don't even remember why. He cares about me. I know it. I feel it when he kisses me and see it in the way he looks at me sometimes. It takes my breath away.

I need him. I want him. He wants to help me, he said so himself. The only thing keeping us apart is me. I need to see him and tell him I'm sorry. That's what adults in relationships do, right? When they fuck up, they man up, apologize, and deal with it.

If Cooper is the man I'm sure he is, he'll forgive me. I brush my teeth, wash the sweat off my body as best I can with a washrag, and head downstairs to his room.

19

COOPER

Despite trying to fall asleep for the last few hours, all I've accomplished is to make the lump of unease growing in the pit of my stomach bigger.

Sean knocks softly at my bedroom door in the wee small hours of the night. "Cooper?"

"Yeah? I'm awake. What's up?"

"Can I come in?" he asks as if he's unsure if I'll say yes.

There's no reality in which I'd say no to Sean in my bedroom.

"Of course." Scrubbing the sleep from my face, I push up to sit against the headboard, making sure the sheet covers me from the waist down. I sleep naked. I click on the lamp on the nightstand as Sean comes in and I get a good look at his face.

He's been crying. It's the first time Sean is in my bedroom and he's crying.

I can see it in his red eyes and in the tracks of tears on his face. He's breaking my heart.

All night I've been fighting the urge to go to him and hold him, chase his demons away with my hands and my body.

But I didn't. Because he asked me not to.

All I can do is love him and wait for him to come to me.

"I need you."

And now he has.

"Anything." He hasn't moved beyond the doorframe.

"Can I sleep here? With you? I don' wanna sleep alone anymore. And I don't know why, but I think you can stop the nightmares." His voice is low and soft and his accent is the strongest I've heard it. It's the middle of the night and he's emotionally exhausted.

Now is not the time for words.

I hold out my hand and he walks over, sinking onto the bed with a sigh. All he's wearing is a pair of old, loose boxer shorts. I run my hand down the graceful line of his spine, feeling the bones pressing in my palm. "You can sleep here any time you want to."

His body relaxes.

"One question first."

He tenses up again.

"I'm in my birthday suit here. Should I put on some pants?"

He laughs softly. "Nah. It's okay. Not like I haven't seen it all already anyway."

"Then lie down." I make room for him on my right side, my good leg closest to him.

Sean fits against me like we're two puzzle pieces snapping together. His head on my shoulder, his arm across my chest, and his leg draped over mine. I wrap my arm around his back. His skin is so soft and my hand glides down his side, settling into the dip of his waist like it was built specifically for me.

He sighs deeply, his breath caressing my skin. "I'm sorry," he says. His face is pressed into my chest, and I feel his mouth moving. I tighten my hold on him. "It's okay. You don't have to apologize."

"But I want to."

"All right. We all have off nights. If you want, we can talk about it in the morning." I shut the light off. "I wish you would let me help you. Not because I think you *can't* handle it alone, but because you shouldn't have to."

He makes a sound as if that hadn't occurred to him. "You shouldn't have to deal with my problems, either, though."

"I'm no expert in relationships," I say. "But I'm pretty sure that helping each other with the tough things is one of those things you're supposed to do."

"I had a nightmare," he says.

"What happened in it?" I'm running my fingers through his hair the way we both love. His hair is thick and silken, and I love the way it feels between my fingers.

"I don't know. Nothing. I was doing dishes. Like tonight. 'Cept I was naked," he says with the shadow of a laugh that dies off quickly. "Why would I be naked?" he asks himself almost inaudibly. "You know when nightmares are scary because of the feeling? Not because of anything that's actually happening?"

"Yeah."

"It was like that." His voice trails off.

Restlessness pours off of him like body heat. He's caressing my chest, pushing the hair against the grain and smoothing it back down. He's avoiding my nipples, not consciously trying to start anything sexual, but his hips are rolling, subtly rubbing his still-soft cock against my thigh.

Now I'm wishing I had put some pants on. Sean is in my bed, touching me, heat pouring off his body, his hands on my body, and the thin sheet over my lap hides exactly nothing.

His fingers are circling closer and closer to my nipples, tracing figure eights around them. He exhales long and hot against my skin.

I let my hand drift from his hair to his shoulder. When his breath hitches, I slide it lower to the curve of his waist.

Of course, I want him, I always do. He's young and beautiful and infinitely interesting. And when he forces his way past whatever hang-ups he has about sex and lets himself get lost in the pleasure, he's impossible to look away from.

But he's skittish. Sometimes it feels like the more he enjoys sex, the deeper his enjoyment, the more he retreats. After the first time he came twice, once while straddling my hips while I stroked him as slowly as he could take, it was two days before he would even lean against me while we watched a movie.

There is no way I'll make any kind of move tonight, but it doesn't mean I won't talk. The next time his fingertips flirt with my nipples, I capture his hand in mine and bring it to my lips. I kiss his palm. "I've pictured you in my bed a hundred times, but not quite like this," I say lightly.

"Huh," Sean says. "I've pictured it a thousand. And this is exactly how I imagined it. It's perfect."

"Yeah, it is."

He lifts his head to look me in the eye. "I'm sorry. I shouldn't have lost my temper and I shouldn't have stomped away like that."

"Up the stairs even." I raised my eyebrows. "You know I can actually walk up the stairs?"

He kisses me quickly on the lips. "I know. But I know you're nice enough not to."

"I'm very nice," I say, my voice gravel-rough.

"You are," he says, voice thick and slow with arousal-laced sleepiness.

"I'm what? Nice?"

"Yeah. You look nice and you smell nice and you feel—"

"Nice?"

"Fucking amazing," he says forcefully. "And so hot. So sexy. I want to touch you, like, all the time," he says like he's confessing his sins. "You should have no shirt on all day every day." Now he drags his fingers across my nipples deliberately, watching for my reaction. He's fascinated with how sensitive I am, so much more than he is.

"You keep doing that, baby, and we're not going to get any sleep."

"Sorry." He stills but doesn't move his hand.

"I'm not. And I didn't say you had to stop."

He resumes his slow, gentle exploration of my body. "I can't help myself 'round you. It's so hard. I know I shouldn't, like, objectify you, and I don't want you to think I only lo—*like* you for your body and your superlative kissin' skills." He rolls onto his back and throws his arm across his eyes. "But, hand to heart, Cooper, it's making me crazy. I swear I'm half hard all the time. I'm sorry."

It takes me a second to process all that, to make sure I'm understanding him. I roll onto my side so I can face him. I manage to hold back the laughter, but a smile tugs the sides of my mouth tight. Sean's eyes are closed, his eyelashes a dark fringe. I trace my fingers along the lines of his cheekbones and over his lips. "Are you apologizing for wanting to have sex with me?"

"It can't be normal how much I want you." He moves his hand and looks directly at me. Even in the almost total darkness, I feel the zap of our connection run down my spine and into my balls.

Daring greatly, I reach for him and pull him tight against me. "Sean, I want it, too. I want you all the time. If it were up to me, we'd never get out of this bed."

His arms wrap around me. "Really?"

I laugh and he slaps my chest lightly. "Stop playing."

"Swear to God, Sean. I have never meant anything more in my life."

With a deep groan, he surges up, his mouth hot and open as soon as our lips touch.

It's far from the first time we've kissed, far from the first time we've been skin to skin. But those previous times were against the wall or on the living room couch with the light from the television illuminating our skin, the sounds of the movie softer than the ones we dragged out of each other.

This is something completely different.

My bedroom is a cave that smells like us. The only sounds are our breaths, the imagined beating of our hearts, and the soft snores of a puppy slumbering unaware in her crate. Remembering how the firelight had played over Sean's skin the night we first kissed, I wish briefly, nonsensically, that I'd put a fireplace in the room.

"Show me how much you want me," Sean whispers.

"I want you all the time." I kiss it into his skin. How much I want him, care for him, love him. Everything is whispers. My words, his sighs and moans. The sound of my hand on him and the sheets sighing across our skin.

Our kisses are slow, languid, hands tracing paths of heat and desire on our bodies. We grind against each other, arousal like molten honey spreading from my center filling me to the tips of my fingers and pounding in my temples.

"Like this," I say when he's spooned tightly against me, his back to my chest. He's got a death grip on my arm where it's wrapped around his shoulders, hand resting lightly against his throat. My cock presses into the sweat-slick space between his thighs, spreading his ass cheeks and sliding against his tight sack.

A shudder racks his body, and his breathing stutters.

"Is this okay?"

"God yes. Why does that feel so good?"

"Like this." I drape my free arm heavily over his hip, pressing his legs even more tightly together as I wrap my hand around his cock.

I roll my hips forward and back. Slowly like the tide, like the waves rolling onto the beach. Each forward thrust forcing a high-pitched gasp from Sean's throat.

Sweat drips from my temples and I struggle to keep my motions slow and controlled, fighting the urge to roll him face down onto the bed and bury myself in his warm, sweet, willing body.

"Cooper," he cries softly, voice straining, as I stroke him from root to tip. His fingers tighten on my arm and he throws his head back, neck arching like an invitation I can't refuse.

I drag my mouth over every inch of his neck and throat I can reach, straining up to lock my teeth into the curve of his neck. I'm riding the edge of explosion but I need him to come first.

My hand on him speeds up, holding almost too tightly as I thrust into him. He gasps, high-pitched and almost pained, in time with my thrusts. Soft *ah-ah-ahs* that threaten to tear me apart. My weight bears him down, rolling him onto his belly and trapping his cock between his body and the bed. He yells as I drive against the soft, glorious muscles of his ass, forcing him into my grip over and over.

Everything in me draws tight as the pleasure grows almost unbearable and my world narrows to heat, sweat, Sean's incoherent sighs, and the sound of our bodies coming together over and over.

Sean draws a ragged breath and holds it, his back arching, body tighter than a bowstring, and his cock throbs in my hand.

"Fuck!" All my weight drops on him and I thrust uncontrollably between his thighs, as he shoots hot and thick over my hand, each thrust forcing another pulse of heat from his cock and a grunt from his throat.

His legs tighten around my cock and the world disappears into a haze of white noise and fading vision as my orgasm slams into me. I come hard, spilling over his balls, the space between his thighs, and onto the ruined bedsheets.

After a timeless moment, my orgasm ebbs, and my muscles unlock. I drop my head against him, sweat dripping from me onto his skin. My heart slams against my ribcage so hard, he must feel it.

With one last full-body shudder, Sean collapses beneath me, muscles lax and breathing deep and desperate.

I roll onto my back with a deep groan. Sean stays face down on the mattress, hands clenched around my arm trapped between him and the bed.

His back rises and falls with the force of his breathing. He presses a soft kiss to my arm.

Heat radiates from his body, his skin glowing in the soft moonlight slipping through the cracks in my curtains. Sweat glistens in the damp curls at the base of his neck and the valley of his spine.

The curve of his ass is irresistible. Marshaling the remains of my energy, I roll back onto my side, sliding my half leg onto his hip for balance. "Is this okay?" I ask.

He exhales, back rising and falling, warm breath spilling over my skin, and he nods. I run my hand down his back, over the wings of his shoulders blades, over the hard ridges of his ribs, to the soft give of his waist. Goosebumps follow in the wake of my touch, and he shivers when I palm his ass cheek.

The inside of his thighs is shiny and slick, coated with my release, and sexy beyond belief. He gasps when I slip my hand between his legs. The gasp turns to a low moan when I caress him, thumb gently stroking the delicate skin of his balls and my fingers sliding through and around the mess.

"Cooper," he sighs, legs tightening and then relaxing. "You're so hot," I say with a kiss on his shoulder blade. "So fucking sexy."

He turns his head in my direction, the improbable blue of his eyes shining like ice in the low light. I can almost feel him debating whether to say something, something he can't take back.

Or maybe I'm just projecting because God knows I'm in love with him. I think I have been for a while, maybe since that first kiss. I want to tell him but I'm afraid. Afraid I'll chase him away. Afraid he doesn't feel the same.

I wonder if Sean knows he has the power to break my heart.

The silence stretches until Sean sighs. "Cooper."

What am I supposed to say to that?

He closes his eyes for a long second, then opens them, smiles, and stretches his neck to kiss me. "I need to clean up," he says, whatever it was hanging between us remaining unsaid.

"I guess you do. I'll change the sheets."

He stops to pet Stumpy through the wires of her crate.

Changing the sheets on my crutches is kind of a pain in the neck but I'm used to it. Sean comes out when I'm halfway through. He helps me finish up. Then I use the bathroom. It's all very domestic and cozy and makes my heart feel tight with all the things I need to leave unsaid.

With a sigh, he crawls under the covers. "I'm exhausted."

"Me, too." I open my arm for him to roll against me. "Let's call in sick to work tomorrow."

"Mmm-hmmm," Sean says in agreement. "I would, but my boss is a tyrant."

"Sounds awful. Why don't you quit?" I ask him with a kiss to his head.

"It has excellent perks," he says with a smothered laugh.

"Damn right," I agree. "Don't worry, I'll call the boss. Tell him to give you the day off."

"You're the best," he says, sleepily. "Can we do something tomorrow?"

"Like what?"

"Boat ride. I want to go out on the lake."

"Absolutely. Now sleep."

"Night," he mutters.

I watch him sleep for a while, wishing I could relax, that I could believe everything will be fine from here on in, but the scene in the kitchen still haunts me. The blank look in his eyes, the anger. It's familiar to me in a way I don't want to think about. So, I don't. I file it away to deal with later.

20

SEAN

"Yes, Mom. I'm eating, sleeping, all the things I've been able to do unsupervised since I was five." I've been ditching my mother's calls for a week now, and I had a feeling if I didn't call her back soon, she was going to show up on Cooper's doorstep one morning. She gives me an update on the family as I walk across the campus, dread and hope both roiling inside of me.

My trepidation isn't due to my mother's call, it's because of where I'm headed; Professor Ito's office. Talking to her about the class is another task I can't put off any longer. It's not quite the end of September. The semester is only three weeks old, and I'm already behind. If I don't get some help, I'll fail the class for sure, and that would be so embarrassing, I'd have to drop out of school.

Cooper promised me a date as a reward if I went today, and I could use a night out.

"Is Cooper still bein' nice?" my mother asks. "You two still gettin' on okay?"

"Oh, we are gettin' along jus' fine," I assure her, managing not to laugh. If she only knew exactly how we were getting on.

"You said he has no family, right?"

"No, he's all alone. It's kinda sad. He doesn't even have a lot of friends in town." I've been trying to get him to reach out to his army buddies, and he's been talking more with that friend he watches *Grey's Anatomy* with. I like her.

"You should bring him with you for Thanksgiving," she says. "We have plenty of space. And Troy and Dmitri will be here."

"Thanks, Mom. I'll ask him." It would be fun to have Cooper meet my family, and I know he'd like to see Troy again. "I gotta go," I tell her. "Meeting with my professor."

"I'm so proud of you," she says. I'm the first one in our family to go to college. That's another reason I can't fail, everybody back home is watching me, rooting for me. I can't let them down.

"Thanks, Mom. I love you."

"I love you, too," she says. "And I'll try not to bug you so much. I jus' worry. It's a momma's job."

"I know," I say. "But I'm fine. I promise. And I really have to go."

It takes a few more goodbyes before she actually hangs up.

Professor Ito's office looks exactly like I thought it would. It's tiny and lined with overflowing bookcases. Books that can't find a home on a shelf are stacked in corners and on any flat surface.

An electric kettle and a selection of teas peek out from the potted plants sitting on the wide radiator under the window. Coffee mugs, papers, and pens cover her desk.

Diplomas from Columbia and Stanford hang on the walls, along with yellowing newspaper articles about awards she's won and talks she's given. I swear there's a photograph of her with Maya Angelou, but I'm too far away to see for sure and too scared to ask directly.

Professor Ito rocks slowly back and forth in her impressive leather chair. Her head doesn't reach the top of the chair and I realize she can't be more than five foot two. Funny, because her aura can fill an auditorium. Her straight dark hair hangs to her shoulders, she wears bright-red cat's eye glasses, and I have no idea how old she is. Thirty-five? Fifty?

"What is it you're trying to say with your writing, Sean?" she asks. "What makes you special?"

Nothing, is the first answer that pops into my head, but I have the feeling she will not be happy with that. I steady myself before I answer, trying to keep the hillbilly out of my voice. It's always stronger right after I've talked to someone from back home on the phone. Stronger still when that person is my mother.

"I don't know, ma'am. I tried, in the assignment. Tried to write about an event in my life that was important to me." I'd written about that trip to Virginia Beach.

She nods. "Yes, you did. And it was very nice."

I flinch at the infinitesimal pause before the word nice.

"But I didn't learn anything about *you* from it. Tell me, what made it such an important moment?"

Oh man. I don't know. It was the first thing to pop into my mind when I read the assignment. It was the only thing to pop into my mind. It's kind of embarrassing that such a simple trip looms so large in my memory. "I guess it wasn't," I confess. "Lotsa...a lot of people go to Virginia Beach every day, I suppose."

"They do. But that doesn't mean it is any less special. As a matter of fact, it is the very ubiquity of the event that imbues it with a specific kind of specialness."

"You lost me," I say.

"There is an art in making the everyday visible, in making the commonplace uncommon so that people can experience it as if it is the first time. So, why, out of every moment in your life, did you write about that one?"

I give a short laugh. "Not like there were many other exciting moments for me to write about. I don't have an interesting life. Maybe I have nothing to write about yet. Not like I've done much."

"Bullshit," she says, enunciating clearly.

I never heard a teacher curse before.

"Excuse me, ma'am?"

"I said that's bullshit. You've had a life."

"Technically, sure. But nothin' interestin', nothin' special." The only unique experience I've had, if you could call it that, is not something I'll be writing fucking poetry about. No, thank you. I can't wait until I never have to think about it again.

Professor Ito's sigh brings me back to her office. She's looking up at the ceiling the same way my ma does when she's praying to God for the patience not to smack me into the middle of next week for being too stupid to live.

"Sorry for wasting your time," I say, and I start to stand up. Not a graceful task, as I'm sitting on a low round stool that swivels with every breath I take.

"Sit down," she says, pointing at the stool.

I sit.

"Where are you from, Sean?"

"Um. Nowhere..." I stop, pinned by her glare. "Clarksville, West Virginia, ma'am. Home of the marble."

"Please stop calling me ma'am every sentence. We don't have the time."

"Yes, ma—Professor."

"Wait, did you say home of marbles or home of *the* marble?"

"Marble. The round glass kind. Used to be a big factory in town, Akro Agate. Close up in the early fifties. Now some of them are collector's items."

"Huh." She rocks back in her chair. "I never thought about marble factories before."

"And the Mothman," I say, since we're talking about weird things from my home state.

"Pardon?"

"You familiar with the Mothman legend?"

"The name is familiar, but I can't say I know much about it."

"Old story from the sixties. They made a book and a movie

about it. Local haint, big flying guy with red eyes and wings. There's a statue of him over in Point Pleasant."

She throws out her arms as if to say *see*? And then shakes her head. "That right there. That's unique."

"But neither of those are things I had anything to do with," I protest.

"How many of my other students are from West Virginia, would you say?"

How would I know? It's a month into the semester, but I've barely spoken to anyone. I take a wild guess. "Three?"

"None. I believe you are the first student I've ever had. I'd venture to say most students I've had haven't even visited your home state."

Huh. That's a weird thing to think about. "Where I'm from, everyone's from West Virginia."

She laughs, a musical sound that I really like hearing. "Perfect. Bring that humor to your writing." She leans forward, studying me. "You're very striking. Interesting combination of features. Dark hair, olive skin, and those bright blue eyes. You don't see that a lot. What's your ethnic background?"

It's been a while since anyone's asked me that. Back home, most people know my whole life story, some better than I do. When people have to guess, they say Irish, or Mexican mixed with my ma's Italian genes. None of them are right.

"Italian and Persian," I say, like I'm confessing a secret.

She nods. "Not one of your more common backgrounds."

"My dad was an engineering student at the college. Mining. He and my mom met at a party when she was in high school and, well." I gesture at myself.

"Did he teach you any of his language? Culture? Did you meet his family?"

I shake my head quickly and rapidly. "No. No. They didn't get married. I barely met him when I was little. And the few times I did, well, I didn't like him."

"Was he Muslim?" she asks.

I'm not sure if she's allowed to ask these kinds of questions, but all at once, I can't hold back. I never talk about my father with anyone outside the family. Hell, we barely talk about him among ourselves. Maybe it's like Cooper said, it's easier to talk to strangers about certain things. And I trust her. "No, ma'am. Well, maybe he was once, I don't know. My mom didn't want to marry him, and he was gone by the time I was around six. Don't know where he went, but he got into some crazy Christian church. Really conservative."

Her perfectly shaped eyebrows Rose. "Now that's interesting. And your family?"

"Catholic. Used to be pretty devout but since, um, me and my uncle Troy, my mom's youngest brother, came out, they've stopped going as much."

"And when was that?"

"Three years ago, Christmas."

"Both of you at the same time?" I nod. "And how did that go over?"

I'm wringing my hands together, just thinking about it. "Well, Uncle Troy, he used to be a solider, and he's got PTSD. And my Uncle Davy took a swing at him, and Troy had some kind of attack and almost beat the crap out of him until his boyfriend and his service dog got him calmed down."

She pinches the bridge of her nose. "And your father? Does he know? Does it matter?"

"Oh, it matters," I say before I can censor myself. The look she gives me is level and quiet. "He, uh, found out. I don't know how. My mom swears she didn't tell him, but she knew way before Christmas. But he, uh, thought, thinks, that gay people are abominations and doing it for attention, and…" Nervous giggles are all that come out when I try to finish and I stare at the thick rug underneath my feet, tracing the swirling pattern of color threaded through it. I think it's a Persian rug, and I bite my teeth against some more giggles.

"Tea?" the professor asks, handing me a mug. Steam and the

sweet smell of mint rises from it. "It's not any fancy Japanese tea, don't worry. Just mint. Twining's, I believe."

I take the tea, not sure I want it, but it would be rude not to. I didn't even notice her turning the kettle on. I take a few sips while she talks about tea and how her mother is appalled at her love of supermarket American teas in bags, no less. And don't even get her started on the atrocity of putting stevia in it.

She putters around the office as she speaks, moving books from one pile to another. She pulls one off a shelf and holds it in her hands as she turns back to me. "Tea always helps, right?" she asks me with a smile. She looks a little concerned as if she thinks I might not like tea.

I realize I've finished most of the tea while I've been watching her. "Yes. Thank you."

She hands the book to me before sitting behind her desk again. *The Essence of Modern Haiku: 300 Poems* by Seishi Yamaguchi.

I open the book, flipping through the pages. Alongside the English translations, the haikus are written in two different languages I can't read. I'm going to go out on a limb and assume at least one of them is Japanese. There are also notes about the context of the poem and the reasons the translator chose certain words over other options. "Thank you." I close the book and wait for her to tell me what I'm supposed to do with it.

The sounds of the world outside come in through her open window. People calling to each other. Birdsong. Distant traffic. A gull screeches loudly and I flinch.

"I'll tell you the most important secret of being a writer. The only thing we have to bring to the table is our unique identity, our unique way of seeing the world. Everything humans experience has been written about. Time and time again. I've heard it boiled down to two main narratives: a man goes on a journey, and a stranger comes to town. Your story is both."

I nod, as if I understand what she's saying. The stupid gull won't stop that high-pitched screeching and it's distracting me.

She leans forward in her chair, shifting to her left to get

between my line of sight and the window. "Your journey is your life. You're a gay, half-Persian Catholic man from a small town deep in the heart of Appalachia. But even if you weren't, if you were a cis straight man from, I don't know, New York City, you would still be the only one who has lived your specific life. Even your identical twin would have had his own journey. And at this point in your story, you are the stranger who rides into town. Use that. Dig deep. Use all of those parts of yourself, even the ones you don't like, or don't want to think about. Sometimes those are the parts you need to reach most of all."

"I'm trying to do that." My voice is small, and I wrap and unwrap my fingers around the book, feeling the edge dig into the soft flesh where my fingers join my palm.

"I don't think you are," she says softly. "I think you're hiding a lot, the way you keep trying to hide that accent."

I don't say anything, but I feel the blush starting in my cheeks.

She throws herself back in her chair, making it rock gently. "I'm only telling you all this because, based only on this conversation and what you have turned it, I think you have potential. I'm not sure what form it will take, and you'll probably spend your life trying different things. But you'll have to be brave enough to put yourself out there with your words."

"Easier said than done," I mutter quietly. Not quietly enough, apparently.

She gives me a small smile. "I didn't say it was easy. Most important things aren't easy."

"So why this?" I hold the book up. "I've never written haikus."

"You know the basics, I assume?" she asks.

I nod. "Three lines, seventeen syllables. Five-seven-five? And aren't they traditionally about nature or seasons?"

"In English, yes, that's the syllable count. And they don't have to be *about* nature or even a particular season so much as be situated in a particular season. Traditionally they contain a *kigo*, a single word or phrase that does that work."

She can tell I don't quite get it. "When I say Thanksgiving in a poem, or even just mention turkey, you know exactly what season the poem is talking about, yes? Just that one word evokes a multitude of sensual associations, visual, emotional, even scent and sound."

I nod quickly. That I understand.

She smiles and continues. "In Japan, *sakura*, the cherry blossom, is a marker for spring. The fewer words or even syllables you can use as signifiers, the better. I want you to look through that book, find some haikus that speak to you. And then I want you to write me five of your own. Five haikus about your life. Make them tiny. Granular. The smallest glimpse into your life."

"Like what? Pepperoni rolls?"

"Yes." She leans forward, pointing a perfectly manicured bloodred fingernail at my chest. "Write a haiku about pepperoni rolls that makes me feel something about them, think about them and what they mean in a way I never did before."

"Find the specialness in the ubiquity?"

"Exactly that."

"In seventeen syllables?"

"I didn't say it was going to be easy," she says with a grin. Her eyes drift to the wall clock and I realize it's almost time for my next class. I don't even have time to hit the food court like I was going to. A candy bar and a Coke from the vending machines will have to do.

I stand up. "Thank you, Professor."

"You are welcome. Not only is it my job, Sean, it's been a pleasure. Are you feeling a little more clear on my expectations for you, for the entire class?"

"Maybe?" I hold the book of haikus up. "This will help, I bet. And I promise to think about what you've said. When I doubt myself, I'll try to remember you think I have something unique to say even if I don't."

"Excellent. And my door is always open. I find the more a student takes advantage of that fact, they better they tend to do. Come back and tell me some stories. Let me hear that accent some more so when I read the poems, I hear them in your voice, in more ways than one."

"I will. I promise. Thank you again."

She waves me out of her office. "Shut the door when you leave, please."

I barely make it to my next class on time and never do get time to hit up the vending machines.

The good feeling from Professor Ito's words fades along with my energy as the day drags on. By the end of the last class, my head is pounding and I'm on edge.

I can't be sure if I'm on edge because of something or if the feeling is making me look for reasons to justify it.

21

COOPER

The combination garage-workroom on the side of the property is one of the main reasons I bought this house. The workroom isn't anything fancy, but the rough-hewn wooden benches down both long sides have heavy duty outlets every few feet and there are shelves and pegboards for storage. The sliding barn doors on the back give me a view of the lake and the matching doors on the front of the structure let in sunlight and a nice cross breeze. It's a hot day, but the shaded corners of the room are cool. It will be cold in the winter, but there's an old free-standing wood stove in one corner with a round tin pipe stuck through a hole in the roof for a chimney.

I'm taking a lunch break from my current job of cutting boards for the siding. Built in the nineteen-sixties, the house isn't old enough to be historic. It's just old. But luckily, it had either escaped being entombed in vinyl siding, or a previous owner had stripped it off, leaving behind the wood.

The entire house needs to be stripped and repainted, but I don't have the funds for that yet, and I really don't want to do it myself. Most of the boards are either easily repairable or in decent enough shape to survive one more winter, but a handful are too damaged to fix. We also need to replace molding and trim around the doors and windows. I have big plans for the kitchen cabinets, but those can wait until the exterior is finished. I'll take my time working on them over the winter.

I've let Stumpy out of her crate so we can eat lunch together. Stumpy scarfs down her food as if she hasn't eaten for a week, and then sits at my feet and stares at my sandwich. "Not happening, dog," I tell her.

How can it be that Sean's only been around for a few weeks and already the house feels empty without him in it? And I feel lonely without him near me.

Every time I see him, I get a jolt right to my core, just like the first time. It's not only because of how beautiful he is, though sometimes looking at him takes my breath away. He's smart, he's funny. When he's passionate about something, he speaks with his whole body, hands in the air, words just spilling out of him like a river tripping down those Appalachian mountains of his.

And if sometimes his bright and shiny youth makes me feel old and scared and damaged, that's my issue, not his. He's never said anything to make me feel that way. He doesn't shy away from the stump or the scars on my shoulders.

"I'm ridiculous," I say, reaching down to scratch behind Stumpy's ears. "But he is something else, right?" She gives me her doggy smile, tongue hanging out, eyes wide and adoring. I can tell she agrees with me.

And then there's the sex.

I'll never admit it to Sean, but I love that I'm the first person that gets to make love to him. If I have my way, I'll be the last. When he comes, his eyes get wide and surprised, like he can't believe how good it feels, like he never knew it could be like that.

Neither can I. Probably because it never has before Sean. God. Maybe I should be the one writing poetry, or at least trying to write some lyrics for my music. I know what I'm trying to say with each composition, but I can never find the words to match. But Sean makes me want to try.

"I'm a cliché," I say to Stumpy. "An older beat-up man in love with a bright shiny new boy." Stumpy doesn't laugh and she doesn't judge. She just listens. "Don't tell Sean," I say, feeding her a piece of ham from my sandwich as a reward for her understanding.

Time to get back to work. Sean and I have a date tonight. I'll have to hustle to get everything finished and still have time to take a shower and shave.

Sean calls while I'm getting dressed after my shower. "Hey, I was just thinking about you," I say.

"Hi."

Just that one word and I can tell something wrong. "Are you okay?"

"I'm fine, just exhausted. Would you be mad if we stayed in tonight?"

"Of course not." I really don't mind. Stay in, go out, as long as we're together, I'm good. Tonight is not the night to bring up my insecurities. Tonight, Sean needs me to take care of him, and it makes me happy to be able to do it.

"Can you pick me up? I am not feeling up to biking home. I skipped lunch and…"

"No need to explain. Tell me where to meet you."

He does. I throw on clean shorts and a T-shirt and take a few minutes to throw together a sandwich and a travel mug of coffee for him before I leave.

"What if I suck? What if I'm fooling myself?" Sean barrels on without waiting for me to respond. "I mean, it's not like a creative writing degree is useful at all. I'm probably wasting my time and money. It's not like I thought I could make a living as a poet. I'm not an idiot. But I hoped, maybe, you know, people would at least read them. Not a lot of people. Maybe say good things about them. Maybe I could be a writing teacher one day. It's stupid. It was a stupid dream. Everyone was right."

Sean holds the sandwich and travel mug I'd handed him as soon as he'd gotten settled in my truck, but despite moving both toward his mouth, has yet to take a bite of food or a sip of coffee.

That's enough of that. His shoulders are up around his ears and tension and sadness radiate from him. "It's not a stupid dream. It's not," I repeat when he gives me a skeptical look.

"All my life," he says staring out the side window, "all my life everyone has said I'm a dreamer. Like it's a bad thing. I should be more realistic. Life isn't scribbling in a notebook. It's hard work and taking care of your family. Why do I have to be so difficult? Why do I have to be different? Why can't I just be normal?"

"That's a load of horseshit if I ever heard one." I may have said that more emphatically than I'd intended, but, God, he's breaking my heart. "Who told you that?"

He shrugs. "Everyone. Teachers. My mom. My dad." He says that last word through clenched teeth, speaking so quietly I almost don't hear it.

It's only a short drive between the university and my house, but I've noticed Sean opens up more when we're driving than if we're face to face, so I take the long way, circling down side streets and back roads. He doesn't notice.

"I want to hear all your dreams. They're amazing. I think you're brilliant. You should chase them with everything you have. Which is a damn lot. A damn sight more than a lot of people I know."

He shakes his head.

"I've never met anyone like you, Sean."

"Foolish?"

Stretching my arm across the space between us, I rest my hand on his neck. When he doesn't flinch away, I massage the spot where his spine connects with his skull, pressing firmly into the rock-hard muscles. Squeeze and release. Repeating it until his shoulders drop and he exhales, his head falling forward, giving me more room to work.

"Sean, what did we talk about?" We've been working on him learning to take a compliment. He hasn't had enough in his life to be used to it.

He sighs deeply. "That you're a New Englander, born and bred, and not in the habit of wasting words so I should save time and believe that you mean what you say." He says it like a kid repeating something his parents have said a thousand times.

"And do you believe *that*?"

He laughs. "Guess I have to."

With a touch to his elbow, I nudge the hand holding the sandwich closer to his mouth. "Eat. It will help."

As he eats, I massage his neck as best as I can with one hand, moving from his shoulders to the base of his skull until he relaxes. "Better?"

"A little." He stretches his neck side to side and then tips his head front to back with a happy sigh. "Thanks for that. Felt amazing. It's been a day, you know?"

"Do you want to know one of my dreams?" I ask.

"Of course."

"They're nothing like yours. I've never been able to think as big as you do."

"Yeah, cause you're normal."

"Boring, compared to you. I want to have a big, traditional Thanksgiving dinner, like in a Norman Rockwell painting, in my own home. With all the trimmings and friends and family and football on the lawn. The works."

"Not Christmas dinner?"

"No, Christmas is too high pressure. Thanksgiving is easy. It's eating food with people you love and taking the time to be grateful for all the good things in your life. My entire life, I've been a guest at someone else's table. I'm grateful to all my friends who invited me, don't get me wrong, but I would love to be the host for a change." All I've ever wanted is a place of my own. Now I have it, and I'm going to make the most of it.

"With your husband and kids at your side," Sean says.

"One day, yes."

"I can make that happen." He freezes mid bite of sandwich, his cheeks flaming red. "The dinner part, I meant. Not, the, uh…"

"Are you saying you don't want to have my babies, Sean?"

He laughs around a mouthful of peanut butter and jelly. "I'm worried about keeping my girlish figure," he says.

I turn on the radio to stop me from saying anything stupid about me and Sean and the future. "You can pick something," I say.

"Dang. I must look like crap if you're letting me choose."

"I'm happy to pick something if you're not up to it."

"No, no. I'm good." Placing the sandwich on the seat next to him, he takes a long sip of coffee and then sighs. "That's so good. Thank you." Humming to himself, he scrolls though his songs on his phone, connecting to the Bluetooth when he finds one he's happy with.

It takes me a second to place the music. "Billy Joel?"

"My grandma loves him. Makes me think of her when I hear him. It's kind of corny, I know. But I love it."

"Everybody loves at least one Billy Joel song. If they say they don't, they're lying."

By the time "Piano Man" is over, Sean's finished all of the food and most of his coffee.

"Sorry I ruined our date night," he says.

"It's not ruined."

"Would have been a nice night to walk around town though."

He's not wrong. On the cusp of September, the sun is still well above the horizon at six in the evening but the worst of the humidity is gone. Right now, it's still warm enough for a T-shirt, but later tonight, people will be pulling out their flannels and fleeces if they're outside. Some of the sugar maples near my house are already considering changing colors, their green leaves shading toward yellow at the tips.

"We can still go," I say.

Sean shakes his head. "I just want to go home. Pet Stumpy."

"That works for me. It's a gorgeous night for a fire on the beach, too. We can pick up some food on our way through town, if you'd like."

"I don't feel like stopping," he says. "I'll cook. Might take you up on that fire, though."

"Sounds good." It sounded perfect. "Speaking of dates, I have an appointment with my prosthetist next week. I was hoping you'd come with me."

"Sounds romantic," he says.

"It's in Boston, smartass. I was thinking we could make a trip out of it. After the doctor, we could get a hotel room, do some sightseeing, have dinner at a swanky restaurant." He wants romance, I'll give him romance. I haven't had a lot of opportunity to do that before, it could be fun.

"In that case, sign me up," he says. "I can amuse myself while you're at your appointment."

"I was assuming you'd come with me," I say. "But obviously you don't have to."

We pull into my driveway, and Sean stops me before I can step out of the truck. "I would be happy to go to your appointment with you. I'm honored you trust me enough for that."

"It will be nice not to be alone for once," I say. "Now let's get this date night started."

22

SEAN

Instead of cooking anything new, we decide to clear out the leftovers from the fridge. A barbequed chicken leg and thigh, a couple of scoops of potato salad, a thick slab of meatloaf, one pork chop, and some roasted broccoli.

I'm still unsettled. I feel like I'm going to come out of my skin. Cooper's in an odd mood, too. Not sure if it's because of me or if he has something on his mind. I could ask, of course, but truthfully, I'm afraid to find out it *is* me. Surely that can wait for another day.

We're sitting side by side on the bench, our backs to the table. Cooper's drinking some nasty IPA and I'm on my second bottle of Shipley's amber cider. Ever since that first night at V and V, Cooper makes sure to keep some in the house. I'll have to bring a bunch home for my family for Thanksgiving.

Speaking of which. I knock my knee against Cooper's. "Do you want to come to Clarksburg with me for Thanksgiving? I think Troy and Dmitri are coming over, too."

"Won't it be weird for me to be there?"

"Why? My mom wants to meet you. She's the one who suggested it."

"Was that before or after we…?" He motions between us with his bottle.

"After." I grin at him. "I mean, this," I copy his motion, "took us a whole, what, three days to get to?"

It's hard to tell behind the beard, but I think he's blushing. I look closer. He is. "You're blushing!"

He scoffs.

"You totally are." I put my hand on his cheek. It's warm. "That's adorable."

"Will you tell them we're dating, if I go?" he asks.

Huh. That's a really good question. "I don't know. I can't imagine talking to my mom about my sex life. Not that I've had one before." I make the gesture with the bottle again.

Cooper gives me a look that I don't quite understand. He looks confused, maybe. And hurt? "What?"

"Telling her we're dating isn't talking about your sex life," he says. Yeah, that's confusion in his tone. "It's telling her that there's someone important to you in your life. Someone new. And wanting her to meet them." There's the hurt.

Oh fuck. I am so bad at this. "Cooper, I'm sorry."

The anger I felt before is starting to come back and I don't want it. I won't have it ruining this beautiful night and this peaceful moment between me and Cooper.

"What are you thinking?" Cooper asks.

"I feel a bit like I've fallen down a rabbit hole. Though gone over the rainbow is probably a better metaphor."

"In what way?"

"My town, my old world, is so straight, so heteronormative. Outside of Troy and Dmitri and some people I met…somewhere else. Do you know, before Troy came out, I'd never even talked to someone else I knew for sure was gay in real life."

"Really?"

I don't look at him, not wanting to see pity in his eyes. "I know, I know. There's gay people everywhere. But let me tell you, they were mighty quiet about it back home. And whenever people talked about 'the gays,' it was like they were this separate breed of humans that only existed somewhere else. In some unsavory big city like San Francisco or New York."

"Not in small towns," he says.

"Exactly. But that's a lie. I'm here. You're here. People like Dr. Moore and Tai and Briar are just…out there. Living their lives. Part of the neighborhood. Like it's a perfectly normal thing."

My voice has gotten higher and louder and my hands are clenched around the bottle. So much for not getting angry again.

"Come here," Cooper says. "Sean, please."

I sit as close to him as I can on the bench. He puts his arm around me, and I lean into his side, taking the silent offer of comfort.

"It *is* normal," he says.

I'm not expecting the tightness in my chest or the tears that come to my eyes.

"*You* are normal," he says quietly but firmly. "We," Cooper taps himself on his chest, "are normal." He kisses the top of my head.

I wrap my arms around him and cling like an octopus.

He gently pats my back.

"I know that in here." I tap my head. "But here…" I tap my chest, not sure how to finish that sentence.

"Knowing something is different from believing it," Cooper says softly. "I get it."

I want him to tell me I'm normal again. Maybe if he says it enough times, I'll believe it. What would happen if I told Cooper everything, everything that happened and all the stupid confusing thoughts that keep swirling around in my head and how I never, ever feel like I belong anywhere? Would he still think I was normal? Or would he say it's too much for him to deal with? I don't want to add to his burdens.

"You okay?" he asks.

"For right now? Yes." I kiss the line of his jaw. "Thank you for not tossing me in the lake or out onto the street."

When he laughs, his chest moves up and down and I feel the rumbling against my cheek. "I would never. You'd track mud and sand and water into the house and I'd have to clean it up."

"I promise I will clean up. If you think I need to be dunked to get some sense into my head, you do it."

"Fine."

I sit up and look at him. "You agreed to that suspiciously quickly."

He shrugs and sips his beer, a Cheshire cat smile on his lips. "You're the one who suggested it."

I settle back against him with a sigh.

He rubs my arm up and down, soothing me. "Not to bring up another touchy subject," he says after a few seconds of watching the sun sinking toward the water and turning the sky orange, "but how did it go with your professor? You were upset when I picked you up."

"Good. I think. I think she likes me."

"Of course she likes you."

"You have to say that. You're my boyfriend."

He smiles down at me, tilting my head up for a kiss. "I am, aren't I?"

I kiss him back. "You are. And of course I will tell my family that. Though the kissing will probably give it away."

We make out a little more. It starts out slow and sweet, but the promise of more is in each kiss. Sadly, the bench isn't the best place for it, and I kind of want to watch the sunset. Tonight's looks like it might be one of the spectacular ones.

Cooper doesn't object when I stop kissing him and lean against his chest again. He rests his hand on the back of my neck and starts giving me another of those amazing massages.

I groan, and let my head fall forward to give him more room. "Don't stop."

"I won't if you tell me what the professor said."

I groan for a different reason. "She wants me to write five haikus about being gay and from West Virginia. Haikus!"

"You can do it," Cooper says. "I'd love to read them, if you'll let me. It's kind of an interesting experiment, isn't it? Trying to fit such a big thing into such a little poem."

That's such a spot-on observation that I sit up straight, shocked into silence. Will he ever stop surprising me? I doubt it. I hope I get a long, long time to find out.

"Yeah," I finally say through a rough throat. "Exactly. How do you always know the perfect thing to say?"

He laughs loudly. "Never before in my life have I been accused of that."

"Maybe it's just me," I say, thumb picking at the cider bottle's label where condensation has made it start to separate from the glass. "Because I think you're just about perfect." Resting my elbows on my knees, I look up at Cooper the way I know he likes. I don't know what he sees, but it makes his breath hitch every time. "You're just about everything good to me."

Sure enough, I get the hitched breath and heat, so much heat, but there's something else in his eyes tonight. Something deeper that scares me a little with all the promises it holds.

"You better be hoping to be kissed if you're going to be saying things like that while you're giving me those eyes."

"I thought you were immune to my eyes." I blink quickly.

"Not those ones," he confesses with a growl that goes directly to my cock.

"Shit, Cooper. Kiss me already."

That earns me another of those sexy growls, and his hands clamp onto my arms as he hauls me onto his lap.

Fuck yes. I grab onto his shoulders and slam our mouths together. His tongue immediately invades my mouth, exploring every inch of it. I let out a manly whimper when he pulls back.

"Sweet," he says. "That cider tastes better on you."

I stretch my arm out and grab my abandoned bottle of cider, taking another long sip, making it sloppy. "More."

I expect him to dive right back in. Instead, he cradles my face in his huge, warm palms, holding me in place, and then he licks the cider off my lips with long, slow drags of his tongue.

My hands close convulsively on his shoulders, and I press against him as hard as I can, like I'll die if I don't get some friction on my cock right this second.

He sucks my bottom lip into his mouth, searching for more, and then releases it with a nip of his teeth. He pulls away, resting our heads together. We're both panting for breath and he's as hard as I am.

Still cradling my face, he rolls his forehead against mine, his beard scratching erotically across my lips and proving once again that my mouth is connected directly to my cock.

"Holy shit," I whisper. "That, that was a fucking kiss for the record books."

He laughs breathlessly.

Stumpy hops over to us, barking sharply, excited by what she sees as us playing.

"More." I grab the back of his head this time and dive back in for more X-rated kissing. Cooper wraps his arms around me, holding me as tightly against him as he can.

Cupping my hands around his face and tilting his head back, I press down, forcing his mouth open, and shoving my tongue halfway down his throat, desperate for him in a way I've never been before.

The table groans as we rock against it, his arms crush me to his chest so tightly that breathing is becoming an issue. The hot, wet suction of his mouth on my tongue is giving my cock ideas, and we're in serious danger of falling off the bench.

Stumpy, tired of being ignored, shoves her nose against my lower back where my shirt has rucked up from Cooper's hands. I jolt upright, pulling myself out of Cooper's mouth and hands. Twisting around, I push her away. "Damn it, Stumps."

Cooper laughs at me, his hands back on my hips.

When I turn back to him, whatever smart-assed comment I was going to make gets lost at the way his dark eyes are shining at me, and the smile on his beautiful mouth. His lips are pink and full from the force of our kisses. He's the most gorgeous man I've ever seen and I am so in love with him I can barely breathe.

I grab his hand and tug him off the table. "Stumpy. Bedtime. Now." Making sure Cooper has his footing, I drag him inside.

23

COOPER

As soon as the door closes behind us, Sean is on me. With a trembling hand, he gently pushes me against the wall. His eyes lock on mine and it's as if the air pressure in the room has shifted.

There's an intensity in his gaze and in the tension in his body.

This is important. This moment means something.

I reach up to touch his face. "God, the way you look at me," I say reverently.

"How do I look at you?" His voice is deep, thrumming with a maturity I've been noticing more and more since that night he came to my room. Something changed then. Something leading to this moment.

"Like you can't believe what you're seeing. Like I'm every Christmas present you ever wanted rolled into one."

"That's how I feel." His thumb traces over my lips, still sensitive from our kissing. His fingers follow the edge of my jaw, slide around the back of my neck.

Gone is the shy, tentative boy of a few weeks ago, and in his place is the confident man I sensed was there. Those first cautious but oh-so-sweet times we touched, where he begged me to teach him, to show him how to give and receive pleasure, are being replaced with something more. Something deeper.

Sean slides his thigh between my legs. "The way you look at me brings me to my knees," he says against my lips.

"How's that?"

"Like you never want to look at anyone else."

"Imagine that," I say. Sliding my hands down his shorts, I grab two handfuls of his perfect ass as I steal the kiss he's been promising.

Sean melts against me with a moan, his mouth opening at my touch. I grind against his thigh, chasing the friction and pressure. He's already hard, pressing against my hip.

Sean pulls off gasping, resting his forehead against mine, hand still cradling my skull.

I reach up and grab his wrist. "Sean."

"I want you," he says.

"You have me. All of me."

"I want you to make love to me."

I can feel the heat from his blush against my lips, but there's no hesitation in his voice. My hands tighten on his ass. "Yeah?" I croak through a dry throat.

He nods, rolling his forehead against mine. He kisses his way down my temple and cheekbone to my ear. "But first I want to get my mouth on you," he whispers, then bites softly at my earlobe.

Jesus. With a hand on his chin, I pull his face to me, so I can look into his eyes. "You're sure?" Not that I think he doesn't know his own mind, but I can't help asking.

"Been thinkin' about it a long time." He makes an almost silent laugh. "A very long time."

"Me, too," I confess.

"Bedroom," he says, grabbing my hand. "We're going to need a bed for this."

"That sounds like an excellent plan."

With a quick look at Stumpy, who's taken advantage of our distraction to curl up on the couch, I let him lead me to my room. Without stopping, he pulls his shirt over his head, tossing it aside. All that warm skin is irresistible, so I don't even try to resist it. I tug him back, wrapping my arm around his stomach. Pressing kisses to the nape of his neck, I push him against the wall next to the bedroom door.

He hits it with a groan, hands slapping against the wall. My hands are all over him, feeling every inch of skin I can. When my fingers slip under the waistband of his shorts, he inhales sharply. "Cooper," he says, drawing my name out deliciously. His stomach draws in with the force of his inhale, his shorts hanging from his hipbones like an invitation I can't refuse. With two quick tugs, they slide over the curve of his ass and down to the floor. I grab him through his boxer briefs. I know the biting kisses I'm pressing into the side of his throat and the curve of his shoulder will leave marks, but I don't care.

I crowd him tighter against the wall, rubbing my thumb over the head of his cock, and grind against him as if I could take him right here.

"Cooper!" he yells, throwing his head back. "Fuck. Stop. It's too good. I'm gonna come." He drops his head back against the wall. "God. The door's right there."

"I'm not the one stripping in the hallway," I growl, giving his cock a squeeze. Then I step away, not touching him anywhere. He whines at the loss of contact, so I slap his ass. "Stop dawdling," I say, moving quickly into the bedroom.

He kicks his shorts away, reaching the door a half-second behind me.

When I hit the bed, I turn, catching him in my arms, checking him out. "Underwear and sneakers. Hot. Like a jock porno."

"Shut up," he says as he tries to take my shirt off. I lift my arms, more than happy to help.

"Leg off or on?" he asks, running his hands over my chest, paying special attention to my nipples the way he knows makes me crazy. Very distracting when I'm trying to take my shorts off.

"Off." I might miss the extra leverage, but all I want in bed with us is skin.

"Then get naked," he orders.

"I've taught you well," I say, shoving my shorts and underwear to the ground and then sitting on the edge of the bed.

"I'm a sex savant." After he's gloriously naked, he kneels and takes the sneaker off my good leg, while I make quick work of the prosthesis.

Sean spreads my legs so he can kneel between them. "Since I'm already here."

He wraps a hand around my cock, something we've done many times before, and gives a slow stroke down and back up. Opening his mouth and sticking his tongue out, he pulls me toward him. And, Christ, isn't that a picture. I know I'll take that image to the grave.

He runs his thumb over the head, collecting the single pearl of pre-cum sitting on the tip. Without letting go of my cock, he looks up at me through his long, dark lashes and leans forward to lick his thumb.

I suck in a breath and my cock jumps in his hand. His mouth curves in a filthy smile. "Not bad," he says, licking his thumb again.

"Jesus, Sean."

He grins and then slides me into his mouth like he's done it a hundred times.

"Oh fuck." I say, grabbing his shoulders.

It's messy, more enthusiasm than technique, and it's the best blow job I've ever gotten. He's touching me everywhere he can reach, palm cupping my balls and fingers digging into my thighs.

I'm clutching one hand in the sheet and the other on his shoulder. An unintentional thrust of my hips shoves my cock deeper into his mouth than he was ready for and he gags. He pulls off, strands of spit keeping us connected. There's spit on his chin, and his lips are shiny and swollen. "Sorry," he says, wiping his mouth.

With a groan, I get a handful of his hair and pull him back onto me. He groans like he's dying and grabs my thighs hard enough to bruise, handing me control of his mouth.

It's filthy.

My mouth is desert dry. Sean's moaning and grunting around me, fisting his cock like a desperate man.

I'm so close, but all I can think about is getting inside him. "Sean," I groan. "If you want me to fuck you, you have to stop." I pull his head off me.

He sits back on his heels, a death grip on the base of his cock, and a huge grin on his face. "Fuck, Cooper. That was so hot, with your hand in my hair and everything. I had no idea I could get off on giving a blow job. I thought it was just fun for the person getting the blowjob."

I laugh, caressing my erection just to relieve some of the ache. "God, no. Believe me, I love getting my mouth on you."

"I get it now. We are definitely going to have to do that again real soon."

"Oh, we will. But for now, get up here."

In record time, Sean is on his back and I'm kissing every inch of skin I can reach.

Without moving my mouth from Sean, I slick up my fingers and reach between his legs. Sean whimpers and spreads his legs wider. With a finger pressed against his entrance, I kiss him. "Is this okay? Is it good? You want me to stop?"

He lifts his head and huffs a small laugh. "It feels so good. So good. Stop, and I'll kill you."

Slowly, but steadily, I push in. Sean hisses through his teeth, and I hold back a groan. He's so hot and tight. I slide my finger steadily in and out, mesmerized by the silken feel, until Sean cuffs me weakly on the side of the head. "More. More. God, Cooper."

I give him what he's asking for, pushing in a second finger, pumping harder and faster. Sean is panting. If he thinks that feels good, wait until he feels this. I crook my fingers up, searching for that magic spot. Sean shouts, almost levitating off the bed. Found it.

"Jesus fucking Christ. Fuck me already," he cries.

"Ooh," I say, kissing his shoulder. "Your grandmother would

not appreciate that language." I ghost my fingers over his prostate again, just to see him shiver.

"I don't think she'd appreciate any of this, so for the love of God stop talking about her."

"Yes, sir. But you're not ready yet."

He grumbles a wordless complaint.

"Trust me," I say, kissing him and slowly shoving my fingers back in him.

"Cooper!" Sean cries.

God, the way he looks. His eyes are wide and wild, fixed on mine. He's clenching the sheets, pulling them up and off the mattress. A pink flush spreads down his golden skin from his cheeks to his chest and his nipples are tight and hard. His cock is dark red and throbbing, shiny with the pearlescent fluid sliding down it. He's so hard it looks almost painful and I can feel his heartbeat against my fingertip.

I angle my wrist, driving my fingers deep inside him when he slams down again. His eyes get impossibly wider and he lifts his hips as high as he can again, arching off the bed. He's clenching my shoulder, and mouthing *fuck, Cooper, fuck, Cooper* over and over like they're the only two words he can remember.

Between his breathless, almost silent whines, the way he's riding my finger, hips pumping like a pro, and the way he looks, I'm seconds away from coming without even getting to the main event.

So is he. I can tell. His cock is hard and his thighs are trembling.

"You have to stop," he says. "I don't want to come until you're inside me."

I pull reluctantly out of his body. "Keep talking like that and it's going to be over before it starts," I warn him.

"Please," he begs.

"Okay, okay." Wiping my fingers off on the sheet, I stroke him from throat to groin. "Hold on." I reach for the condom.

"Do we need to use one?" Sean asks. "This is my first time."

I hesitate. During my lengthy hospital stay, I was tested and retested for everything six ways to Sunday. All negative and I haven't been with anyone since then.

But Sean should get in the habit of using them, especially with other people. God, I hate the idea of him being with anyone else.

"Cooper?"

"It's not completely necessary," I admit. "But it's a good habit to use one. Especially with…" I can't finish that sentence.

He reaches up and touches my cheek. "Hey. With someone else?" he asks.

I nod.

"There isn't anyone else and I not looking for anyone else. I only want you."

I have to kiss him, then. I'll never hold him to that, of course, but I love hearing it. "Thank you," I tell him between kisses.

"For what?" he asks.

"For letting me be your first."

"I can't imagine anyone better," he says. "Of course, that assumes we're actually going to get to the sex sometime this century," he says, grabbing my hand and dragging it back between his legs.

"Anything for you, baby."

"How, uh, should we do this?" he asks.

"We could do it like this, spooning, both on our sides. Remember?"

He turns to face me and touches my cheek. "I'll never forget it."

I kiss his palm. "Or I could lie on my back and you could ride me." Wrapping my arm around his waist, I pull him closer. We kiss like it's the last time we're going to get the chance. The way he grinds on me, sliding our bodies against each other, threatens to make the question of positions a moot point.

Sean pulls off, gasping for air. He rolls onto his back, chest heaving, and grabs himself to stave off his orgasm. "Okay. Okay."

"Ride me," I say. "I need to see your face."

"God, you're brilliant," he says, sitting up and pushing me onto my back. Before I can blink, he's straddling me. "Oh God," he says, bracing himself on my chest and rolling his hips over my cock.

I grab his hips. "More lube."

"More?"

"Can never have too much." I find the tube, and he grabs it out of my hand.

"Let me." With an evil smile, he squeezes a nice size blob onto his palm. Coming up to his knees, he reaches behind him and slicks me up.

"Cold!"

"Don't worry, I'll warm you up."

I let him get a few strokes in before stopping him.

"Let me help," I tell him. I hold myself as he leans forward. "Slowly."

His eyes are locked on mine, his hands on my chest. There's a little fumbling and a few false starts before we get it right. Sean gasps at the first breach and grimaces.

"Okay?" I ask, voice strained.

"Yes, just a lot bigger than fingers," he says breathily. "Are you sure it's not bigger now?" He's rocking gently, sliding down almost imperceptibly with each motion.

"Keep doing that and it will get bigger."

"Stings," he says with a grimace.

"Do you want to stop?" My arms shake from holding him up.

"Not if my mother walked in," he says.

I laugh. "I thought we weren't talking about her."

Sean bears down, taking me deeper with a shout. "Fuck."

"Good?"

He nods quickly. "Jesus."

I lie still until the need to move is almost unbearable. "Sean." With a hand on his thighs, I urge him up. He goes willingly, and then back down so slowly my eyes roll back in my head.

It takes a minute to find a rhythm and then we're rocking

together gently to the sound of our breathing. My heart beats so loud, I feel my pulse in my throat and my stomach and my wrists.

Sean arches backward, resting his hands on my thighs. "Oh my God." He's doing most of the work, thrusting his hips up and down, each stroke punching the most gorgeous sounds out of him.

He rides me relentlessly until all I can do is hold on, arms trembling, and a fire burning in my blood. He's so gorgeous like this. The most beautiful thing I've ever seen. He's flushed from his cheeks to his chest and his eyes are wide with wonder. "Sean," I whisper. "Sean."

Is this what it's like when you have sex with someone you love? Because if it is, I don't know how people survive it. I feel like I'm going to fly off into space.

Sean falls forward onto me, breathing heavily. His forehead rests against mine, his sweaty curls ticking my skin. His hands clench and unclench on my shoulders.

"Sean?" I ask, a little concerned. "You okay?" I cup his cheek.

Sean pushes into the touch, rubbing his head against my palm, kissing wherever he can reach. "Yeah. Yeah." His voice is shaky. "It's just...just..."

I wind my fingers through his hair and tug gently. Sean hisses at the sensation. "Yeah," I echo.

"It's just, I fucking love you so much. And it's never...I never..." He stops, inhaling with a shudder as I caress his body from shoulders to ankles, following the curve of his body.

"Yeah, Sean." I tilt my head up to capture his beautiful mouth. "Me, too. Never like this. No one." I kissing him long and deep. "God, I love you."

That is all I can take. Groaning, I wrap my arms around him, holding him in place. Bending my good leg, I brace my foot on the bed and thrust into him as hard and fast and deep as I can.

One, two, three thrusts, and my orgasm slams into me. My back arches and I've got an iron grip on Sean's shoulders. His legs tighten around me, and he comes without a touch.

24

COOPER

It feels like it takes forever for the world to creep back into my consciousness. Sean's still on top of me and we're in danger of sticking together. I kiss the side of his head. "So? Was it everything you hoped?"

"Can't speak. Dead," he mutters into my neck.

"That's too bad," I say. "I was hoping we could do this again."

He pushes himself upright, grimacing at the mess we've made. "Oh, we are so doing this again. All the time. That was..." He shakes his head. "Perfect. Thank you."

"Thank you for letting me be your first," I say. I push his hair back from his face. "I can't believe I'm the only one who's ever gotten to see you like this. You're so beautiful." My inner caveman wants to make him promise that no one else ever will.

"So are you," he says, and then rolls off me, stretching out his legs with a groan. "Oh my God. I feel so good."

I nod. That was life-changing.

He turns his head and smiles shyly at me. "So, you, uh, love me?" he asks softly.

Since he looks as if he likes the idea, I'm not going to lie, or claim it was said in the heat of the moment. "Yeah. I do."

"I love you, too, then," he says.

"You don't have to say it just because I did."

"A, my brain is currently off-line, but if I remember correctly, I said it first. And B, I've been thinking it for a long time."

"Yeah? Since when?" I ask.

"Since I saw you playing your guitar," he answers. "I know it's not new for you." He looks away.

I can't let him keep thinking something so false. "Sean, look at me."

He does.

"I swear, I've never felt this way about anyone before you."

"Really?"

"Cross my heart."

His smile is blinding. He kisses me. "I'm totally going to tell my mom you're my boyfriend when we get home. I'm gonna kiss you on the front stoop right in front of God and my gigi and everyone."

He lays back on the bed. "God, I need a shower."

"Don't go," I tell him, grabbing his arm to hold him still.

"We're pretty gross," he says.

"It's the price we pay."

He laughs, all the shadows driven from his eyes for the moment. "But I'm gross," he says trying not very hard to wiggle out of my grip.

"Good point. But I still don't want you to leave," I say, meaning it in more than one way.

"How about if I promise to come back?"

"And stay?" I ask with a kiss between his shoulder blades.

"And stay," he says.

I take his chin and turn his head toward me. "Stay with me."

"I said I would." Pink touches the tops of his ears and his cheekbones.

"Stay with me," I repeat. "Don't move out."

"For how long?"

"For as long as you want."

He wrinkles up his nose. "Or until you get tired of me."

So forever, then? "So, yes?" I try not to hold my breath while I wait for his answer.

"Yes. Of course. If you're sure." His eyebrows draw together as if he doesn't dare trust I am.

"Completely sure." Sure that he'll fly away one day, but in the meantime, I want as much of him as I can get.

"Jus' to be perfectly clear, we are talking about me staying here, in the house with you, not just staying in your bed, right?"

"Yes. Stay with me."

His smile is as blinding as the sun. "Well, a'right then." He turns so he can kiss me, giving me a sweet, deep kiss. If I was fifteen years younger, that would be the start of round two, but sleep is tugging at my eyelids and my bones want to yield to the siren song of the mattress.

"We really have to clean up, though," Sean says after a few minutes of cuddling.

"Yeah. I know. We left food outside on the table, didn't we?"

"Birds probably ate it already," he says, but he sits up. "Get up."

I get up, grumbling the whole time.

We shower, separately, and clean up the mess from dinner together, stealing kisses the entire time. I take care of my leg while Sean gets Stumpy ready for bed. It's all terribly domestic and I love it.

Falling into bed with Sean is the perfect end to the day.

Stumpy's whining wakes me up, but it's Sean that gets my attention. He's turned away from me, curled in on himself like a child with his knees and elbows almost touching. His shoulders are shaking under the thin sheet.

"Sean?" I whisper.

Nothing. I'm not sure he's awake.

Stumpy whines again. I can't see her in the dark room, and I'm worried she's hurt. Sean makes a choked sound. Moving slowly, I touch his arm. "Sean?" No answer. I think he's asleep. He sniffs a couple of times.

Grabbing my cell phone to use as a flashlight, I get out of bed and crutch myself over to Stumpy's crate. She's awake, and standing up, her face pressed against the wires. "You okay, sweetie?" I ask, shining the light at her. It's not easy for me to bend down and check her more closely, but from here, she looks fine. I stick my fingers through the wires and pet her. "Go to sleep," I tell her.

On the bed, Sean tosses and turns, breathing heavily. Stumpy barks. "Shh," I tell her. "You'll wake him up."

Sean makes a sound a lot like the ones Stumpy was making. Risking waking him up, I point the phone to the bed. His eyes are closed, but something shimmers on his eyelashes. Is he crying?

Stumpy barks again. I sigh. "Fine." I open her crate and she heads directly to Sean's side of the bed. She reaches both paws up to the mattress, tail wagging. "Come on," I say, lifting her onto the bed. I know it's a terrible habit to get into, but I really want to sleep.

She crawls over to Sean, stretching out against his side.

He has been crying. I can see tear tracks on his cheeks. I run my fingers through his hair and Sean sighs without opening his eyes, and then rolls on his side, draping an arm over Stumpy. I pet him a few times, and then her.

Since I'm up, I might as well use the bathroom. By the time I slip back in bed, they're both sound asleep. It takes me a bit longer, Sean's tears haunting me for a long time.

The morning goes smoothly. I cook breakfast for us while Sean gets ready for school. We make our plans for the day. Stumpy sticks close to him the whole time.

"She likes you better than me," I tell him as he sits at the table.

"She likes me better than you like me, or she likes me better than she likes you?" he asks. He sounds a little tired, and a little distant.

"Right now? Both." I say, handing him a cup of coffee.

"I can't believe you let her on the bed last night," he says.

"You were both whining. It was the only way I could get any sleep."

"I wasn't whining," he says.

"You were. Bad dream I think." I sip my coffee, watching his face. My gut is telling me something's off, but he'd kissed me when he woke up, telling me he loved me and how special last night had been.

He shrugs, seemingly unconcerned. "I don't remember any." He stands up, having not eaten anything. "I should get going."

"Aren't you going to eat?"

"I'm not very hungry this morning. Sorry."

"Well at least take something for later." I hand him the sandwich I made him.

"I promise to eat." He picks up his backpack, gets his keys off the key rack, and kisses me gently on the way out.

He doesn't come home.

25

SEAN

It's raining again. Almost as hard as it was the night I came to town. Headlights from the trucks headed the opposite direction from me flood my cab seconds before their tires send sheets of water cascading over my windshield. Rusty's wipers are no match for the sheer volume of water, so for a few seconds, I'm driving virtually blind.

It seems fitting. It's not like I know where I'm going.

I should be at school, but I've already missed two classes, so why bother worrying about the rest?

Instead, I'm driving aimlessly down highways, trying to figure out why I feel so blank.

I woke up this morning feeling mostly normal. The slight soreness in places that had previously never felt sore was a constant reminder of what I had done last night.

I'd had sex with a man. Specifically, I'd had anal sex with Cooper. Then he told me he loved me and I told him I loved him, too.

For all intents and purposes, I'm living with a man who loves me and our dog. It's everything I've always wanted but thought I could never have.

All of those are good things, right?

I should be walking on air. There should be little cartoon hearts flying around my head, just like Richie said.

Somewhere inside, I'm ecstatic. I can see it, but that ecstasy seems to have gotten trapped behind the same pane of glass that keeps the anger and sadness at bay so I can function.

I'm sure that can't be good, but I don't know what to do about it. If I let the happiness out, the bad feelings will get out, too.

I can't go to school. I can't go back to Cooper. He was so perfect last night, and so loving this morning. He brought me coffee in bed and kissed me awake.

I think I said and did all the right things. I've gotten good at acting the way a normal person would be expected to act. I smiled and kissed him. I helped make plans for the day and evening. Gave my opinion on dinner options and paint colors for the kitchen. Then I took the sandwich he'd made me for lunch, kissed him goodbye, and reassured him that last night was amazing and I had no regrets at all.

That part isn't a lie. I will never regret any of my time with Cooper. The only thing I will regret is how I can't be the person he needs me to be, the person he deserves.

Cooper's a good man. He deserves someone kind and gentle like him. Someone who can bring light to his life. Not someone constantly a hair's breadth from cracking.

He thinks he loves all of me, but he doesn't know all of me. He only knows the me in front of the wall of glass.

Behind it, there's a deep well of anger inside me. Behind the glass, a twelve-year-old boy screams in rage, railing at the unfairness of the universe; a terrified teen, helpless in the face of torture, cries for someone to help him. And present me stares at them, so angry I scare myself with the things I might be capable of.

God, I am fucking tired. Tired of being sad, tired of being angry, and tired of apologizing for who I am. Tired of trying to be something I'm not.

Pain like a fist squeezing my heart slams into me, and the truck slews right. *Enough*, I think. With an ease born of years of practice, I shove everything—the good, the bad, and the truly ugly—back behind the glass.

There's nothing to be done. Can't change anything. Gotta keep going.

So hands at ten and two, eyes on the road, I drive.

It's all I can do.

―――――――

By the time I get to Richie's house, I'm worn down to my bones. My memories of the drive are vague, at best. It's a blur of highways, rain, and darkness alternating with the blinding glare of gas station lights. What little sleep I got was in rest stops and parking lots, pulling over only when I couldn't keep my eyes open. I have no idea what time it is, my phone's dead. It's night, that's all I know.

I stagger up the stairs of the crappy fourplex to his apartment and take a deep breath. The music pouring out the open windows tells me he's home, so I knock hard on his door.

I'm still knocking when he opens the door.

"Sean? It's one o'clock in the morning, what the hell are you doing here?"

Well, that answers that question.

"Fuck if I know, Richie. I don't have the least idea what I'm doing," I confess. "I just had to go. I couldn't stay one more minute, and I didn't know where else to go. You gonna let me in or not?"

"Yeah, a'course." Richie throws a look over his shoulder at some guy standing in his living room. I don't know who it is and I don't care. I push my way past Richie and sink down onto his couch without so much a look at the guy.

Richie comes and sits on the couch next to me, ass half off the cushion like he's ready to bolt if I do something crazy. "What happened? Did Cooper kick you out?"

If only. That would be simpler. "No. He told me he loves me."

"That asshole," he says, deadpan.

"But he can't really. He doesn't understand, doesn't know how fucked-up I am." I close my eyes, pressing my fists against my eyelids for good measure. I don't want to see Cooper's face even in my mind. I don't want to think about it.

I'm not. I'm not thinking about it. God, I'm tired.

"Sean. Sean?" Richie's got his hand on my shoulder and he's shaking me. I shove him off harder than I mean to.

"Fuck. Sorry."

"You're scaring me, dude," he says. "I'm gonna call your mom."

"No," I bark. "Don't. Just, fucking, don't."

Richie looks less than thrilled. "Does Cooper know you're here?"

"No. He texted me at some point but I didn't answer it. Couldn't. Didn't even know where I was headed 'til I was halfway through New Jersey."

"I'm going to go," the other guy says. "Call me later?"

Who is he and what is he even still doing here?

Richie jumps up. "Oh, yeah. Probably a good idea." Richie takes a step toward him, stops, and shoves his hands in his pockets. "Later."

The guy leaves with an awkward wave in my direction.

That all probably meant something, and normally I would be all over Richie about it, but right now, I can't deal with it.

The white noise buzzing in my brain is getting louder. My body is still vibrating from God knows how many hours on the road, and my hands and wrists hurt from how hard I was gripping the steering wheel. I could curl up right here on the floor and sleep. "Can I just stay here for a little bit?" I ask Richie, suddenly not nearly as sure of my welcome as I'd been five minutes ago.

"Yeah, of course," he says. "Go sleep on my bed."

I nod. "Thanks." Feeling like I'm wearing a suit of lead armor, I muster up the last of my reserves and stand up. "Please don't tell anybody I'm here."

"I won't," he promises. "But you're gonna have to hide that truck."

I dig the keys out of my pocket. "Take it. Do what you want with it."

I crash face first onto Richie's unmade bed and I'm asleep before he's out the front door.

26

COOPER

It's Saturday afternoon and Sean's been gone almost thirty-six hours, and I'm going out of my mind with worry and fear. All I keep thinking is that he could be dead.

I've gone through so many worst-case scenarios the last day and a half. He got into an accident with his truck. He got stabbed by a mugger in an alley and no one has found him yet. Maybe he went hiking alone, twisted his ankle, and ended up in the bottom of a gully. Neither the local hospitals or police stations have any record of him, but I'm not sure what they can legally tell me.

There's not going to be a good reason he's disappeared. The best case scenario I've come up with is that he freaked out after last night, went to a club somewhere, hooked up with someone. He's still with the guy, and he's trying to figure out the best way to let me know it's over and he's moving out.

I can't believe it. Granted, I haven't known Sean that long, but that seems implausible at best.

What a horrible thing it is to realize that you could kiss someone goodbye in the morning and never see them again. I've served in war zones, for God's sake. You'd think I'd have learned that by now. But I've never been in love before. Love changes everything.

What's really frightening is that I don't believe that any of my worst case scenarios are true.

My heart is telling me that the past Sean's been running from has finally caught up with him.

I could kick myself for being cowardly. I knew he was having nightmares, outbursts of temper, and episodes of depression. There were times when he'd get lost in his head and I'd have to call his name more than once to get his attention.

Those are all classic signs of PTSD, and I let it go because I was afraid that if I pushed Sean he would run. I guess the joke's on me, because he's gone anyway. I can't even imagine what happened to him to have caused it.

Twenty-two veterans a day. That's the suicide rate, and many of them were diagnosed with PTSD. Sean isn't a vet, but depression doesn't discriminate.

My pacing is upsetting Stumpy and she's trying to stay as close to me as possible, which means she's constantly in the way of my crutches as I pace the living room.

My phone rings and I check it immediately. The damn thing might as well be grafted to my hand, I haven't put it down since last night. I slept with it, if you can call drifting in and out of consciousness on the couch sleeping. To make things worse, I fell asleep with the prosthesis on and somehow fell trying to stand up, twisted the hell out of my knee. Hence the crutches.

The phone keeps ringing while I stare at it. It's not Sean, but Troy. I have to know if Sean is alive, and Troy's my best bet.

"Troy," I say brusquely. "Have you heard from Sean?"

"No," he says. "But he doesn't call me a lot. Matter of fact, that's why I was calling. My sister's bugging me. Says she hadn't been able to get a hold of him for a week and asked me to call him and tell him to call his momma."

Well at least there's been no call to Sean's mom from a hospital. No call yet.

"He's not here," I say.

"Well, when he gets home, tell him to call his mom," Troy says.

Fuck fuck fuck. I hate that I'm about to ruin his good mood. "Fuck," I say into the phone. "What I mean is that I don't know where he is. He left the house yesterday morning, and I haven't heard from him since."

There's silence for a long second as Troy tries to process what I just told him. "What? Where did he go?"

I laugh bitterly. "That's the question. He left for school and then just…didn't come home."

"Well, fuck," Troy says. "Do you think he's, shit, hurt or something? Think someone grabbed him? Damn. Mary's gonna lose her shit. She can't go through this again."

Again? "He's disappeared before?" I ask, not sure if I want the answer to be yes or no.

"Fuck," Troy says softly. I hear a voice in the background asking him what's wrong. "Sean's missing," he says to the person I assume is his husband. "Again?" Dmitri asks.

"Troy. You gotta tell me right fucking now what you are talking about."

"I will. I'm putting you on speaker. Crap. I need a drink."

"It's eight a.m.," Dmitri says.

"Put it in my orange juice, then."

"Troy, for Chrissake." If I could strangle him through the phone, I would.

"Okay, but first I gotta say chances of it being the same thing again are like zero. A coupla years ago, when Sean was eighteen, nineteen, Sean's dad, well, he had someone grab Sean from his bedroom in the middle of the night and take him to some fucking gay conversion camp in the middle of nowhere Alabama."

"Jesus. How bad was it?" Now I need to sit down. I've heard nightmare stories about those kind of places, but I thought they were illegal now.

"I don't know," Troy admits. "I was still in the Army when it happened, and Sean and Mary don't talk about it. I only found out about it when Sean was twenty. What I do know is that he was there for weeks before Mary could find him. The police and the FBI were involved. It's a big deal."

"Jesus. And somehow no one talks about it? Did Sean ever get therapy or talk to anyone about it outside of the family?"

"Not that I know of," he says. "I didn't even know Sean was gay until Christmas three years ago. I fucked up, didn't I?"

"Troy…" I have to bite my tongue against all the things I want to say. "Sounds like a lot of people did." I could slam their heads together. "He told me about the Christmas, and I know you were having a hard time of it when you were his age. It doesn't sound like it's an easy thing to come to terms with in your world. Did you even call him or talk to him about being gay at least?"

"We weren't that close. I moved out when he was eight," he says defensively.

"I didn't either," Dmitri adds. "We fucked up, Troy. Cooper, do you think it has something to do with why he's gone now?"

"I have no fucking idea why he's gone now. For all I know he's a John Doe on a slab somewhere." Troy gasps, his breath hitching.

"Jesus," Dmitri says. "What should we do?"

"Should I fly out there?" Troy asks.

A second call beeps though and my heart stops when Sean's name pops up. "He's on the other line right now."

Dmitri and Troy exhale simultaneously. "Call me back as soon as you know what's going on," Troy demands.

"I will. I promise." I hang up on him and pick up the other call. "Sean?

"Uh, no," a man's voice says. "It's Richie. Sean's friend."

"Is he with you? Is he okay?" Obviously, they're together or Richie wouldn't have his phone.

"He's here at my place," Richie says. "I took his phone, figured you would pick up. And you deserve to know." He sounds angry; I don't know if it's for me or at me.

"Oh, thank God." Closing my eyes, I let my head drop to the top of the couch, the muscles in my neck and shoulders unclenching for the first time in days. Tears prick my eyelids, and I blink them away, taking a few seconds to pull myself together.

"Is he okay?"

"Depends on how you define okay. He ain't dead, but he's been sleeping since he got here. He was kind of out of it when he got here. I can't believe he didn't crash, driving like that. He won't eat anything and he won't say two words to me. What happened?"

Hearing Sean's accent from Richie and Troy makes me miss him even more. There's a hole in my heart at the thought of him being gone. We had such a short time together.

But I just want him to get help.

I make a split-second decision to tell Richie everything I know and suspect. He's Sean's best friend. If Sean doesn't feel safe living with me and letting me help him, he'll need someone in West Virginia on his side.

"How much do you know about PTSD and what happened to Sean at that fucking place?"

"His fucking piece of shit dad," Richie spits out. "I'd kill that fucking guy if I could find him. You think that place fucked him up more than he's sayin'?"

"That's exactly what I think."

"So what do I do? I'm in over my head here, man. Should I try to make him get up? Make him call his mom?" Richie asks.

"I'm glad he has you," I say. "You're a great friend."

"Thanks, but I don't know how to help him now."

"I'm coming down," I say. "Give me your address and phone number."

"Oh, thank God," he says.

Checking the time, I do some quick calculations. "If I leave soon, I'll be there in the middle of the night, so I'll get a motel. Don't do anything until I get there."

"Should I call his mom? He really doesn't want me to. Tell you the truth, I'm kind of still pissed at her for how she handled this."

"That makes two of us," I admit.

"He really loves you, you know. Like, I've never seen him so happy as long as I've known him. You ain't gonna yell at him when you get here, are you?"

The tears threaten to fall again. "No. I'm not going to yell at him. And I love him, too. Though I know he has trouble believing it."

"Yeah, well, sometimes it's not an easy thing to believe."

Despite everything, I laugh quietly. "You're not wrong. Okay, let me get my stuff together."

"Okay, Cooper. I'm really glad I called you. I'll text you from my phone. Let me know when you get in town, no matter what time it is."

"I will. And you call me for anything you need. Tell Sean I'm not mad at him. But maybe don't tell him I'm coming down."

"I won't. And I won't let him do anything stupid. Stupider."

We hang up.

I call Troy back and tell him my plans. "I'm booking a flight, too," he says. "See you there."

"See you in West Virginia."

An hour later I've decided driving will actually be quicker than flying and has the bonus of allowing me to bring Stumpy. I think it will be good for both of them. I'm also not thrilled with the idea of putting the prosthesis back on because of my knee, and flying without it is a pain in the ass.

I stop at the diner on my way out of town.

"Hey, Cooper," Dewey says when I enter. "Where's your young man?"

"That's what I need to talk to you about. I need a favor from you and Debbie." I take a seat at the counter, and Debbie brings over a cup of coffee without me asking.

"Of course we'll help," she says. "Anyway we can."

I fill them in on the situation and what I need from them and get back on the road with enough food for three people.

Make no mistake, I intend to bring him back.

Of course if Sean needs to stay in West Virginia, I'm not going to force him to come home, but from the first minute I saw him, I knew we were meant to be, and I'm not going down without a fight.

SEAN

Little by little the worst of whatever was going on fades away, and I'm finally able to get out of bed for longer than it takes to pee. The ancient radio alarm clock on Richie's nightstand says it's nine thirty-seven. The light streaming through the bent mini-blinds tells me it's daytime.

Either I slept all night or I've slept away two days, and I'm afraid to find out which it is. But I have to pee like a racehorse, and for the first time since leaving Vermont, I'm hungry. For a minute, I contemplate peeing and crawling right back into bed where I won't have to deal with all of the shit I know is waiting for me out in the world, but then I remember I owe Richie some kind of explanation. And I know damn well lying in bed isn't going to solve anything.

I make myself get up. Though I don't remember changing my clothes, I'm wearing some shorts and a T-shirt I recognize as belonging to Richie.

Time to face the music.

I don't take my phone with me. Don't even look at it, too afraid to see all the missed calls and texts from Cooper I know will be there. God, I'm an asshole. I need to call him. Soon.

Richie's sitting on the couch watching TV and looking at

something on his phone. When he hears me coming down the hall, he turns around, hanging his arm over the back of the couch. "Look who decided to rejoin the living. Feeling better?"

I shrug. "A little."

"Well, you still look like shit," he says bluntly, "and you smell worse."

He's right. I can smell myself, which is never a good sign. My hair feels about ready to crawl off my head and my skin itches from sweat and God knows what else. "Can I shower?"

With one last look at his phone, he tosses it on the couch and stands up. "Dude, I am begging you to shower." His tone is light, but I can see the concern in his expression. He looks like he's worried that if he says the wrong word, I'll bolt.

I can't blame him.

"And can I borrow some clean clothes? Some more clothes, I guess. I, uh, kind of didn't pack." Standing in the hallway feels awkward, but I'm not sure what I should be doing.

"No shit." He walks over to me and looks me up and down like he's checking for injuries. "I'm surprised you made it all this way in one piece. Do you even remember the drive?"

Honestly? No. The blood drains from my face and I grab the doorframe for support. God, it is a miracle I didn't kill myself or, God forbid, some other poor soul unlucky enough to be on the road with me.

"Some of it," I lie. "I remember stopping at one of those service plazas and crawling into the back of the truck to sleep."

He shakes his head. "Shit, Sean." I know he wants to ask me a whole shit-ton of questions, I can see it in his eyes. I owe him some kind of explanation. I just don't know if I *can* explain it. Luckily, my stomach growls loud enough for the neighbors to hear.

"Hungry?" he asks. I nod. "No wonder. I couldn't get you to eat anything but a few bites of toast and half a Pop-Tart."

"Cherry?"

"Strawberry. Unfrosted. I grabbed it by mistake last time I

went shopping," he explains when I give him a look. Eating unfrosted Pop-Tarts is like eating jam-filled cardboard.

"Well, that's why. Strawberry is nasty."

"When did you last eat real food?"

"I think I grabbed something on the road. I know I got a coffee and egg sandwich when I left ho—Cooper's house on Thursday morning. What day is it?"

"It's Sunday," Richie says, staring at me to gauge my reaction.

"Holy shit," I say. "And I got here sometime Friday, right?" I've been more or less passed out in his room for two and a half days. I haven't talked to Cooper in three. He must be frantic. *Oh, God. Oh, shit. Now I know I've fucked it up.*

"Yeah, you asshole," Richie says. He punches me, hard, on the arm. "You scared the shit outta me."

"I'm sorry."

"You should be." He turns and walks toward the tiny galley kitchen.

I follow slowly behind him.

He's digging through the cabinets, and when I come into the kitchen he shoves a silver-foiled package at me. "Here. Frosted cherry, princess. Eat the fucking Pop-Tart and take a shower. I'll make us some real food and then you'll get talkin', *capisce*?"

I throw my arms around him, hugging him in a way we don't normally do. "You're not even Italian."

"Ugh, get off me, you reek." His words say get off, his arms around me say stay. I stay.

"Love you," I whisper into the top of his head. We've never said it before, but I know he knows, like I know he loves me.

Scoffing, he pushes me away. "You're still not getting in my pants, Johnson," he says.

"No, but Joel might be," I say with a campy eyebrow raise, trying to make things normal again. "That was him I saw, right?"

Joel is the new guy at his dad's company. Over the last few weeks, his name has been popping up more and more in our conversations.

"Bite me," Richie says.

"Only if Joel won't be mad."

He tries to yank the Pop-Tart out of my hand but I hold it over my head as far as I can reach. Given that I've been five inches taller than Richie since tenth grade, it's my go-to move for keep-away.

"Dick." He crosses his arms over his chest in defeat. "Shower. Food. Talk," he repeats.

"Coffee?" I ask as I skate by him, out of pop-tart grabbing distance.

"You don't deserve coffee," he says.

"That's not a no." I rip open the Pop-Tart package and cram one into my mouth as I walk away.

In Richie's room, I grab some clothes before heading to the shower: sweat pants, a T-shirt, and underwear. I'm feeling better than I have the last few days, but that's not saying much. My phone sits on the nightstand. Dead as a doornail and it still manages to glare at me accusingly.

I stare back at it for a few seconds as I slowly chew the remains of my prebreakfast snack. Damn these things are dry. I should have grabbed something to drink.

On the nightstand, a glass of milk sits next to a plate with a cold slice of toast with two bites taken out of it.

The milk is warm, but when I pick it up and take a cautious sniff, it smells fine, so I drink it. Beggars can't be choosers.

Seeing how Richie took care of me when I showed up at his door in the middle of the freaking night, makes me want to cry. I don't deserve him. He's a good friend. The best.

I don't deserve Cooper either. I'm sure at least one of the messages on my phone is telling me where I can pick up my stuff.

Richie keeps a phone charger plugged in by the bed, and luckily it fits my phone. I wait as it powers up and, as I suspected, it starts pinging its brains out with text notifications. I see a bunch in a row from Cooper, then Troy. Then Cooper again.

I don't have the energy to read all the texts now, but the least I can do is let him know I'm alive.

I'm okay. At Richie's. I'll call when I can.

I send the text and stare at the phone, waiting for a response that doesn't come. Oh, yeah. He is done with me. I don't blame him.

I make my plodding way to the bathroom.

As I stand under the hot water, I let my mind drift, trying not to think about anything. I know I won't be able to avoid facing my shit for long, but I can at least wait until after I eat.

"Do you wanna talk about it?" Richie asks over breakfast.

"I suppose you won't believe me if I say I'm fine?" I give him a fake smile.

He just stares at me.

"Fine. I think all that," I wave my fork in the air, "with, you know, my dad and, and that place, is starting to get to me."

"You think?" Richie asked.

"I've been having nightmares and I'm angrier and sadder and just more everything. And I keep thinking about it. I can't stop thinking about it."

"You think it's because of Cooper? Because you finally actually did stuff with a guy?" he asks.

"Did stuff?" I say sarcastically. "Like fishing?"

Richie is not impressed with my sarcasm. "You know what I mean. Fooled around with."

"This, uh, might be TMI, but we had sex. Like, actual…" I trail off, hoping my meaningful expression will convey enough.

"You fucked," he says.

I can't keep the smile off my face. "Oh, yeah, we did." I look down at my plate. "And he told me he loved me." I don't know why that feels harder to admit than the fact that we'd had sex.

"Told you so," Richie says smugly. "And why wouldn't he?"

"Because I'm a disaster of a human who freaks out and runs away like a coward," I say more bitterly than I planned on.

"You gotta cut yourself some slack, man. You're awesome. You just have," he searches for a word, "baggage. Like we all do."

"Baggage?" I raise my eyebrows and force a smile. "Been reading relationship books or something?"

He doesn't rise to the joke. "Yeah. Baggage. And you know exactly what I'm talking about."

"Yeah, I do," I admit. I push my plate away and rest my head in my hands, elbows on the table like a hillbilly, as my grandma would say. "Why won't it just go away?" I ask. "It's fucking over and done. I just want to get past it."

"I don't think you can," he says.

"When did you get all wise and shit?"

"I read. I watch Lifetime TV with my mom," he says. "And I think you gotta let it out. You gotta talk to someone."

"I'm scared to," I confess, not looking at him.

"Scared of what in particular?"

"Everything." I shoot to my feet, shoving the chair away and it tips to the floor. "Of myself. I'm so angry, Richie. I don't know how I can stand it. I don't know what will happen if I let it all out. If I start talking, I'm gonna say things I can't take back and what will that do to my family? To me and Cooper?"

"I think you need to be asking what holding it in has done to you, because you are not good, dude."

I snort. "You're not wrong."

He watches me as I pace the tiny kitchen. "It's more than just what happened to me there, I think."

"What do you mean?"

Some of the fractured thoughts I'd had over the last three days are starting to come together. Surprisingly, they are somewhat coherent. "I have the feeling that I was kind of messed up before. Way before. But I just didn't know it."

"How?"

"I'm not sure. I gotta think. No, I gotta write. I need to write some stuff." If I can get these flashes of images in my mind out on paper where I can read them, maybe they'll make more sense.

"Isn't writing just the same as thinking?" he asks.

I shake my head. "No. It's hard to explain. It's like sometimes my fingers write things my head didn't even know we were thinking about."

"Weird," he says.

"Tell me about it." Even thinking about writing is calming me down. I'm still buzzing with nerves, but the fog that had settled in my brain weeks ago lifts a bit. "Okay, here's what I'm going to do. Sunday, right?"

"Yep." He eats and follows my progress across the floor.

"So that means after church, my mom will probably go to my grandma's house for Sunday dinner."

"Prob'ly."

"I'm going to meet her there."

His eyebrows raise. "Are you sure you want to get into it in front of everyone?"

"I think I need to. Like you said, hiding how I'm feeling only made things worse. And I ain't proud of it, but I kinda want her to feel bad."

"Not for nothin', I know you're mad at her, and you should be, but it was your asshole dad who started all that shit."

I shake my head. "No." I'm so close to understanding something, I can feel it on my tongue. "He made it a thousand times worse. Hell, I'm afraid he broke me for good. But she started it."

"How?" he asks.

"I don't know," I yell through gritted teeth. "Sorry. Guess I'm still mad."

He shrugs like he's good with whatever I need to be.

"Okay." I glance at the clock on the microwave. "That thing right?" I ask.

"More or less," Richie answers.

"Here's the plan. I'm going to do some writing, try to think. And then I'm going to go to my grandma's house and raise some hell."

Richie raises his eyebrow and shakes his head as if questioning my life choices. Get in line. "Do what you gotta do. I'm always here if you need a place to crash."

"I know you are. You're the best. Be right back."

I run to his room, grab my backpack, and go back to the kitchen. It's got the only table in the apartment.

Richie refills my coffee and I scarf down the rest of the eggs and bacon. I miss having real maple syrup to dip the bacon into.

"Guess I should leave you alone," Richie says.

"Just for a bit." I point at him with a piece of bacon. Richie always did like his more well-done than I did. "But don't think we're not going to talk about Joel later. That blond hottie was him, right?"

Richie shrugs again with feigned nonchalance but won't meet my eyes. "You think he's hot?"

"Uh, yeah. Even half outta my mind. He looks like he was Prom King and starting quarterback on his high school football team."

"He was," Richie says with a fond smile.

"Oh God," I say with an eye roll.

Richie flicks some scrambled eggs at me. I duck and they hit the floor. It takes me a second to realize Stumpy isn't going to come hopping over to grab it. God, I miss home.

"We're just friends," Richie insists. "We're just hanging out. No big deal."

"Uh-huh. Sure. So that's *not* a hickey on your neck?"

Richie's hand flies to his neck, and I laugh out loud for the first time in days.

"Oh, screw you," Richie says. "And I went out and got Pop-Tarts special for you."

"I'll leave that for Joel."

Richie panics, leaning forward, eyes wide. "Sean, dude, you gotta help me. Seriously. I don't know what I'm doing here!"

"Does he?"

Richie nods, eyes getting even wider. "Uh, yeah."

"Then you'll be fine. Trust me."

Richie grabs my hand. "Please. I need more than that. I need details. I don't know what I'm supposed to be doing, you know?"

"Hell yeah, I know," I tell him about the first few conversations I had with Cooper. "I'm lucky he didn't kick my ass out of his truck day one. We'll talk. I promise. I don't know what I'm doing either, but we can do it together. After I drop a bomb on my family and see if Cooper is still talking to me."

"He'll talk to you," Richie says.

"How do you know?"

Richie picks up his plate and carries it to the sink. "I just have a feeling is all."

Well if that ain't as shifty as all get-out. "Mmm-hmm. What did you do, Richard Spellman?"

"I didn't do nothing," he insists. "I can just tell by the way you talk about him."

"I hope you're right." Do I ever. I really messed up with Cooper. My running away like that hurt him. But even people who love each other do that, right? They hurt each other, and then they apologize, talk about it, and keep going. Cooper's the best thing in my life. I love him, and I'm not going down without a fight. So, I'll bare my soul, show him all the dark places, the weakness in me I've been hiding, and hope he still loves me.

If he won't pick up the damn phone, I'll haunt his doorstep when I get home until he has to talk to me. I've been told I can be very annoying when I want to be.

28

COOPER

The ringing of my phone pulls me out of sleep so deep, it takes me a solid minute before I realize where I am. Right. Holiday Inn. Clarksburg, West Virginia. I'd texted Richie at three in the morning after I'd checked in, body aching from sixteen hours on the road. I'd driven straight through, only stopping for gas and to let Stumpy out. I caught a few fitful hours of sleep in the back seat of the cab. He told me he'd call in the morning with an update.

"Richie," I say, wiping the sleep out of my eyes. Stumpy doesn't budge. "What's up?"

"Sean, for one thing," he says. "Finally got his ass out of bed. Even showered and ate. He's writing now."

Thank you, universe. "That's great."

"Yeah, well, after that he's going to his grandma's house to put the fear of the Lord into his mom."

"Oh, hell."

"I know," he agrees.

"Do you think it's a good idea?" I ask him.

I can practically hear him shrug. "Beats the heck outta me. Not like he can make it worse, right?"

"Your guess is as good as mine. Do you think I should go there?"

"Yeah. It might not be the best, but he's gonna need you there. Wish I could be there. I kinda want to watch him lay into his momma."

"What happened to Sean's father, after the police found him? Sean never mentions him."

"I don't know," Richie says. "Seems like he should have gotten arrested, but I don't rightly know what happened to him. Could probably Google it," he suggests.

"I'll ask Sean first."

Richie gives me Sean's grandparents' address and tells me Sean will be there around one. "I'm going to get to meet you before you leave, right?"

"Absolutely," I tell him. "I'm looking forward to it."

"Me, too," he says. "I need to talk to you about your intentions concerning my boy."

"Only the best, I swear."

"Good luck, Cooper," he says. "Text me after the fireworks."

"Will do."

I hang up and check the time. If I hurry, I've got time for a shower and breakfast.

———

Seeing Rusty parked in the driveway lets me know without a shadow of a doubt I'm at the right house. His grandparents live in a well-established neighborhood lush with mature trees, green lawns, and houses build in the seventies. I pull up to the curb and shut off the engine. Stumpy whines softly to get out, but I need a minute to get myself together. Mentally girding my loins, I hop out of the car. Holding onto the doorframe, I grab my crutches from behind the seat.

As soon as I step out of my truck, I can hear the faint sounds of an argument coming from behind the house. I can't tell who the woman is, but the man is definitely Sean, so I assume she's his mother.

Stumpy barks at me. "I'm coming." I walk around to open her door, unclip her harness from the seatbelt, and clip on her leash. The leash is a new development and she's not quite sure what to make of it.

She hops toward Sean's grandmother's house, shooting me a look of betrayal when she reaches the end of the lead. *Well?* she seems to ask.

"Just give me a second," I tell her. "You try walking a dog on crutches. What do you think he's going to say when he sees us, girl?"

Sean still has no idea I'm coming. He'd texted me an hour or so before Richie had called, but what needs to be said between us can't be said over text.

I'm nervous, of course, but in my heart, I don't think he'll tell me to leave. Only a few days ago, he told me he loved me, and I'm holding on to that. Of course, he'd said it right before he walked out on me without a word.

A curtain in the front window is pushed aside, and I get a flash of a face and a hand. Too late to turn back now, even if I wanted to.

"Time to meet the family, Stumpy."

I breathe a sigh of relief when Troy opens the door. "Hey," he says. "Damn, it's good to see you."

"Good to see you, too, TJ. Wish it were under better circumstances."

"Me, too."

It takes a bit of maneuvering to get me and the crutches and the dog into the house, especially when Stumpy runs over to the brown Labrador sitting patiently at Troy's side, wrapping her leash around Troy's legs as she does.

"Sorry about Stumpy," I say as he untangles everyone. "She's not too trained yet."

"Stumpy?" he says with a laugh. "Like father, like daughter, eh?"

"How could I resist?" I ask. "Funny story, I met Sean and Stumpy at the same time. Of course, she had four legs then."

"Did he hit her?" he asks.

I shake my head. "Rescued her after a hit-and-run."

Troy keeps hold of Stumpy's leash and opens his arms. "C'mon. Bring it in. It's been too long."

"You got that right."

We give each other the back-thumping not-quite-a-hug greeting you give your army buddies whenever you meet.

Except for the yelling coming from the back door, the house is suspiciously quiet, though something on the stove smells delicious. The house looks exactly like I'd thought it would. It's neat as a pin. The living room has a working wood fireplace and floral-patterned sofas flanked by rosewood end tables. Photographs on the walls show off the three generations of Johnsons who have lived in this house.

I love it.

"Where are your parents?" I ask.

"Hiding in their room," he says with a grin. "My brother's here, too. Not the homophobe one. Paulie."

"Does Sean know you're coming?" Troy asks as he leads me through a dining room to the back of the house.

"No. You?"

He shakes his head.

"What are they fighting about?" I ask.

"I just got here, so I missed the beginning. But if I had my guess, I'd say it's about his dad and that shit."

"Yeah, I wouldn't be surprised."

I feel a little guilty eavesdropping on Sean and his mother. Is it even technically eavesdropping if the people you're listening to are yelling at each other at the top of their lungs?

Troy stops at a set of half-open sliding doors. We can see Sean and his mom clearly through the opened vertical blinds, and the screen door lets in the sound.

Sean's mother looks a lot like Troy. Same coloring, same hair. She's wearing a nicer outfit than I expected, a skirt and a blouse. From the way she's pacing, I think her heels are sinking into the grass.

"Fuck the neighbors!" Sean is yelling. "I don't care if they hear!" He turns and makes a megaphone of his cupped hands. "I'm gay!" he yells in the direction of the house next door. "Sean Johnson is a homosexual."

When she hears Sean's voice, Stumpy whines and does the hunching-wagging of the entire back half of her body thing she does when she's excited. Troy's lab doesn't even blink.

"I've never heard Sean yell," I say. "Have you?"

Troy shakes his head. "I've seen him all brooding teenager, but never all het up like that."

"Congratulations?" a woman's voice calls out from the other direction.

"Jesus, Sean. You don't have to announce it to the whole world," she says, looking around to see who heard.

Sean throws his arms up in the air. "Are you even listening to me, Mom? Hiding is what caused all this!"

"No, this is all your father's fault! From those horrible people." Mary crosses her arms over her chest and looks away.

"Whatever happened to Sean's father?" I ask Troy.

He shrugs. "No idea. Hasn't been around since then. I think my grandmother would shoot him if he came around."

Sean stalks closer to his mother. "That sucks, yeah. And it's part of it. But just this morning I realized that you started all this."

That's news to me. Sean's only ever had good things to say about his mother. I look at Troy and he shrugs. "News to me," he says.

"You don't even know how much it fucked me up!" Sean continues.

"Sean!" his mother objects.

"Seriously? That's your issue? My cursing?"

"Well, I don't know what you're talking about. I never did anything to hurt you. I wouldn't! I love you." She looks ready to cry.

"Yeah? If that's true then how come when I was kidnapped and tortured…" His voice breaks, and I want desperately to go to him, but he starts talking again and I can't interrupt him.

Sean takes a deep breath. "Can you imagine how scared I was when I woke up to a grown man sitting on my back and zip-tying my hands together? When he dragged me out of my bedroom and threw me into the back of a van, I thought I was going to be killed."

Troy's grip on my arm is the only thing keeping me from running outside and doing something I would regret. "Let him get it out," he says.

I know he's right, but it's killing me.

Mary covers her mouth with her hand, her eyes wide.

"If I was fine before that moment, if you never made me feel bad about myself, tell me why then, when my own father paid someone to drug me and haul me to some, some fucking *torture* chamber where they tried to beat the gay out of me and a handful of other kids, I was the one to feel ashamed, Mom?"

Mary's crying and shaking her head. "I didn't do that, Sean. You know that. I don't know why you felt like that."

"I do. Because part of me, a stupid fucking part of my brain that I can't shut off, *believed* them when they said I was unnatural, a freak. Because that's what you told me." He's yelling by the end of that.

"I know how he feels," Troy says quietly.

My heart is breaking.

"When, Sean? When did I ever say something that awful?" Mary yells back at him, not backing down.

He shakes his head. "Maybe not in so many words," he

admits. "But you all made damn sure I knew being gay was not allowed. Remember that trip to Virginia Beach?" he asks.

"Of course," she says. "What's that got to do with anything?"

"Do you know what he's talking about?" I ask Troy.

He shrugs. "No. I must have been gone already."

I have a feeling that whatever Sean is about to say is a crucial part of his story. He lowers his voice and I strain to hear.

"Remember the boys, Mom? The ones who rented the beach house? And the ones who were playing volleyball on the beach every day?"

"Not really," she says, looking away from him.

"Yes, you do. We saw two of them kiss, you made a face, and the next day we moved to a different motel."

"I was trying to protect you. Why did they have to do that in public?" Mary says.

Sean thrusts his finger at her. "There! That attitude right there. I was fascinated by them, and you knew why, didn't you? You already suspected I was gay."

She nods.

"Well, that makes two of us. Up until that exact moment, I didn't know. The moment I first really understood what being gay meant and realized that I was gay, that very same moment, I knew from your reaction that if ever wanted people to accept me, if I wanted my family, my own *mother* to love me, I would have to hide this part of me. Deny something intrinsic to who I am."

"I couldn't help it! That was the way I was raised! I don't think that now," she says.

"It's too late. Do you understand what that meant? I was twelve years old when I started hating myself. Half my life, I've been dealing with this bullshit."

Oh, Sean. You're killing me, baby.

"I'm sorry!" she says again, voice full of pain. She's crying now.

Sean is too, and he's shaking so hard I can see it through the screen and the blinds.

Troy and I exchange glances. I open the screen door and Stumpy runs directly to Sean. "Stumpy?" he asks. On autopilot, he reaches down to pet her even as he's looking toward the house.

29

COOPER

When Sean sees me, his expression guts me. It's full of yearning and need.

I'm out the door in an instant. Sean runs toward me, and I brace myself for impact. I stagger when he hits me, but I wrap my arms around him and he's strong enough to keep me from toppling.

He buries his face in my shoulder. "Cooper, oh, my God. Cooper." His hands are clenched in my shirt.

"Don't ever leave me again," I whisper in his ear and then kiss the side of his head so he knows I'm not angry.

"I'm sorry. I'm so sorry."

"It's okay."

A weather-worn loveseat-sized swing catches my eye and I start to maneuver us in its direction. "Come here."

Sean's mother passes behind us silently and slips into the house.

We sit on the padded swing and rock gently back and forth. The green and white striped awning is worn on the seams.

I arrange us so my back is against the arm, my good leg up stretched out across the seat and Sean curled up against my chest. It's a tight fit, and Sean's legs hang off the side, but neither of us care. With my good foot on the ground, I push gently to keep us rocking.

Sean's crying almost silently now, his body shaking as all the anger and adrenaline that had fueled him dissipates. I run my hands up and down his arms.

Stumpy eyes the swing with some trepidation, swaying like she wants to jump up but isn't sure of the physics involved.

"There's no room," I tell her.

Giving me a look, she reaches up with her front paws, resting them on Sean's thigh, and stares soulfully at him, her tail thumping softly against the ground. She whines when Sean doesn't react, nudging him with her nose.

He gives a small, broken laugh, but it's better than crying or yelling. With an infinitesimal smile, he reaches down to pet her. "It's okay, baby. I'm okay."

She gives him one of her rare woofs, pushing her nose against his palm. He pets her head and she crawls over his legs, arranging herself on top of him as best as she can.

He pets her, fingers carding through her thick fur the same way mine push through his waves.

We rock and cuddle and pet the dog and gradually Sean calms down. My heart settles back into my chest, beating normally for the first time in days now that he's in my arms where he belongs.

"I can't believe you're here," he says. "How did you even know where to go?"

"Richie called me," I admit.

"And you came," he says with disbelief.

"I can't believe you think I wouldn't," I tell him. "I love you, remember?" I sigh heavily when he doesn't answer. "Oh, Sean. You don't believe me, do you?"

"I want to," he says quietly.

I give the swing another push. "So, can we assume your family is watching? And that they may have guessed I'm more than your landlord?"

This time his laugh isn't so biting. "Yes, and I reckon."

"I really want to kiss you. How do you feel about that?"

He runs his hand down my chest. "I feel very positive about that."

"And your family?"

"Can go scratch, if they have any problem with it."

I tilt his head up, and kiss him. He tastes like tears and home. "I love you. If you believe anything, believe that."

"I'll try." I pinch him and he squeaks. "I do. I do. I just don't understand why."

"I don't think love needs a reason," I say.

He sighs and lays his head on my chest. "Well, I may not deserve it, but I'm going to take it. I love you, too. You know that, right?"

"I do." I kiss his head and hug him, all the worst-case scenarios I'd envisioned running through my head like a slide-show of nightmares. He grunts as my arms tighten almost painfully around him.

"Sorry," I say.

He shakes his head vehemently. "No. I'm sorry. I'm so sorry I ran away. Sorry for breaking down."

"Don't," I say. "Never apologize for that." I close my eyes.

"I scared you, didn't I?"

"To my bones," I confess. "I thought you were dead in a car accident or something," I tell him, voice catching.

"My driving's not that bad," he says.

"You could have been and I wouldn't have known. I'm not your emergency contact, no one would call me."

"Actually, you are," he says sheepishly. "For school anyway. I forgot to tell you. I figured if I was ever in an accident or got hurt, it wouldn't do much good to call my mom, would it? Might as well call you. Is that okay?"

I take a deep breath. "It's fine. But I don't even have your mother's number. The only number I have is Troy's."

"I'm sorry. I'll make sure you have them," he promises. "It

238

didn't occur to me that you'd think I was hurt until Richie said it. Of course, I wasn't thinking clearly at all."

"That's another thing that scared me. Richie was very worried about you. Said you were barely responsive and he was afraid to leave you alone," I say, hugging him tighter. "That was terrifying."

"Why?" he asks. "I would have been fine on my own."

"Sean, baby, we were both worried about the same thing."

"What?"

Can he really not know? I guess that's a positive sign. At least his mind hadn't gone straight to where mine had. "We were both worried you were going to," the words get stuck in my throat. "To do something stupid," I finish.

"Something..." He pulls away just far enough to look me in the eye. "Kill myself, you mean. You were worried I was going to kill myself?"

I nod, pause, and then shake my head. "Not really, not convinced or anything. But it happens, baby. Especially with PTSD." I wait for him to deny it. I've never said the words out loud, but it's the only conclusion I can come to, especially after what Richie told me about Sean being kidnapped and tortured for weeks.

"You think I have PTSD?" he asks in a small voice.

"I do."

He's quiet for a long time. I put the swing in motion again, and we rock and listen to each other breathe for a few minutes.

"I do, too," he says eventually.

"Good."

"Good?" he asks.

"Naming it is the first step. Now we can make a plan how to deal with it."

"We?"

"Yes, we. I love you, remember? I'm not going to make you handle it alone. Not because I don't think you can't, but because you shouldn't have to." Neither of us mentions that his family thought he should. I'm particularly angry at Troy. I know he lives far away, but damn it, he must have noticed something at some point.

The brown lab that had been sitting next to Troy ambles over to us, followed by Troy. "Hey," he says.

Sean looks up but doesn't move from where he's lying on me. "Who called you?" he asks.

"Richie," Troy answers. He doesn't seem to know where to look. His eyes cut to us and then back to the yard or down to the dog.

"I kind of love Richie," I say.

"He's a cute kid," Troy says.

"Not a kid," Sean and I say at the same time.

"Sorry."

"You really didn't have to come all the way here," Sean says unenthusiastically.

"I did," Troy says. "I need to apologize and we need to talk. But after dinner."

Sean groans. "Oh, God. I don't want to do dinner. How'm I supposed to sit there with Grandma and everyone without yelling at them?"

"Why would you yell at your grandma and pop-pop?" Troy asks.

Sean sits up, dislodging Stumpy, who hops over to make friends with the lab. The lab, for the most part, ignores her.

"Because I'm fucking pissed at the lot of them, Troy," Sean says.

Troy nods. "Me, too?" he asks not meeting Sean's eyes.

Sean sighs heavily. "Yeah, if you really wanna know. You're right below Mom on my list."

"I deserve it," he says. He looks at Sean. "For what it's worth, I really am sorry. I didn't know things...well I didn't know a lot of things, and I should have called you more after that Christmas."

"Yeah. You should have."

"How 'bout we schedule in a nice long yell for after dinner?"

Troy suggests. "You can yell at me, too, Sergeant Hill. I can see it in your eyes that you want to."

"Shut it, Detroit."

Sean runs his hand through his hair. "You know what? I'll say what I need to because I have a feeling it's going to be a long time before I come back here."

Troy makes a face.

"Oh, like you come back all the time," Sean says. "We're lucky we see you once a year since you moved."

He nods. "You're right. You're right and I'm sorry."

Sean holds out his hand to me. "Want to meet the family?"

I look from him to Troy and back again. "Do I?" I ask.

"I don't know. Are you and Sean a thing?"

"A thing?"

"You know what I mean," he says.

"Yeah, we're together," Sean says. "Got a problem with that?"

Troy holds up his hands. "No problem. I'm sure Cooper is treating you right. He's a good man. And he drove all the way here for you. My sister, she might have something to say."

Sean glares in the direction of the house. "My mother has no say in my life anymore."

Okay. Best to get this over with so Sean and I can figure out what we're going to do from here. "Can we eat before you start laying into everyone?" I ask. "I'm running on gas station coffee and heat-lamp biscuits."

"What's for dinner?" Sean asks.

"Sausage and peppers. Spaghetti. Garlic bread."

"It did smell really good in there," I admit. "I wouldn't say no."

"Come in," Troy says to Sean. "Please?"

"Fine." Sean stands up.

Troy looks at him and nods. "Sean?"

"Yeah?"

To Sean's surprise, Troy hugs him, cupping the back of his

head. Sean is stiff for a second and then relaxes, hugging his uncle back. "I really am sorry," he whispers.

Sean nods.

"Love you," Troy says roughly, patting Sean on the back. When they separate, both of them have tears in their eyes.

"See you inside," Troy says.

"This is going to be so much fun," I say to Sean with a wide grin.

"Let's just get it over with," Sean says, holding out a hand for me.

"My thoughts exactly." I squeeze his hand and we walk to the house like we're going to court.

As it happens, we don't end up eating dinner with Sean's family after all. Stumpy and Rose, Troy's service dog, are happy running around the back yard, so we leave them to it. Sean takes me to the kitchen to introduce me to his great-grandmother, whom I instantly like.

We're talking about the thirty-foot RV she drives around by herself, when his mother comes in.

Her eyes are still red from crying, and she's changed into jeans and a T-shirt. It makes her look ten years younger, and I remember she's only three or four years older than me. Crap. It's so easy to forget the age difference between Sean and me when we're alone. Not so easy at the moment.

Her expression when she looks at Sean is so sad and confused that I feel sorry for her. I'm still angry with her, but I know she thought she was doing what was best for Sean even if she got it completely wrong.

She doesn't make eye contact with me as she makes for the refrigerator I'm standing in front of. "Sorry," I say, swinging out of her way.

She doesn't acknowledge me.

Sean looks at me and frowns. I shake my head. It's not worth it. His eyes narrow and he gets a determined look on his face. I sigh mentally. This isn't going to go well. At least I know where Sean gets his stubbornness from.

It's been interesting to see this side of him. Though I hadn't realized it, he was still trying to be on his best behavior around me. Despite the yelling and the emotions running high, he's more relaxed and outspoken here. More vivid. I like it. I hope I get to see more of it at home.

Mary pulls two bottles of salad dressing and a pitcher of iced tea out of the fridge.

"Mom," Sean says.

She freezes.

"Aren't you going to say hello to my boyfriend?" He saunters over to me (something else I'd never seen him do before) and wraps his arm around me.

"In front of God and Gigi," he whispers in my ear before kissing me. I have to bite my cheek to keep from laughing.

Mary looks like she wants to hurl the salad dressing bottles at my head.

"Isn't my son a little young for you?" she says. "How old are you? Forty? Can't find someone your own age? All this is probably your fault anyway, isn't it?"

Sean bristles and steps in front of me as if he's putting himself between me and danger. I love that, too. I love a lot of things about Sean.

"Cooper did more to make me feel good about myself in the first three days I knew him than anyone in this family has ever done," he says, fists clenched at his side.

"I bet you have," Gigi whispers in my ear as she opens a cabinet near my head. I choke back a laugh, and the tops of Sean's ears turn red. I do like her a lot.

Mary isn't amused at all. She crosses her arms and glares at Sean. "If he's so great, then why did you run away? Why are you having these breakdowns now? That didn't happen when you lived at home!"

"I don't know," he says, uncertain for the first time.

"It's because he feels safe with Cooper," Troy says from the doorway. "With his body safe, his mind finally feels like it can start processing. You do realize that's what the T stands for? It's *post*-traumatic stress disorder. It hits you after the trauma is over, just when you think it's safe."

"Yes. Exactly. That's exactly what it is." He turns to me, wrapping his arms around me. "You make me feel safe," he says, looking up at me with such love in his eyes, I have to kiss him.

With a loud sound of disgust, Mary storms off.

"I think that's your cue to leave, boys," Gigi says as she scoops an alarming amount of sausage and peppers into plastic tubs. "Detroit, honey, take one of those loaves of garlic bread and wrap it in some foil. You can take it with you."

"Gigi, shouldn't I stay?" Sean asks. "Deal with this?" He's turned around but he's leaning against me, my arms around his waist as best I can with the crutches.

Gigi pulls out a handful of plastic bags from the cabinet under the sink and loads them up with containers. "Rome wasn't built in a day, and neither was this mess." She turns and walks over to us and reaches up to cup Sean's cheek. She's tiny, barely five foot tall.

"Go home with your handsome man here. I'll talk to your mother and my daughter. Everything will be okay, I promise."

Sean sniffles and wraps her up in a tight hug. "I love you, Gigi."

"I know you do, sweetie. And your mom loves you so much. You two will eventually work it out." She pats his cheek before going back to her bags.

"Take these and get out of here," she says, holding the bags out to Sean. "Now you call me," she says, pointing at Sean. "I haven't had one call from you since you left. I cry myself to sleep every night clutching a picture of you to my chest."

"No you don't," Sean says with a laugh.

She turns her attention to me. "And you, you make sure he gets some help with that PTSD, okay? Sean, I'm so sorry I didn't notice before now."

"Don't be, Gigi. I hid it from myself," Sean tells her.

She nods. "So, Mr. Cooper Hill, I'm trusting you with my favorite great-grandson. Treat him good."

"I'm your only great-grandson," Sean says.

"Only so far," she replies with a finger wag.

"I promise," I say. "It's kind of all I want to do."

She smiles. "Good. Now get the hell out of here. You think I want to wash three extra dishes if I don't have to?"

"You never do the dishes, Gigi," Sean says. She swats at him with a dishtowel. "Get out. And bring that Tupperware back before you leave!"

With kisses and hugs, we grab the dogs and escape without having to talk to anyone else.

SEAN

A quick call to Richie to make sure he's around, and we're on the road. It's a bit of a convoy, with my truck, Cooper's truck, and Troy's rental car. Troy makes a detour to pick up some pepperoni rolls for Cooper to try.

Richie nods at Cooper when he comes in. Cooper smiles broadly and holds out his hand. "Nice to finally meet you."

"You, too, man. Really good." Richie looks at me. "You're not mad I called him, are you?"

Shaking my head, I put down the bags I'm carrying and hug Richie. "I'm so glad you did. I owe you big time."

He pats my back. "Nah. You'd do the same for me."

I pull away. "I'll always be there for you, you know that, right? Just say the word."

"Same for me," Cooper says. "I can't thank you enough."

Blushing, Richie waves us both away and turns his attention to Stumpy. "Who's this baby?" he asks, crouching down to pet her. "Hey, girl. Aren't you a cutie?"

"Her name is Stumpy," I say.

"Seriously?" he asks, raising his eyebrows at Cooper.

"It was his idea," I explain. "I swear."

Richie catches sight of the plastic bags. "Is that Gigi's food?"

"Yep."

"Excellent," he says, and swoops them up. "Let's eat."

The kitchen table is too small for four people, so Richie grabs plates and utensils and we head to the living room. Cooper and I sit on the couch. Richie sits on the floor. Stumpy lays down next to him.

There's a knock on the door and Troy lets himself in, Rose following behind. "Hey," he says. "Hope you don't mind me walking in."

Richie waves him in. "Nah, it's okay. You bought a dog and beer, so it's all good."

"And pepperoni rolls," Troy adds, holding up the bag. He joins Richie on the floor, leaning his back against the couch by my legs.

We pass around the food and drinks until everyone has a plate full and their beverage of choice. I take the first bite of sausages and moan. "Man, I missed this."

"You had Gigi's food like six weeks ago," Troy says. "I bet she made you a feast before you left and gave you a care package for the road."

"Yeah, but still."

"It's delicious," Cooper says through a mouthful of food.

"How about the pepperoni rolls?" I ask.

"Good, but nowhere near this," he says, pointing to Gigi's food.

"They're better when you're drunk," Richie says. Troy and I agree.

Four grown men can eat a lot, and we finish off every bit. Troy and Cooper have a silent stand-off over the last piece of garlic bread.

"I'm the guest," Cooper says.

Troy knows his beaten. You can't trump the guest card unless, possibly, you've been in the hospital. "Fine," he sighs.

"How long are you here for?" I ask him.

"Two more days," he says. "I didn't know how long I'd need."

"I bet you can convince Gigi to make you more before you leave. Tell her it's for Dmitri, and she'll make two loaves."

We're on our second beers and stuffed to the gills when Richie breaks. "So? How'd it go?" he asks.

Troy, Cooper, and I exchange glances, each hoping the other will answer.

"It went really well," Cooper says decisively.

"Did you yell at your mom?" Richie asks.

"Oh, he did," Troy answers for me. "Very loudly."

"How'd she take it?"

"Well, she hates me," Cooper says.

"She tell you you're a cradle robber who's corrupting her son?" Richie asks.

"Pretty much," I say.

"But you guys are good, right?" Richie asks Cooper and me.

I lean against Cooper and he puts his arm around my shoulders. "We're great," I say. "Thank you for calling him."

"I told you he wasn't mad," Richie says. "So what's gonna happen now? Like, what's the result of all this?"

I lean forward, spinning the beer can between my palms. "Well, I think I have to face the fact that I'm dealing with some PTSD."

"From that place where they made you watch porn and then shocked you? And stuck your hands in boiling water?" Richie's voice is heated and he's primed to go on, but I don't want to relive each individual thing. "Yes. Stop."

"Sorry," he says. "I'm just so mad. I've wanted you to say something, to do something for *years*. I've been telling him," he says to Troy and Cooper.

"I know you have, Richie. And you were right. But it's more than that." I tell him about my revelation and how I'd internalized all the homophobia I'd been surrounded by until I hated who I was even as I was fighting to prove that there was nothing wrong with me.

"Do you have any idea how many times I prayed to God to make me normal?" I say.

All three of them start to object. "Hush," I say, waving them down. "I know it's normal. But all that twelve- and thirteen- and fourteen-, hell, all sixteen-year-old Sean knew was what his family and their friends taught him."

"I hear that," Troy said.

"Did you know you were gay before you met Dmitri?" Richie asks him.

Troy starts to shake his head no, then shrugs. "Maybe? I think I tried to convince myself I wasn't. Told myself all guys had those feelings, and that a lot of guys appreciated other guys' bodies."

"They don't?" Richie says eyes widening slightly. He looks to me for confirmation.

I shake my head. He deflates and then nods firmly. I know what he's thinking, but it's not my place to bring it up in front of Troy and Cooper. We can talk about it later.

"You have PTSD, right?" he asks Troy. "That's what Sean said."

"I do," he admits.

"And you're gay and from the same family. Sounds like you guys should have been talking a lot more after you found out about Sean, then. Kinda dropped the ball there," Richie says with a stern look.

"No shit," Cooper says.

I squeeze his hand. Even though I was mad at Troy, too, I love him and he's kin. "I appreciate the support, guy. But cut Troy some slack. He had his own crap to work through and it's not like I called him either."

Troy shakes his head. "I should have done more, reached out more. I'm older. I'm supposed to protect you."

I drop my hand onto his shoulder and give him a squeeze. "I wouldn't have talked about it anyway. I was in denial, remember?"

Cooper isn't as forgiving as I am. He glares at the back of

Troy's head. "He should have forced it. The people around you let you down."

"Yeah, well, that's life, ain't it?" Richie says. He finishes his beer and slams the can on the coffee table. "Past is past. It's what you're gonna do now that matters. Now, excuse me while I go make room for more beer."

Troy cranes his neck to follow Richie's departure. "When did he get so smart?"

"He says it's from watching TV with his mom."

"He's not wrong," Troy says. "But we don't have to make any decisions today, We'll talk later, though, right?"

"We will," Cooper answers, reminding me that I have a partner in this and anything else life throws at me. How did I get so lucky?

Troy stretches his legs out with a groan. Rose raises her head to check on him and he pats her to reassure her he's okay.

"What happened to Sweetie?" I ask. I loved his old service dog.

"Nothing. She's just getting up there. I'm out and about too much now. She's sleeping on the couch all day loving life."

"I think Stumpy would be a good dog for Sean," Cooper says.

"Yeah? Like we should train her?" Sean asks. "I don't have the same issues in crowds or anything that Uncle Troy has, though. Do I need an official service dog?"

I love the idea of service dogs, but having one would mark me in public as someone who has problems. People would ask me about her and why I need one.

Oh. I turn to Cooper. "I suddenly completely understand why you would want to cover up the prosthesis in public."

He grins at me. "You just imagined people coming up to you and telling you look fine and asking you what you need a service dog for, didn't you?"

"Yes," I confess.

"It will happen," Troy says. "Only you can decide if it's worth it."

"I've noticed she's very sensitive to your moods," Cooper says. "Whenever you're angry or upset, she sticks close to you. I think she feels it before you do."

"And she hates when I have nightmares," I tell Troy. "She starts whining in her crate, and the only thing that stops her is if we bring her into the bed." Admitting Cooper and I sleep in the same bed makes me blush but I don't try to hide it.

"Sweetie sleeps with me and Dmitri," Troy says. "I can get violent in my sleep. It's safer for her to wake me up than Dmitri. Sometimes just feeling her cuts off the bad dreams before they start."

"I don't think I do that. Do I?" I ask Cooper.

"Not to me," Cooper says. "I don't know if it happened when you were alone. But letting her sleep with us still sound like a good idea."

"Did you hear that, Stumps? I think you just got a free pass to sleep on the bed."

She gives me a doggie smile.

"I'll call my friend Roy and get you two in touch. He trains service dogs, and he'll be able to give you better advice. Stumpy might not even work out. I have a friend, Benny, former Marine," he says as an aside to Cooper. "You'd like him. He's hilarious. Good artist, too. Anyway, he's got this crazy dog, Poochie."

Richie rejoins us right then. "Poochie? And I thought Stumpy was bad."

"Poochie is a trip," Troy says and then launches into a few stories Benny and his labradoodle who flunked out of service dog school but can sense impending seizures before his owner can.

"So what's one piece of advice you have," I ask Troy.

"Are you still writing?" he asks without hesitation.

"I am. Wrote this morning, as a matter of fact."

"Keep that up," he says. "I know my photography is one of the things that keeps me sane. You're a writer. Use it. You know I started this whole art therapy program out in Red Deer for vets with PTSD. We do a little of everything. People seem to really like it."

"My poems are terrible," I say. Sadly, the more I learn about poetry and writing, the worse my own writing seems to me. Professor Ito assures me that's a normal part of learning something and it will come and go throughout my life.

"They don't have to be good. You're writing them for yourself. No one ever has to see them if you don't want to show them. Sometimes you need to put your pain outside of you so that you can see it clearly."

"That's basically what you told me this morning," Richie said.

"And you don't have to censor yourself when you're writing. You need to speak it somehow. Whether that's telling somebody, or whether that's doing some art when words aren't enough."

"Or I'm feeling something embarrassing or wrong."

"None of your emotions are wrong, Sean," Cooper says as he pulls me against him. "Some of them might be more helpful than others. I can tell you that you have nothing to be ashamed of until I'm blue in the face, but it won't matter until you believe it with your whole heart."

"That's the whole problem, isn't it? How do I do that?" I ask.

"I don't know exactly, and I know it's not going to be easy but I know it'll be worth it," Cooper says.

"You're worth it," I tell him.

"You're worth it," Cooper says.

"You're both gross," Troy says.

"Like you can talk," I say. "You and Dmitri are all over each other when I see you."

Troy points to Cooper and me snuggling on the couch. "You were making out in the backyard," he says. "In front of Grandma Jean!"

Richie laughs. "Busted."

"Richie has a boyfriend," I blurt out in a desperate attempt to deflect attention away from my love life. "And he has a hickey."

It works. We get into all kinds of discussions about many

subjects, included, but not limited to, the ethics of outing people in public, whether Cooper and Troy count as the public, and where you draw the line between friends with benefits and boyfriend.

Eventually, exhaustion hits me and I can't stop yawning. We wrap it up with a promise to get breakfast tomorrow before Cooper and I hit the road. I can't wait to get home. I'd leave tonight if I wasn't so tired.

"Are you going to see the family before you leave?" Troy asks.

"No. I can't deal with them right now."

He nods. "I get it. I'll tell Mary you're okay and to lay off you for a while. I'll also talk to her about everything, if that's okay with you."

"Please," I say.

Stumpy is reluctant to leave her new friends, but eventually we're all out the door. I follow Cooper to his hotel, and wonder how he feels about some reunion-slash-makeup sex. I bet he's a pro.

31

SEAN

"Ooh, indoor hallways, swanky," I say as I follow Cooper to his room.

"I just needed a bed," he says.

Does he think I'm criticizing his choice? "I'm serious. This is the nicest hotel I've ever stayed in. Not that I've stayed in that many. Three? And they were all the kind you drove your car right up to the door."

"I like those," Cooper says. "Don't have to carry your suitcases far."

"Yeah, but this one has an indoor pool and a restaurant."

"You'd love this hotel in Montreal I saw. The Auberge du Vieux-Port. It's in Old Montreal, right on the St. Lawrence River. A lot of rooms have a fireplace, exposed stone walls, and balconies that look over the river. The rooftop restaurant looks beautiful." He pulls out the keycard, opens the door, and maneuvers on his crutches like they're a part of his body.

"Sounds expensive," I say even as I'm dying to stay at this hotel I never heard of in a city I never dreamed of visiting before.

He shrugs. "We'll splurge. It can be our Christmas present. The city is beautiful at Christmas."

"Have you stayed at it before?"

"No." He sits on the end of the bed closest to the door, resting his crutches against it, and reaches for me. Tugging me forward by the belt loops, he positions me between his knees. My favorite place to be. "It's a very romantic hotel and I never had anyone I wanted to stay there with before."

"Good," I say, resting my hands on his shoulders. "It sounds perfect. I can't wait." I push his shoulders until he's lying flat on his back, and climb on top of him. "Now I want a real kiss. And then I'll think of a way to make up for scaring you."

I lean down to kiss him, and I'm stopped by the look in his beautiful brown eyes. It's sweet, full of affection and amusement, no hint of the fear he's been living with the last few days.

The first night we met, he stared at me with this intense look, angry and wanting at the same time. The intensity in his gaze captivated me, burning me to my bones. Not gonna lie, that was super-hot, but I like this look better.

"The way you look at me," I say softly, running my hand over his hair.

"How do I look at you?" he asks, hands on my hips and his thumbs sneaking under the bottom of my shirt to caress my skin.

"Like you love me."

"Imagine that," he says.

I kiss him. I bend down, and, finally, I'm kissing Cooper.

Kissing. Such a simple word. It doesn't sound like a big deal. Friends kiss. I kiss my grandma. Before Cooper, I'd expected to like kissing. After all, it must feel good or people wouldn't do it, but I assumed it would pale in comparison to the "real" stuff.

Before Cooper, I was an idiot.

Kissing Cooper is an experience in and of itself. It's so much more than simply a prelude to sex.

His hands are in my hair, which seems to be his favorite place for them to be. I used to get frustrated with the waves that wouldn't stay where I wanted them, would tangle instantly, and stick up in whichever gravity-defying direction they chose, so I kept it short. Now I want to let it grow down to my shoulders if it will keep Cooper petting me.

Cooper's tongue explores every inch of my mouth, and I need more. I need to be pressed against him so tightly not even air can get between us. I pull off, gasping for oxygen. "More," I say. "I need to feel more. "Slide up the bed so I can lie on top of you. Ooh, better, you lie on me. Please." He laughs at me as I wiggle backward off him. "Shirt off, too," I order as I bend down to untie his shoe. I pull my shirt over my head, kick my shoes off, and throw myself on the bed, rolling onto my back. "Come here." I hold out my arms.

He pulls his shirt off and I ogle his wide back appreciatively. Sliding into his crutches, he examines me and the bed, and then walks to my left. He pats the mattress near him. "Scoot closer."

I do, and, in a fairly impressive display of strength and balance, kneels on the bed with his good leg, lets the crutches fall, and then swings his other leg over me, caging me between his arms and legs.

"Happy now?" he asks.

"Almost." I wrap my arms around his waist and tug. "Lie on me. I need to feel you."

"I'll crush you," he says, not budging an inch. He's smiling, but I catch a hint of pain in his face.

"This is hurting you," I say.

"My stump," he admits. "I fell. That's why I'm not wearing the leg."

"You fell?" I shove him gently to the right. "Then get off me, you idiot. I was going for sexy, not hurty."

He goes down easy, landing on his back. He stuffs a pillow beneath his head. "I wanted to give you what you want."

I turn onto my side so I can fondle his chest. "I want it all. You can lie on me when your stump is better," I promise. "Did you go to the doctor?"

"No. But I have that appointment next week, remember? It will be okay until then. I'll ice it, keep off of it. Not to brag, but I am an expert faller now. I know when it's serious and when it's just annoying."

"Fine. I'll trust in your superior falling ability." I spread my hand out on his chest, loving the feel of his hair against my palm, and the hard muscles beneath it. "I love your hairy chest. It's so hot."

He laughs and pulls my hand up to his mouth so he can kiss the palm. "I think you're prejudiced in my favor."

"And I think we might as well get naked now," I say.

The way he hesitates and kisses my palm again makes me anxious. "What?" He's staring at me now, looking for God only knows what. "Cooper, we have to use our words now."

He sighs softly. "I'm a little worried," he admits.

I push up so I'm sitting cross-legged on the bed next to him, my knees pressing against his side. I think I know what he's worried about, but I'm going to make him say it. I trace circles around his navel. "Worried about what?"

"That sex is what's been upsetting you," he admits. "When I thought back, I realized that every time you've had a nightmare, it's been after some kind of jump in our physical relationship."

I pick up his hand and thread our fingers together. "I can see how it looks like that, but you're missing a few things." He waits for me to continue. "One, it's not every time. And two, those are only the nightmares you know about," I say, a little reluctantly. But if I'm going to get better, I need to stop hiding.

"You have them a lot?"

"How do you define a lot? Weekly, maybe? And the random, out-of-nowhere anger, too."

"I wish you'd told me," he says softly.

"I'm telling you now." I go up on my knees and straddle him. "And we'll talk more, I promise. But for now, I want to make it clear that I love having sex with you in all its wonderful variety, most of which I have yet to experience, and I'm not going to spend the rest of my life being afraid of it. I can't. I won't let them take that from me, too. I won't let them win." My body is braced for a fight, my hands in fists, shoulders tense.

Sensing it, Cooper runs his hands up and down my thighs to soothe me. "Okay. I get it. I don't want that either. But—"

"No buts. Okay, fine, there will be butts involved if I have my way."

"Which you know you will," he says with a smile.

"Really?" I grin, showing all my teeth, and he shakes his head. "Anyway, now we know what could possibly happen, we'll be prepared for it. And we can deal with it better."

He doesn't look completely convinced. Reaching up, he pushes my hair behind my ear as if it stands any chance of staying there. "I just hate the thought of hurting you in any way."

"Treating me like I'm damaged, breakable, will hurt me more than anything. I know you understand that." He nods. "Do you trust me to—if not know my limits, not yet—be able to tell you when I'm starting to feel bad or if I feel something might trigger me?"

"I do now, yes," he says.

"I know I won't always be able to tell. And things might be shitty sometimes." I look away, drawing a pattern on his chest with my fingertip. "Remember how I said I didn't know anything about being gay?"

"I will take those conversations to my grave," he says.

I smack him on the stomach. "Don't make fun," I say.

"Sorry," he says, not looking sorry at all.

"Well, I don't know how to be in a relationship, either. I feel like all my emotional development stopped four years ago. Or maybe it was all those years ago on the beach when I made the decision, however unconsciously, to hide who I am."

"I think you're not giving yourself nearly enough credit," he says.

"And I think you're prejudiced in my favor," I tell him, echoing his comment.

"Probably," he said. "It's a side effect of the whole being in love with you."

"You have terrible taste in men."

He shrugs. "What can you do?"

God, he's so good to me. And good for me. I hope I never take it for granted. "I know I might not be in the best place to be in a relationship right now. I'm going to need help. Therapy. I'll have bad days, maybe bad weeks. I can't expect you to want to deal with all this."

He starts to interrupt me, and I cover his mouth with my hand. "Let me finish. I'm kind of a wreck, as you may have noticed. But, even so. Even so, I want to be with you, and I really want to come home."

He pulls my hand away. "Can I talk now?" I nod. "I really want you to come home. I drove seven hundred miles to come and bring you back. With our dog."

"Our dog?"

"I'm not the one that hit her with my truck," he says, the big jerk.

"I didn't hit…forget it. I changed my mind." I try to slide off him and, laughing, he grabs me, pulling me down on top of him. I sigh and melt against him, my head nestled on his shoulder.

"I need you. I need us," he says, running his hands down my back. "My life before you feels empty. Being without you, was the worst two days of my life."

"You've literally fought in a war," I object.

"I built things in a war zone," he correct, then he shakes me gently. "Worst. Two. Days. Of my life."

"I think you're the one who needs the therapist," I mumble into his shoulder, secretly ready to explode with happiness.

He taps my chin until I look at him. "I'm not joking. I've never met anyone like you. I've never felt like this about anyone else. I told you I want you to stay with me as long as you want, remember?"

I take a deep breath like I'm getting ready to jump off a high diving board. "So forever then?"

His eyes light up and he pulls me tightly against him, his fingers digging into my back. "Sounds perfect."

SEAN

THANKSGIVING

I double-check the table. The new dishes we bought a few days ago look great with the silver candlesticks and a centerpiece of silk chrysanthemums and maple leaves. All of which were courtesy of the local thrift store. We'd gotten a great deal on a full set of silverware at an estate sale. Leaf-shaped napkin rings cradle the cloth napkins we found on clearance at the local home goods store.

Dinner is still a few hours away and already the house smells delicious from the slow cooker full of hot spiced cider and the apple and pumpkin pies we'd baked earlier.

Since neither of us had baked before, we'd done a lot of practice baking and cooking. I think I've gained ten pounds this month.

"The only way it could be more Thanksgiving-y in here is if we had people dressed up as actual pilgrims," I tell him. "It's going to be perfect. Our friends are going to have a good time."

We'd worked hard over the last few months to get the house ready and it looks amazing. We'd even gotten the back deck finished and picked up a nicer patio table and chairs set at an end-of-season sale at the hardware store.

My entire goal had been to give Cooper the Norman Rockwell Thanksgiving he'd always wanted.

When I first brought it up, he was hesitant for some reason. After some persuading of the naked type, he admitted it was because he didn't think anybody would want to come.

I correctly interpreted that as Cooper thinking people would have better options for the holiday than spending time with him.

It's taken me a while to realize it, but Cooper has a hard time accepting that people actually like him and want to be his friend. The kind of friends who choose to spend time with him on Thanksgiving.

Well, luckily for him, he has me. Anticipating this exact reaction, I'd checked with a few select people before bringing up the idea to Cooper. Enough people had said yes that we'd have a nice group even if no one else could make it.

Troy and Dmitri are already here, having flown in yesterday. They volunteered to make a beer and wine run into town. Dmitri said it was because Troy wanted an excuse to drive Rusty again. Rose was not thrilled with the idea of going out in the cold, so Troy had taken pity on her. She and Stumpy have curled up in front of the heater in the living room.

Dewey and Debbie are coming along with two of Dewey's kids who are older than me. Cooper and I think Dewey and Debbie are dating. We're just waiting for them to announce it.

A few people from Vino and Veritas said they would come, and four friends I made at school who couldn't afford to go home for the long weekend were thrilled to be invited.

It's going to be great. It has to be.

I'm determined to make this the best Thanksgiving ever. I need to do something special for Cooper to show him how much I appreciate everything he does for me.

Like how he goes out of his way to make me feel welcome in the house.

When we got back from West Virginia, I'd gone upstairs to my room to get some clean clothes and I'd gotten the surprise of my life. And given the last few weeks I'd had, that was saying something.

Somehow, in the short space of time I'd been gone, Cooper had fixed up the entire top floor for me.

My bedroom had a bed frame with a real mattress. There was a dresser and a nightstand with a table lamp. Dark green curtains hung over the window and a cozy armchair sat in the corner under a new reading lamp.

Even better, the previously empty second bedroom had been turned into a writing room. A battered but sturdy table now sat beneath the window, giving me a view of the tree-lined street below. Three low bookcases lined one wall.

"I thought you could put some pictures up," Cooper had said nervously as if he was afraid I wouldn't like it.

"It's perfect," I'd said, awed. There were a couple of books already on the shelves, and I'd gone over to check them out.

They were perfect, too, of course. Books of poetry, a few romances, and travel books to some of the places I've dreamed of visiting one day.

He'd shrugged when I asked him how he'd managed to do all this in a few days.

"Dewey and Debbie mostly. I had a bunch of stuff delivered and they came over with some of Dewey's grandkids, apparently, and put it all together. Debbie said Briar helped her with the romances. I ordered the rest."

I'd hugged him, which turned into us christening the arm chair and then the new mattress.

It's a great mattress. Of course, I don't spend much time in my own bed anymore, but there are nights when I need it, or when Cooper's feeling restless and tells me I'll be better off sleeping alone.

"Everything is perfect," I tell him again. "Grab some cider and let's go outside and relax before everyone gets here." Yeah, it's freezing out, but the cold is worth braving for the view.

We bundle up and walk down to the old picnic table. We'd moved it closer to the water after we'd finished the deck and gotten the new furniture, but it is still my favorite place to sit.

Wood sits piled in the fire pit, waiting for the kiss of a match to set it blazing. S'mores around the campfire are part of the dessert menu. We've asked everyone to bring a beach chair if they can.

We sit on the bench, and I shiver as the cold goes right through my jeans. I bump my shoulder against Cooper's. "Happy?" I ask him.

"More than I've ever been," he says, putting his arm around me.

"I'm glad. You owe me twenty dollars, by the way."

"Oh? Why?"

"You bet me twenty bucks I would want to move out before Thanksgiving," I remind him.

"I did, didn't I? I've never been happier to be wrong. Can I put it on my tab? I'm a little short of cash at the moment."

"You can Venmo me like the kids do these days, old man."

We watch the waves lap at the shore. The snow from last week lingers in the shadows under the trees. A gull cries, her call loud and lonesome in the cold air.

It's been two months since I left West Virginia for the second time. September turned to October, bringing the cold and snow I was promised. Can't say I'm a fan.

We haven't talked much about my revelations about that beach trip with my mother. I'm in therapy, which has been helping. I've been reading and meditating and doing all the things I should. I have good days and bad days. But the gulls' calls will always take me right back to Virginia Beach and the beautiful boys kissing in the sunshine.

It feels like a good time to talk about it. "You know why I kept thinking about that beach trip over and over?" I ask Cooper.

"No, why?"

I point my mug at the sky. "It's the seagulls. Lake-gulls? Just gulls, I guess. They were everywhere that week. I'd never seen so many, and they sounded so lonely and yet wild to me. Kind of like I felt, you know? Like they knew all about the 'endless immensity of the sea' and it haunted them the way all the places I want to see and all the things I wanted to be haunted me even then."

Cooper looks at me with wonder in his eyes. "You're amazing."

I kiss him, our lips cold and breath streaming into the air.

"You wrote a lot about them and the beach in your poems," he says.

I'd forgotten I'd given him my old journal, and he hadn't mentioned them before. "You read them?"

He pats the chest pocket of his coat. "Of course I did."

"Do you have it on you now? You carry it with you?"

"All the time. Everywhere I can. I love them," he says. "There's one I've been meaning to talk to you about. I think it would fit perfectly with this new song I've written."

I blink away the tears that ambush me. "Cooper." I squeeze his hand tight, hoping it can somehow convey everything I feel for him.

"Do you think living on the lake will be a problem?" he asks, surprising me again. "There are gulls here all the time. We could move."

"You would do that for me.?"

"It's just a house," Cooper says as if he hasn't wanted a home of his own forever.

"But it's your house. Your *first* house. You love it."

"I love you more." He says it like it's self-evident. Like it's an immutable law of nature. The sky is blue, gravity pulls things down to the earth, and Cooper loves me.

"Silly man." I stand up, slotting myself between his leg, and hold his face in my hands. "Silly wonderful, amazing man."

Sooner than I like, the cold drives us inside. We have just enough time to clean more of the apparently never-ending mess cooking Thanksgiving dinner creates.

"What about the future?" I ask Cooper as I try to find a spot for the roasting pan. "Where do you see yourself?"

He thinks about it while he checks on the green bean casserole. "I don't know. I'm not very good at planning for the future. The way my life usually goes, I make a decision, not necessarily a well-thought-out one, and then I just kind of ride it to the end. I joined the Army because the recruiter who came to the high school made the military sound like the answer to all my problems, so I enlisted as soon as I could."

"You sound like Troy."

"I'm not surprised. I picked my OMS because one of the guys sitting next to me did and I thought it sound fun." He closes the oven door and leans against the counter, deep in thought. "I left the Army because they made me. I came to Burlington because I didn't know where else to go."

"But you like it, right?" I ask.

"Yeah, It's nice. I never gave the future much thought." He snags me as I pass him, my hands full of pots. "Until you and your dreams came into my life," he says. "You make me want to take charge of my life. To make a plan. To be better."

"You couldn't be better," I protest. "Besides, I don't know what I'm going to do with my life."

"The specifics don't matter to me," Cooper says. "I've never had a big dream. Mine are all small, commonplace. I just want a life. I want to be around people I love and have enough money to take care of them and feel secure and maybe travel a bit. Mostly I just want to be with you, wherever that is, and whatever that looks like."

I reach around him to drop the pans on the counter. "For real?"

"For real."

"What if I want to live in a big city, like New York, or Boston?"

"I know you do." He rubs the back of his neck. "I have a confession to make. I read your notebook."

"I know. I gave it to you."

"Not that one. The little one. The one with all the lists."

"Oh, that one." The one I carry all the time, the one that has every stupid thing that's crossed my mind written in it. Once I would have been embarrassed, but not anymore.

"I thought it was mine," he explains. "They look the same."

"It's okay," I tell him. "You can look at it anytime you want."

"Thank you, but I won't. Everyone needs privacy. But anyway, I saw your list of places to visit or live. And I want to do that with you, all of it. It might be cool to live in a big city or another country."

"We could hunt alligators down in the Everglades," I say, getting into the idea. "Sip margaritas on the beach in Mexico. Move to Colorado with Troy and see real mountains."

"We can go where the wind takes us," Cooper says.

I can't possibly deserve this man. For the millionth time, I vow to do everything I can to make him as happy as he makes me. "So, if I want to live in the Sahara desert?"

"I'd buy a camel," he says with a grin. "I love you," he says. "Where you go, I go."

"I love you so much," I say. "Now you tell me again."

"I love you," he says with a kiss to the tip of my nose.

I sigh. "I'll never get tired of hearing that."

The sound of Rusty pulling up the driveway cuts off any thoughts I have about sneaking in a quickie before company starts arriving.

Troy bursts through the door, bringing with him the cold and a case of wine. "It's colder than a witch's tit out there," he says.

"What does that even mean?" Dmitri asks, paper bags rattling in his hands. "Why would a witch have cold tits?"

"Beats me," Cooper says, taking the case from Troy. I grab the bag from Dmitri and finish up getting ready for company.

Dinner is a huge success. Much food is eaten, much wine and spiked cider are drunk, and people huddle around the campfire longer than I'd predicted. Despite our vociferous protests, Dewey organizes a cleanup crew of him, Debbie, and my friends. They don't seem to mind, judging from the peals of laughter coming from the kitchen.

Stumpy and Rose are asleep, and Troy and Dmitri have disappeared as I'd expected. Troy still isn't thrilled about being in groups of people. They're staying in my room, so we'll see them tomorrow.

Cooper is beaming from ear to ear and I'm exhausted by the time we say our last goodbye.

"God, I'm dead on my feet," I say. "Let's go to bed."

"No argument here," Cooper says.

"Tell me the story," he asks as we're lying in bed after making sleepy, sweet love. "Tell me about your trip to the beach. I love your voice and I want to hear a story."

"It's not a very happy one," I say, kissing his fingers.

"Maybe not," he concedes. "But I happen to know it has a happy ending."

"Yes, it does. A very happy ending. Okay." I take a deep breath. "Once upon a time there was a little boy who had never seen the sea."

He falls asleep before I finish telling the tale of the beautiful boys kissing under the blazing summer sun on a day I'll remember forever.

But that's okay. Like he said, we know how the story ends.

33

SEAN'S HAIKUS

Pepperoni rolls
    On my favorite Christmas plate
    Alone in my room

The tortellini
    Taste like ashes in my mouth.
    Church on Christmas Eve

Seagulls scream out loud
    Two boys kiss under the sun.
    The world stops turning

Cradled in his arms.
    Atlas must have looked like this
    When he held the world

Things I cannot do:

Kiss under the mistletoe
A wish for next year.

I watched the boys kiss
My mother was watching me
How I learned to hide

He sang take me home
Whither thou goest, I will go
Home is where he is

The weight of the past
Follows me into the future.
A toast to old fears.

34

SEAN'S STORY

Once upon a time, a group of young men rented a house on Virginia Beach, in the same spot my mother and I were staying. They were bright as butterflies, young, happy, and it was worlds away from anything I'd ever seen, from anything I'd ever imagined.

The men wore very small bathing suits and outrageous shirts. They had pitchers of multicolored drinks that looked like fruit juice, but I could tell they had alcohol in them by the way the men were acting. They'd have these midday dance parties, and I was just mesmerized.

My mom would hurry me past, muttering how they shouldn't be acting like that in public, in front of children. I thought she was talking about the drinking. I barely knew what being gay meant, outside of it being something bad that you definitely did not want to be. I pretended I wasn't interested when she was around, but every chance I got, I would make an excuse to walk past them. The men would smile at me and wave. Sometimes I was brave enough to wave back and they would laugh, but it never felt like they were making fun of me. It felt as if they were acknowledging me in a language I didn't speak yet.

In hindsight, I must have been the most oblivious baby gay in the world.

There was a second group of men who also had caught my eye. A group of very buff men who played volleyball on the beach every day. Looking back, I know they were probably college kids on Spring Break. My mom didn't have a problem with me watching them playing. In fact, she encouraged me. Some of them were flirting with her, I realize now. She was a young-looking thirty.

One day, my fascinations collided when one of the hot guys I'd been watching jogged past the house the gay guys had rented. The men on the deck hooted and hollered, toasting him with their fruity drinks. The deck wasn't that high off the beach, maybe three feet.

One of the prettiest boys I'd ever seen, the one I'd been watching clandestinely, leaned over the railing and called to the jogger. The shirtless college kid gave a smile that blinded me and ran over to the deck. Wild horses couldn't have dragged me away from watching as he pulled himself up by the top rail, muscles bulging, tiny shorts riding up. He balanced on the railing, grabbed the pretty boy around the neck with one hand, and pulled him in for a deep, long kiss.

It was the first time I'd ever seen two men kiss, and I remember three things clearly. The man's hand around the pretty boy's neck, the muscles on the jogger's back, and how desperately I wanted to be that boy on the deck.

The moment broke and the college guy jumped down to the sand and jogged away. The pretty boy's friends cheered and whistled at him as he did.

The whole thing couldn't have taken thirty seconds, but my world shifted on its axis. My mom snapped my name like she'd already tried to get my attention a few times. When I looked back at her, I could tell she was angry. I had no idea why, but we never came back to that part of the beach again.

And that is the story of my gay awakening, something I'd

repressed so deeply, I hadn't even remembered it until now. When I think of it, and I do often, all I can see is the faces of the men, and all I can hear is the screaming of the seagulls. They sound like they're warning me to *beware, beware.*

THE
END

Printed in Great Britain
by Amazon

37481279R00159